I0601063

The Year
of the
Butterfly

Published by Alouette Enterprises, Inc.

ISBN — 978-0-9799922-0-9

To my beloved
Ralph

ONE

Hearing a loud thud, I glanced down at the book that had just fallen from a top shelf in the bookstore where I stood, browsing for a new book. The title was *Hello from Heaven*. I shook my head and smiled.

Wasn't I surprised that a book with such a title had landed at my feet, seemingly for no apparent reason? Not really. In fact, no book could have been more perfect. Unusual coincidences and synchronous events, often providing me with insights about my life, happened to me frequently these days. Or perhaps it's just that I notice these signs now, whereas in the past I had been unaware of them or chose to ignore their guidance.

Sitting down in the nearest chair, I opened the book to the first chapter and couldn't stop reading. The after-death experiences described by people who had lost their loved ones seemed so familiar to me. I wondered what might have happened if I had found this book years ago. Would I have felt so compelled to tell our story?

Yes—I had to write my story...actually, the story of Ralph and me. I felt guided by a force beyond myself. It was something I knew I had to do. When I heard some women talking in my health club about a resort that was located next to an ancient sacred burial site about an hour from Guadalajara, Mexico, it sounded like the perfect getaway for writing.

As soon as I arrived at the resort in Mexico, I found it to be unlike any I had ever stayed at...no imposing lobby, no manicured garden, no welcoming Mai Tai...just many little cabins stuck on top of a mountain in the middle of the desert...and so very quiet and peaceful. My small, one-room cabin didn't have a television, telephone, or electricity but had just enough room for a desk and single bed—the bed with faded sheets and a blanket showing wear from being washed hundreds of times. No frills, no distractions…nothing but me, my pen, and writing paper.

Outside the one window of my little cabin, I could see miles of desert. I had been warned about poisonous insects and snakes, but that was okay because I only planned to go out once a day for a meal in the community hall. Then I began to write—something I had never done before or ever contemplated doing. I wrote for twelve to fourteen hours a day, in the faint morning light of dawn, and by candlelight at night. I wrote until I was exhausted and could barely see the blurry notes in front of me. The words poured out of me…I didn't pause to reflect on what I had written. When I left the resort ten days later, I had a stack of paper.

My story begins shortly before I met Ralph, during the 1970s, when I was a young, highly ambitious, single woman living in Chicago. While visiting my parents' home, Mom and I were having an all too familiar conversation.

"I might as well have the words 'Old Maid' tattooed across my forehead," I said to my mom, who was standing in front of the sink, peeling potatoes.

"But you're not even thirty years old yet," Mom said.

"I don't care," I said, feeling close to tears of frustration. "All my friends have been married for years, and I feel as if I'll never meet the right man. It seems that if someone likes me, I don't like him, and if I like him, then he doesn't like me."

"That's ridiculous, Donna. You just haven't found the right man. Of course, you'll get married, sweetheart. But, as I've told you before, I think many men are intimidated by your job."

"Well, I'm certainly not going to give up my career. You know how hard I've worked to get into the business world and how I love working with computers."

"All I'm saying is that most people don't know anything about computers, and even if they do, it's considered to be a man's job. Maybe you should wait until you know someone for a while before you tell him what you do…especially if he seems interesting."

I pursed my lips, shook my head, and gave Mom an exasperated look. She was my best friend; we looked alike, talked alike, and often wore the same style of clothes. I could tell her anything, but sometimes I didn't like her advice.

My concern was not entirely unfounded, because in the 1970s, women who were not married by the time they were thirty were often considered to be old maids—or, at least, that's what I believed. The closer I came to reaching thirty, the more panicky I felt.

The truth is, at some level, I knew I was afraid of making a commitment to marriage even if I did meet the perfect person. Having witnessed the contentious relationship between my parents for years, I had good reason to be cautious. How did I know the same thing wouldn't happen to me? I also realized that I usually picked the wrong men—men who treated me badly, who were afraid themselves of making a commitment, or who were just immature. Consequently, I felt a great deal of inner turmoil—fearing I would never get married, on one hand, while also fearing I might end up in a bad marriage if I did get married. My fears had only been reinforced by several difficult romantic relationships over the past dozen years.

Several months after that conversation with Mom, I started a new job and noticed many interesting men working there—including Ralph, a man I had met on a previous consulting engagement who had seemed attracted to me at the time, but he had been married, and I had been involved with another man. Now, he was divorced, and I was free, too.

"Donna, I'm amazed at how quickly you've understood the business requirements," Ralph said, as he came over to a table where I sat alone, sipping a cup of coffee. His dark eyes seemed to penetrate my soul as he looked at me.

"Well, that's because you explain the business so well," I said, returning the compliment. I couldn't help but think what a smart, handsome man he was every time I looked at him, and so different from the men I usually fell for. He didn't exhibit any of the macho, bravado behavior of the men I was normally attracted to.

"Did you grow up around this area?" he asked.

I felt a distinct flip-flopping in my stomach as he looked at me. Although we had engaged in many business discussions, Ralph hadn't previously asked me any personal questions.

"Actually, I grew up in the country about an hour from here," I said. "My family was pretty self-sufficient in that we grew our own vegetables and raised chickens. My dad hunted pheasant and duck, and my brother and I caught fish in the river behind our house. We even had a vineyard, and my grandfather, who lived next door, made wine in his basement."

"That's interesting because I grew up on a farm as well. Fortunately, we were able to feed ourselves off our land because my dad had a hard time keeping a job. He drank a lot."

Ralph's openness about his father's drinking surprised me. My dad drank too much, too, but I wasn't about to admit that to him or anyone outside of my family.

"Where did you go to college?" I asked him instead.

"I was very fortunate to have received a basketball scholarship to a small college in Missouri where I majored in mathematics."

"Really? That was my minor."

"Isn't that unusual for a girl?"

"Yes, what I really wanted to do was to study drama, but my dad said he would only pay for my college tuition and expenses if I got a math degree and a teaching certificate; with those credentials, he said I should always be able to feed myself. My math background is what led me to get interested in computers."

"I received my computer training when I was part of an intelligence group during the Vietnam War. By the way," he said, changing the subject, "several of us are going over to Byron's for a drink after work. Would you like to join us?"

"Just for a short time. I'm staying at a girlfriend's home tonight because my new apartment is being painted. I've just moved out to the suburbs to escape from being around so much crime and violence in the city."

During the get-together at Byron's that evening, I noticed how Ralph's colleagues focused on him and everything he said, whether telling a joke or talking about work. I found it impossible not to stare at him myself and be drawn into the aura of his personality.

When I stood up to leave, he gave me one of his beautiful smiles. "I'll see you tomorrow," he said.

Driving to my girlfriend's apartment, I continued to feel the warmth from Ralph's smile radiating inside of me. Although I'd had many boyfriends, I couldn't recall ever feeling as comfortable with anyone or as drawn to anyone as I was to Ralph; I felt as if I had known him my entire life.

After parking my car, I opened the passenger door to retrieve my suitcase and noticed a man walking out of the apartment building in front of me. He raised his arm toward his face with an exaggerated gesture, as if straining to see his watch, and then placed his hands on his hips, looking perturbed.

"Do you have the time?" the young man asked as he walked toward me. "My watch seems to have stopped working."

My heart beat quickly, as the dishevelled-looking man stood right in front of me. Although frightened, I was accustomed to being polite and doing what I was told. As soon as I glanced down at my watch, I felt the tight grip of his hand on the back of my neck, and then he pushed me to the ground, scraping my cheek against the pavement, as he yanked my purse off my shoulder by the strap. I watched in shock as he ran with my purse across the parking lot.

I lay on the ground crying, not even thinking about whether I had been hurt or not. Suddenly, I was startled by the sound of running footsteps. I screamed as loud as I could, afraid the man had returned to attack me again. When I dared to look up, I was surprised and relieved to see Ralph's face, as he knelt down beside me.

"He got away," Ralph said. "I followed you in my car to be sure you reached your friend's place safely, because I know this is not a good part of town. Are you hurt?" he asked as he peered intently into my eyes with a concerned look.

"No, I'm just upset," I said, continuing to cry. "I finally moved out of the city to get away from being afraid all the time. And, now…now…this happens during my first night staying in the suburbs," I said, unable to stop sobbing.

"Let me help you inside," he said, as he gently stroked my hair and then helped me to my feet. "We can call the police from your friend's apartment and get something for your face."

"I can't believe you followed me."

"I know. I can't believe I did either. When you left the pub, I had a strange feeling I needed to see that you got to your friend's home safely. I can't explain it, but I'm glad I listened to my intuition."

In those few moments together, I knew without question that Ralph was the man for me. We were inseparable from that night forward. I was thirty, and Ralph was thirty-two.

Ralph wanted to get married soon after we started dating, but he patiently waited for me to get over my fear of marriage. We lived together for almost two years, and the following year, we got married, although my fears generated much drama leading up to the wedding ceremony… saying things like "I knew this was a mistake" when I didn't like the place that his mother had chosen for the civil service and crying much of the time before and during the ceremony.

As soon as we were married, I relaxed. I couldn't believe I had ever been so afraid of marriage.

"I'm the happiest one of all," Ralph would say when he woke me up every morning.

"No, I'm the happiest one of all," I would banter back at him.

Both of my parents adored Ralph. Before I knew it, they were visiting us on our third wedding anniversary.

"Donna," my mother shouted, "you'd better get out here right now!"

When I looked out the kitchen window, I saw my father standing next to Mom, shaking his finger at her. I sighed at the familiar sight of Dad lecturing Mom and finished sweeping the kitchen floor before going outside.

As soon as I stepped out the back door, our three dogs, Chip, Cookie, and Cupcake—fondly referred to by us as the "junk food kids"—greeted me enthusiastically by jumping up against my legs with their tails wagging and licking me.

"Okay, guys," I said, patting each one on the head and giving Chip a kiss on his nose. Our dogs were used to being treated like precious children rather than mere household pets. Then they turned around and ran toward the swimming pool.

"What's going on?" I asked, walking toward my parents who were standing next to the pool. The sparkling blue water looked inviting as it shimmered in the sunlight. Chip reinforced my thoughts by jumping into the pool.

"You'd better talk some sense into your husband," my father began in his familiar, disapproving tone. "He has no idea what he's doing. He bought wood at the lumberyard without any idea of how much he needs. Then, as soon as we came back, he tore down the old fence and started building the new one without measuring or laying out a plan of any kind."

I could tell that my dad was upset by the reddish color of his face and the set of his jaw—a look that my mother, brother, and I had long since become used to. In that regard, he was the direct opposite of Ralph. I couldn't imagine anyone being more up-tight than my father and anyone more easy-going than Ralph, which made the close relationship that developed between the two men difficult for me to understand.

Having finished his swim, Chip climbed out of the pool and ran toward us, shaking his body vigorously and spraying us with water.

"For Christ's sake, Chip, get away from here!" my father yelled.

Even though I had seen Chip coming toward us, I knew it wouldn't have done any good to holler at him because he did exactly what he wanted to do when he wanted to do it. Ralph and I had reluctantly accepted the fact that our dog was impossible to train, though my brother Bill told us the problem was always with the owners—not the dog.

"C'mon, Chip, let's go find your father," I said, knowing his two sisters would follow right behind him.

As I walked through the backyard, relishing the beautiful summer day and admiring the expansive landscape with its lush green grass and towering trees, I still found it hard to believe this place was really ours. The first time Ralph and I drove up the long, winding driveway and saw the majestic white house, setting atop a small hill in the middle of five acres of land, we both knew this was the home for us. This was how Ralph and I reacted to most things we really wanted—identically, as many soul mates do—although I couldn't imagine anyone not falling in love with the house and the beautifully landscaped property. But then, I was crushed to find out the property was already under contract.

Over the next two years, we looked at many properties, but nothing compared to that place I had dubbed my "Tara", because it reminded me so much of Scarlett's home in *Gone with the Wind*—on a much smaller scale, of course. From time to time, I would drive up the long driveway just to see the house I had loved and lost. And then one day, I found a young man working outside in the yard who told me the property had gone into foreclosure. Within a week, Ralph negotiated a contract with the bank.

What was it about this place that attracted us so much? Everything. It had all the old-world charm that is difficult to reproduce today. The house was custom-built in the late 1920s by a wealthy man who had been a landscape designer for European estates. Inside the house, there were polished wood floors in every room, a carved wooden staircase leading to the second floor, and a living room three times the size of what was typical of the day, not to mention the pedestal sinks with genuine gold-plated fixtures, and the unusually large and curvaceous bathtub in the master bath.

When I walked across the lawn to the outskirts of our property to find Ralph and saw he was working on building a new pen for the dogs, I felt the usual surge of delight that enveloped me whenever I saw him. He had inherited the striking good looks of both his parents; his thick, black, wavy hair and slightly olive-toned skin reflected the Cherokee blood in his ancestry. Whether he was dressed in a sharp-looking business suit or wearing jeans as he did that day, his six-foot-four frame was an impressive sight.

Chip ran ahead of me and jumped on the back of Ralph's knees, causing them to buckle. Swinging around to give Chip a nudge with his leg, Ralph saw me and gave me one of his beautiful smiles.

"Hi Donna-Girl," he said. "I was wondering when you were going to venture out here to help me," he said jokingly, because we both knew I would be no help at all with his project.

"My dad seems a little concerned about your measuring and planning techniques," I said, with a smile on my face.

Ralph rolled his eyes. "Would you go to the store and buy some steaks and sweet corn for tonight?" he asked, changing the subject.

Normally Ralph did all the grocery shopping and cooking for us. I detested both tasks: grocery shopping bored me and cooking made me nervous. For Ralph, cooking was relaxing, and he was a great cook. It was unusual for a man to be the primary cook back in those days, and I think the fact Ralph's family couldn't afford to buy much food when he was growing up accounted for why he enjoyed shopping so much. Furthermore, although Ralph was a high-level executive, he believed I had a better chance of making it to the top…a belief shared by my father, and one that was almost impossible for a woman to achieve in those days. Ralph thought that if he took care of many of the chores in our daily lives, then I could more easily focus on my career.

"I'll go to the store and leave you alone so you can finish," I said, giving him a kiss on his cheek. As I walked back to the house, I thought about the challenge it would be to keep my father sober and awake until Ralph finished working on the dogs' pen and came in to cook our dinner.

It was nine o'clock before we sat down for dinner that night. As predicted, Dad filled his stomach with peanuts and beer, and grumbling about how late it was, he climbed the stairs to bed an hour before we were ready to eat.

After dinner, Ralph and I went out to the backyard and lay together on a single lounge chair beside the swimming pool. We were both fairly thin, although I had gained ten pounds over the past several years from his good cooking.

Ralph had been quite thin since his early twenties when he had experienced a severe case of Crohn's disease—a chronic inflammation of the digestive track. In fact, his doctors had given him only two years to live at that time. He showed me some pictures of himself after he had an operation to remove a large piece of his intestine. Ralph was so gaunt he looked like someone from a concentration camp. Other than being quite thin now, however, he seemed to be in pretty good health. His thinness, he had explained to me, was because he couldn't eat much at any one time.

We hadn't talked much about his prior health problems, because he hadn't experienced any serious illness since we met. Occasionally, he had stomach cramps that went away if he skipped a meal or two. So I wasn't worried, and I rarely thought about his Crohn's disease.

"Aren't the stars beautiful tonight?" I asked, cherishing the peaceful quiet of the night and the feeling of Ralph's body next to mine as we snuggled together. "I think they're twinkling just for us because it's our anniversary."

"I think you're right, Donna-Girl. How lucky can two people be? I know I'm married to the most beautiful girl in the world," he said and then kissed me gently.

Ralph was the only person who had ever made me feel pretty, let alone beautiful. Even though I had been homecoming queen in high school, in part, because I fit the general standard of the day as a cute, petite blonde, I had never felt exceptionally attractive. I worked hard on my grooming and dress, but I had a tendency to focus on my flaws, whether it was a blemish on my face or some extra fat on my thighs. In that way, I was a perfectionist like my father. When Ralph first told me he liked me best without any makeup, that's when I knew he really thought I was pretty.

Suddenly, I was startled by a piercing cry. "Ralph, do you hear those coyotes?" I whispered. "It sounds as if they're attacking something out there in the woods."

As nature enthusiasts, Ralph and I loved to study animals. We had gotten into the habit of naming each year for a different animal species, whichever one seemed to be unusually prolific in our area that year. So far, we hadn't named this year. Last year had been the year of the fox.

Ralph shivered beside me.

"Are you cold, honey?" I asked. "Do you want me to get a blanket?"

"No, I'm fine," he said, stifling a yawn. "I think I'm just tired after working outside all day. I probably should go to bed so I can get up early and finish the puppies' pen. Let's wait 'til later to name this year. I'm not fond of thinking of it belonging to the coyotes."

"Okay, babies, let's go to bed," I said to the three dogs lying underneath our chair. The five of us always went to bed at the same time. I wanted to be with Ralph, and the puppies wanted to be with the two of us, happiest when they didn't have to choose between us.

Ralph fell asleep immediately, but I lay awake for a while listening to the owls hooting and the crickets chirping outside our open window. Before I drifted off to sleep, I felt grateful that I didn't hear any more coyotes howling.

TWO

The night of our third anniversary, I woke up a little before midnight to the sound of Ralph vomiting in his bathroom. My body immediately tensed. The sound of anyone vomiting always made me extremely anxious. When I was a child, on many Saturday nights I would lie in bed, shaking from the sound of my father throwing up after drinking too much.

A long time seemed to pass, as I listened anxiously in the dark. When Ralph finally returned to bed, his face looked ashen in the moonlight, and his body trembled.

"Are you all right?" I whispered.

"I'll be fine," he said, lying down on his side of the bed. "I just need a good night's sleep." Then he turned away from me, which I took as a sign he didn't want to talk.

Less than an hour later, I heard him throwing up again, while I lay in bed with my heart pounding, thinking about how terrible he must feel. This same scene repeated itself almost hourly until daylight, when he returned from the bathroom and finally fell asleep.

Later that morning, Ralph and I sat waiting in the office of Dr. Williams, our general practitioner. Usually, Ralph went to see the doctor by himself, so I was glad he had agreed to let me go with him this time.

"It's hard for me to tell without seeing an x-ray, but I think there is a good chance your intestine is blocked," Dr. Williams said after examining Ralph. "You remember we talked about that possibility in cases as severe as yours, Ralph. If that is the case, you will need surgery to remove the blockage and free up the intestine. Of course, we will need to take x-rays to be sure, but I think you should go as soon as possible to a major university center and be prepared to stay."

The look of resignation on Ralph's face made me think that he was not surprised by the doctor's diagnosis. But I was shocked.

"How can this be, Dr. Williams?" I asked in an unsteady voice. "He's been fine since I've known him for the last several years. It can't be that serious. Maybe he ate something that didn't agree with him."

"I've been surprised myself at how well he's done over the past few years. I actually expected he would have another blockage by now. Some people with mild cases of Crohn's disease never have a serious enough problem to require having surgery. Ralph's case, however, is quite severe."

"He told me about that surgery and how he had been given two years to live, but I thought because he's been doing so well, there wasn't anything to worry about."

"There's always uncertainty with Crohn's disease. We don't know the cause of the disease and don't have a cure for it at this point, although we think it may be hereditary. Most patients don't have the extensive damage Ralph had during the early stages of the disease, but research is going on in many university hospitals throughout the country, so hopefully we will find a cure soon."

"I haven't told Donna much about the disease," Ralph explained, "because I was hoping it wouldn't be necessary. I didn't want to worry her."

"That's understandable, Ralph, but I think you're going to need all the support you can get from her now," Dr. Williams said in a solemn tone that scared me.

"Maybe surgery won't be necessary, Ralph," I said, as we were driving home. "Maybe, there isn't a blockage, or, maybe, it will go away."

"I hope you're right, Donna-Girl, but I feel just like I did before I had my last surgery. I don't think I can even keep water down."

"Well then, if you have the surgery, you'll be all right again," I said, trying to encourage him as well as convince myself. I had never seen

Ralph look so dejected.

"What is your worst fear?" I asked, although I wasn't certain I wanted to hear the answer.

"I'm not afraid of dying, but I am afraid of living like a vegetable or with a feeding tube. I'm also afraid that as a result of this surgery, I may need a colostomy bag."

His last comment surprised me because Ralph was not a vain person. "Why would you be afraid of having a colostomy bag? You could still do and enjoy all the things you like. As long as you are alive and we can be together, that's all I care about."

"I don't know. I think I would feel self-conscious. It might be irrational, but I just hate the thought of a colostomy bag."

I decided to drop the subject, since it might not be a problem anyway.

After we got home, Ralph lay down on the sofa in our den, his face frequently contorting with pain, while I cleaned several rooms of the house in a nervous frenzy. Although I generally didn't enjoy cleaning, physical activity of any kind seemed to calm me when I was anxious.

My foot tapped with impatience as we waited at the university hospital for the results of Ralph's x-rays. Ralph sat calmly next to me, holding my hand, until a nurse came into the waiting room and showed us into an office.

Two doctors in white coats rose to greet us. "Hello, I'm Dr. Franks, and this is my colleague Dr. Ray from our surgical unit," the older-looking of the two men said. "Dr. Williams was accurate in his suspicion about a blockage. There really aren't any options for you at this point—you must have surgery to free up the blockage."

I was immediately struck by the lack of warmth in Dr. Franks' voice, which was so unlike Dr. Williams' manner.

"Of course, we will try to minimize how much intestine we remove so you will be able to eat without a feeding tube," Dr. Ray said. "Furthermore, a case like yours will probably require future surgeries…and I'm sure you know there is a limited amount of intestine that can be taken out."

I was extremely disturbed by his ominous tone of voice but stayed silent.

"What about the possibility of a colostomy bag?" Ralph asked.

"That's a distinct possibility, but we will avoid it if we can," Dr. Ray said.

"What other risks are there with the surgery?" I asked.

"Well, there are the usual risks with any major surgery, but based on his history your husband has a strong heart, and we expect he will make it through the surgery," Dr. Franks said. "We can schedule the surgery for tomorrow, in fact, because we just had a cancellation. We'll need to perform some pre-op tests and start cleaning out your system immediately. Do you have any further questions?" Dr. Franks asked, looking at Ralph.

"Not at this time," Ralph responded.

I felt as if everything was happening much too quickly. Surely this is a nightmare from which I will awaken and find Ralph smiling at me in bed as he does every morning, I thought to myself.

I looked over Ralph's arm as he filled out the hospital admittance papers. When I saw that he was about to sign a form, indicating he didn't want to be put on life support or resuscitated, I put my hand over his to stop him from signing it. "Why would you sign that?" I asked with alarm. "You know I want you to live no matter what."

"I wouldn't want to live like a vegetable or in severe pain. I really mean that, and I wouldn't want you to override my intention," he said in a firmer tone than I had ever remembered him using with me. Despite my objection, he signed the form.

I started crying.

"Everything will be all right, Donna-Girl," Ralph said, as he put his arms around me and hugged me.

After Ralph was settled into his hospital room and a nurse had started his IV, I went to find my room on the floor designated for patients' families. As I unpacked my bag, I felt so cold and nervous; I couldn't shake off my feeling of terror. You've got to be strong for Ralph, I told myself. You have to be positive and believe he will be fine. I lay down on the bed and tried to rest, but it was hopeless. I couldn't stop thinking about Ralph, so I decided to go sit with him.

When I got back to Ralph's room, I saw a young black man being pushed on a gurney into the room next door. I noticed there was no one with him—no family or friends. Although he was moaning with pain, the nurses seemed to pay little attention to him.

I sat in a chair next to Ralph's bed that night, unable to sleep and wishing the long night would be over, yet dreading the surgery to come. I couldn't believe how tense and terrified I felt. The moans coming from the man in the room next door didn't help. Gratefully, Ralph had been given a sedative and was sound asleep.

"Good morning, sweetheart," Ralph said, when he awoke early the next morning. "Donna-Girl, I want you to tell me the truth about the outcome of the surgery. No matter what happens, I want the whole truth."

Before I could say anything, a nurse came into the room to begin prepping him for surgery.

"He's not scheduled for surgery until eight," I said, feeling things were moving much too fast and wanting to put off the surgery for as long as possible.

"It'll take a while to get him ready," she said. "Would you mind stepping outside the room?"

As I walked into the corridor, I heard the young black man in the room next door, moaning even louder than he had the previous night.

"I think that man needs some help," I said to a passing nurse who barely looked at me when I spoke to her.

"We'll get to him shortly," she said curtly and walked past his room.

Before long, two large men pushing a gurney entered Ralph's room. As soon as they lifted him onto the gurney, I burst into tears. I was shocked at how quickly I had fallen apart and upset with myself because Ralph needed me to be strong, not acting like a whimpering child. But I just couldn't stop sobbing, as I walked alongside the gurney, holding Ralph's hand tightly. The doors to the surgical room swung open, and I barely had time to choke out the words, "I love you," before he disappeared into the operating room.

Ralph's surgery took over three hours, followed by another hour of closing his incisions.

"Your husband's surgery went far better than I anticipated," Dr. Ray told me after Ralph had been taken to the recovery area. "We removed a large piece of his intestine, but not as much as I initially thought would be necessary, so he will not need a colostomy bag. You can see him back in his room in a few hours."

I felt I should have asked the surgeon some questions, but he stood up and left so quickly that I hardly had time to think. For the first time in several days, however, I felt my body relax, thinking that the worst part of the ordeal was over.

In reality, the worst part to the surgery was just beginning for Ralph— the recovery. When the staff attendants wheeled him back to his room, where I was waiting anxiously, his face looked ashen. He groaned in pain as they lifted him onto his bed, and his body was trembling as he opened his eyes.

"You just need to rest, baby, and everything will be fine," I said. "No colostomy bag."

Ralph closed his eyes again and didn't respond. He looked so weak and pale and vulnerable. Other than my father, I had never seen anyone who had just come out of a major surgery. That look of having had a brush with death permeated Ralph's being, and I remembered how similar my father had looked after his last surgery. The terrifying thought that this is how Ralph will look when he dies entered my mind.

Stop it! a loud voice screamed in my head. Why are you thinking like that? The mere thought of anyone close to me dying terrified me.

Ralph seemed in extreme pain, so I asked his nurse to give him a higher dosage of morphine. After he was given more pain medication, his face seemed to relax, but then I noticed that the machine pumping his stomach had stopped working. I called the nurses' station every five minutes for an hour before someone finally came to replace it. This place is scary, I thought to myself. What if I weren't here hounding the nurses?

After the hospital quieted down for the night and Ralph seemed to be resting peacefully, I walked into the adjacent bathroom. It was a relief to be in another room, even for a few minutes, away from the stench emanating from Ralph's body. As I sat on the toilet, resting my head in my hands, I heard the man in the room next door moaning loudly again, sounding much like a wounded animal in pain.

After leaving the bathroom, I walked outside of Ralph's room and saw a nurse nearby. "The young man in 321 needs attention," I said to the nurse.

"He's addled in the brain," she said, pointing her index finger toward her head and moving it in a circular motion. "There's nothing seriously wrong with him."

Although I didn't believe that was true, I was still at that stage of my life where I respected authority. Like many women who grew up during my era, I had been taught to be submissive and not to cause any problems. So I didn't push other people too much, and I often doubted my own intuition. I went back to Ralph's room and fell into a deep sleep, exhausted from the events of the past several days.

The next day was difficult for Ralph. He developed a fever and an infection. I knew the doctors were concerned about him, because an intern rather than a nurse checked on him frequently.

Early that afternoon when I walked into the hallway, I noticed that the room next door was empty. I walked over to a desk where Ralph's nurse was sitting. "Can you tell me what happened to the young man in room 321?" I asked her. His moaning from the night before had continued to haunt me, and I felt concerned about him.

"He must have been moved to another room," she said.

"Well, can you tell me what room he was moved to?"

"I have no idea," she said, seeming to be uninterested in finding out.

"I really want to know what room that young man was moved to," I said, taking a much firmer stance with her than I normally took with anyone. "You must have some idea."

Then I became annoyed as she looked down at some papers on her desk and ignored me. I continued to stand quietly in front of her while she shuffled papers.

"He died early this morning," she said in a subdued voice without looking up at me.

"What?" I asked, shocked at her admission. "That shouldn't have happened."

"I know," she said, finally looking up at me with somewhat of a contrite or guilty look; I wasn't sure which.

"He didn't get the help he needed last night. I just knew he needed help," I said, feeling both upset and guilty myself.

The young man's death would bother me for the rest of my life. As far as I knew, he had never had any visitors. I didn't blame myself for paying more attention to Ralph than to the young man, but I often wondered whether he would have received help and possibly survived if I had been more demanding on his behalf.

Several days after Ralph's surgery, I was sitting next to his hospital bed one afternoon, reading a book.

"What did you do with my Kleenex?" Ralph asked in an accusatory tone, startling me.

"Nothing, Ralph. They're right here," I replied, handing him a tissue.

"You keep moving my things around, and I never know where to find them," he said, sounding thoroughly irritated with me. "How many times do I have to tell you to leave things exactly where I put them on the night stand?"

I was so taken aback that I didn't know what to say. Even though I knew that the combination of drugs and pain made Ralph act different than usual, I felt hurt by his tone of voice. This was the first time he had ever sounded even slightly annoyed with me.

Thankfully, after a few more days, Ralph's personality returned to his usual happy, kind, good-humored self.

"You know, honey, you really seemed irritated with me a few days ago," I said later that week.

"What do you mean, Donna-Girl? I don't remember being upset with you."

"Don't you remember accusing me of moving your things around on your table?"

"No, I don't. To be truthful, I don't remember a lot about the past several days."

I decided not to pursue the conversation further. Perhaps I was being overly sensitive. I had become so used to thinking of Ralph as a saint that any deviation from that kind of behavior upset me terribly.

After two weeks in the hospital, Ralph was released for three months of recuperation at home. Although I was relieved the surgery had been a success, I now understood how potentially devastating Ralph's disease could be. According to my medical book, in about one-fourth of all cases of Crohn's disease the symptoms, which include cramps, abdominal pain, diarrhoea, and a general sense of feeling ill, only appear once or twice; other more severe cases like Ralph's can continue for years and cause a deterioration of bowel function, inability to absorb nutrients, and intestinal obstructions. Ralph's surgery was not a cure; it was a short-term remedy to treat the symptoms and the internal damage already caused by the disease.

Ralph's three best friends from high school came to see him as soon as he got home. They had played with Ralph on the winning basketball team that put their small town of two hundred people on the map. Mack, Ralph's best friend, owned an insurance and real estate business that was doing quite well, and his other two friends owned large farms.

As I listened to the men talk, I thought about Ralph's upbringing compared to mine. Probably, the biggest difference was the financial status of our families. Although my family had only average means, I had been given most of the material things I wanted, whereas Ralph had sometimes gone to school with holes in his shoes. Fortunately, his basketball stardom had helped to diminish the negative effects of his poor upbringing and alcoholic father. I couldn't help but wonder if Ralph's difficult childhood was a factor in his current health problems.

As I sat with Ralph and his three friends, watching them laugh and share the good times they used to have together, everything seemed so normal again. It was almost hard to believe the nightmare of the past few weeks had ever happened.

THREE

"We're having fried chicken tonight," Ralph said, as I walked into the kitchen after a long day at work. Ralph had continued to cook dinner for the two of us most nights, but, since his surgery, his energy usually waned soon after dinner.

"I'm so happy you're recovering so well," I said, putting my arms around his waist. I squeezed him gently and rested my face against his shirt, while he stood at the stove, turning the chicken.

As Ralph and I were carrying our dinner to the table, he bumped into an antique pedestal that was standing in front of our dining room table.

"Donna-Girl, we have to get rid of some of these things. It's hard to walk around this house," Ralph said more insistently than usual.

I spent a lot of my time and energy on the weekends buying antiques. By now, we had furnished our home with as many antiques as practicable, but I had continued to collect glassware, furniture, and anything else that seemed like a good deal to me. Boxes of antiques were stacked from floor to ceiling in our basement, and I placed excess furniture throughout the house wherever I could find room for it.

"You can't even appreciate most of the things you buy because they're hidden in boxes," Ralph said, as we began eating our dinner.

"I know, honey, but I hate to part with anything. You know antiques are a good investment, and I'm sure I can sell everything for twice what I paid. But, maybe you're right. Maybe I could start by selling just a few things. I know it's the thrill of finding that unbelievable bargain that keeps me hooked, as much as my appreciation of the antiques themselves."

"I'm glad you have fun going to garage sales and auctions, but just think how many more things you could buy if you sold some things first."

"Very funny, Ralph. So, you think you can talk me into clearing out the house by luring me into thinking I could buy more?" I said, smiling at him.

His tactic worked. The next week I rented the second floor of an existing antique shop near our home, spending hours arranging and rearranging the displays. Sometimes I moved a piece more than five times before I found the perfect place to display it.

Two weeks later while on a business trip in Atlanta, I was speaking in a meeting when I was interrupted by a phone call from Ralph. My legs felt weak as I stood up. Ever since his surgery, I feared Ralph would become terribly ill again. I didn't think the secretary would have interrupted the meeting unless something urgent had happened.

"You'd better sit down, Donna-Girl," Ralph said, as soon as I answered the phone.

At least, he sounds okay, was my immediate reaction to the tone of his voice.

"The antique shop has burned down," he said calmly, "and it doesn't look like anything can be salvaged. Unfortunately, the insurance contract hasn't gone through yet."

Although I was upset about the shop burning down, I was relieved there wasn't something wrong with Ralph or my parents.

After flying home the next day, I immediately went to the shop, and I saw that, indeed, almost everything had burned in the fire except for a few pieces of glassware. These are just things, I told myself. They're not that important; they can be replaced.

"Why don't I try to pull some things out of the ashes tomorrow?" Ralph asked when I returned home.

"You can't be serious, Ralph. You haven't even been outside of the house that much. You're supposed to rest for another month."

The next morning, I drove over to the still smoldering building before going to work. I hadn't been there more than a few minutes when Ralph drove up in his car, wearing a hard hat and smiling.

"I feel fine, Donna-Girl. Honest! It's been two months since my surgery. I'm a quick healer."

How could I be mad at him when he looked so happy, acting like his old self again? Maybe he's right about healing quickly, I thought.

"I'll be fine. Let's see what we can pull out of the rubble," he said, as he placed a small ladder against the remaining frame of the building and climbed up to the second story. Then he crawled on his hands and knees on top of the second-floor beams and handed me a few pieces of glassware that were charred but not broken.

I called into work to say I would be a little late; there was no way I would leave him alone up there. After a few hours, we had salvaged several boxes of blackened glassware.

The next day, which was Valentine's Day, I came home to a turkey dinner with all the trimmings and two small boxes waiting to be opened: the first had a red two-piece bathing suit in it, and the second contained a beautiful necklace with a small, heart-shaped ruby surrounded by diamond chips.

"Oh, Ralph, you shouldn't have gone to all this trouble shopping for me. You must be exhausted. But I love everything and you, too," I said, giving him a long, lingering kiss.

He smiled when we parted. "I love you so much, Donna-Girl."

I guess I shouldn't have been surprised by his lavish presents. Ever since we had been together, he had always given me the perfect gift for every holiday. Actually, what surprised me most was his ability to guess my clothes' size. I hardly knew what size I wore myself, having gone from size two to ten and everything in between on numerous occasions. Somehow, he always guessed correctly.

After the fire, I was discouraged about ever owning an antique shop again, so I was surprised when Ralph came home one day, excited about an old Victorian house that was for sale on the main street of a neighboring village.

"I think the house would be perfect for an antique business," he said, "and behind the house is an old barn that could be used for storage. Do you want to take a look at it tonight?"

I suspected that Ralph was suggesting we open another antique business mostly for my sake. Even though he gave himself vitamin shots every week because his body couldn't absorb nutrients easily, his energy level remained low, whereas I needed something other than my executive job with the airline to keep me busy.

Surprisingly, the house was in immaculate condition, particularly since it was almost one hundred years old. The small foyer was large enough to accommodate a desk for a receptionist to greet customers, as well as a display case for some of our finest antiques. The front and back stairway could facilitate customer traffic flow through the four-story structure, especially on busy days. Thick, oak, pocket doors separated the downstairs sitting room from the inviting living room. Ornate stained-glass windows enhanced the top three floors. Old, brass hardware gleamed on every door, as the owner had had his children polish it for many years. And, as Ralph had noted, what was most remarkable was a small barn behind the property—great for storage and so unusual on the main street of the well-developed village.

Within minutes I envisioned the antiques that would fill each of the charming rooms: Christmas decorations on the top floor and some country-style reproductions in the adjacent restroom; antique rope beds, patchwork quilts, vintage clothing, and hand embroidered linens in the bedrooms of the third floor; brightly colored glassware (my specialty), sofas, and marble-topped tables on the main floor; and farm implements and rustic items in the basement, which even boasted a cistern that years ago had caught rainwater. I had no doubt the shop would be the talk of the town.

Sale of the old house had fallen through numerous times over the past ten years, because the current owner had raised his family in the home and had always found a reason to back out of the contract at the last minute, most likely for sentimental reasons, I suspected. Fortunately, the owner and I developed an immediate rapport, as I explained my vision to him and told him he would always be welcome to stop by for a visit and a cup of tea.

Ralph and I had fun decorating the old house together. The day we wallpapered the dining room, each of us alternating putting up strips of paper, was the day I knew we could do anything together. That old house may have been charming, but we soon discovered that its walls were far from straight. When we got to the last corner of the room, we looked at each other in disbelief.

"How can there be six more inches on the bottom than the top?" I asked incredulously.

"Let's just pretend we don't notice the difference," Ralph said, and laughed as he overlapped the last strip of paper onto the wall.

I named the shop "Alouette," the French word for lark, a bird noted for its singing and the name of a popular French children's song I learned in school. Having spent my junior year of college in Paris, I was fond of French words, but I also liked the idea of a free-spirited, adventuresome bird that flitted around enjoying life. And that's how I felt about my life with Ralph; I had never imagined I could feel so fulfilled in so many ways.

On opening day for Alouette, Ralph took off work to support our new manager and make sure everything went smoothly. I arrived later that afternoon.

"Everyone loves the shop," our manager said excitedly. "You can't believe the compliments we heard about the house and the displays, and, of course, the beautiful antiques."

"Yeah, everyone was talking about how they couldn't wait to bring their friends and out-of-town guests here," Ralph said, equally enthusiastic.

"And sales were pretty good, thanks mostly to Ralph," the manager said. "You should have heard how he talked about how rare an antique was, when anyone showed interest in a particular item."

Putting my arms around Ralph, I didn't think I could feel happier or more in love. "Thank you, sweetheart," I said. "Mom may have been right about a lot of things, but she was wrong when she said I would never find a man who would tolerate my obsession with antiques. You've helped me build a business around my passion. How lucky can any girl be?"

We eventually would have two claims to fame: For her movie *A League of Their Own*, Penny Marshall directed her wardrobe assistant to purchase some vintage clothing from our shop. We also won a much-coveted award in the village's Fourth of July parade. Ralph and I, along with our employees, dressed in old-fashioned clothes and posed in multiple vignettes on a large hay wagon that showcased our furniture and antiques. I will never forget how Ralph smiled proudly, in his top hat, suspenders, and ruffled armband, when he accepted our prize.

After Alouette had been open for about a year and was functioning smoothly, Ralph and I took the opportunity to visit my parents who were now living full-time in Venice, Florida. I lifted my face to soak in the sunshine as Ralph and I walked hand in hand from the Florida airport to my parents' car.

"I wish you two would move down here," my father said. "We could start a business together…maybe open up a dog kennel."

Later that day my dad and I went crabbing in a small inlet by the ocean. As a child, I loved to fish in the river behind our house. I would sit on a rock and watch the river flow by, escaping from the tension I always felt at home into nature's calm embrace, not realizing at the time that I was doing a form of meditation.

I felt the same kind of peace when I went crabbing, and I was especially glad to spend some tranquil time with my dad for a change; he was contentious by nature and often provoked me. We sat quietly together, listening to the early evening sounds of nature—the frogs croaking, the cicadas singing, and the cranes calling to one another. My dad didn't seem as if he was trying very hard to catch a crab. His eyes were focused on my line, ready with a net, should I bring a crab close to shore. "Do you really think Ralph is all right?" he asked, breaking the silence.

"I don't know, Dad. He seems to be doing better than before his last surgery, but I'm always worried about him."

"What do the doctors say about his future?"

"They mostly say the disease has no known cause and no known cure. I don't think they know what to expect," I said, as I felt a little tug on my line. I had attached a chicken leg to a long piece of string. Most likely a crab had grabbed the bait with its claws and was trying to drag it away. Very slowly, I started drawing the string into shore, placing one hand over the other as I pulled the bait and crab toward me. Whenever I felt the line slacken, I immediately stopped pulling and waited for the crab to firmly grab the bait again. After about five minutes of slowly leading the crab ashore, my dad leaned over with his net, scooped up a medium-sized blue crab, and placed it into the bucket beside us.

"We need to catch a lot more crabs if we're going to have enough for hors d'oeuvres tonight," he remarked, looking at the one lonely crab in the bucket.

We stayed until dusk, catching five more crabs. The slow, tedious process of crabbing was a refreshing respite from my fast-paced life in the business world.

When we returned to my parents' home, Ralph was lying on a couch, watching television. Leaning over to give him a kiss, I noticed that his forehead seemed unusually warm.

"How are you feeling?" I asked. "You seem a little warm to me."

"Pretty good. My back is just bothering me a little bit."

Ralph's back continued to bother him all week, to the point that he rested on the couch, watching television most of the time. He did his best to act upbeat and insisted that only his back bothered him, although previously staying off his feet usually cured his back problems within a few days. So, even though I was concerned about Ralph's lethargy, Mom and I kept busy, walking on the beach, swimming, bicycling, and shopping. All in all, it was a pleasant week, although I was concerned about Ralph and wished he could have joined us in more activities.

Ralph didn't eat or drink anything during the flight home. "Are you sure you're all right?" I asked him.

"No, I'm not sure," he finally admitted. "I feel so strange, different than I have ever felt before. Other than the pain in my back, I don't have much discomfort, but I'm not sure I could walk a block if I had to…I feel so tired. I'm afraid I should see Dr. Williams."

It was a cold, sub-zero day with a dampness that hung in the air and penetrated our bodies, as we walked to our car after the plane landed at O'Hare airport. The sky was a mantle of grey, the kind of cloud cover that usually lasted all day with little chance of sunshine. Such a drastic change in climate from the sunny warmth of Florida to the dull winter weather of the Midwest always depressed me on these trips.

The weather and worry about Ralph's health weighed heavily on both of us as we drove to Dr. William's office the following morning. After the doctor examined him, Ralph sat in a chair next to me while the doctor wrote some notes.

"I think your backache is actually a result of your intestinal problems," Dr. Williams said, "so I'm not too concerned about your back. I am, however, very concerned about your temperature. Do you know that your temperature is 103 degrees? No wonder you look like you're sunburned and you're feeling so tired. Although I can't be sure, I'm afraid the fever is related to an infection in your intestine. I know you won't like to hear this, Ralph, but I think you should be admitted to the hospital immediately."

"I don't feel that bad," Ralph protested, seeming shocked at Dr. Williams' suggestion.

"I'm not saying you need surgery, but I do think it would be wise to put you on strong doses of anti-inflammatory drugs and antibiotics. You also appear to be dehydrated from the fever. You'll get better much more quickly if we put you on an IV in the hospital. I don't think you'll be in the hospital long."

Reluctantly, Ralph agreed to be admitted to the hospital.

"It may take hours before the paperwork is completed and I'm actually in my room," Ralph said to me. "Why don't you leave and get the puppies before the kennel closes? I'll be fine."

"Okay," I acquiesced, giving him a kiss. I didn't say anything to Ralph, but I planned to come back to the hospital that evening.

It had snowed lightly during the brief time I had been in the hospital, and as I drove down the winding road from the hospital, my car skidded and hit the side of a curb. I got my car safely back on the road, and then a few miles later, while driving down a nearly deserted road in the countryside, the car started shaking. I pulled over to the side of the road and stepped out of the car. Just as I suspected; the left front tire was almost flat.

The wind stung my sunburned face, as it raced over the cornfields and blew snow across the road in front of me. Looking at my watch, I knew I had only an hour before the kennel closed. Fortunately, it wasn't long before a former neighbor recognized my car and stopped. After we talked about Ralph's health problems for a few minutes, he offered to change the tire.

What is he doing? I wondered, after more than fifteen minutes went by. I stepped out of the car to see what was going on; my feet hurt from sitting in the cold.

"I can't get this one bolt unscrewed," he said, as the wind howled around us.

"Please, just go get some help!" I begged.

"No, I can do this," he said, trying without success for another half hour.

It was dark by the time a tow truck arrived to haul my car to a gas station. While I huddled on a chair inside the garage to wait for my car to be fixed, my feet really began to hurt as they thawed, and I took off my shoes to rub them.

An elderly man walked over to where I sat. "Is there anything I can do for you?" he asked.

I burst into tears, and the startled man took a few steps back. I didn't cry often, but when I did, I cried for a long time, unable to stop. The strain from Ralph's sickness that week, the tense plane-ride home, the hospitalization, the flat tire, the painful cold—it was overwhelming.

"Can I get you some hot chocolate or tea?" the man asked.

"No, but thank you for your kindness," I stammered and continued to cry. As the man walked away, I wanted to scream at no one in particular that there were a lot of things I needed—most of all, a healthy husband and everything back to the way it used to be.

Since it was too late to pick up the puppies, I drove home after the tire was fixed. I don't remember ever feeling as lonely as I did that night when I walked into our dark house, which seemed so quiet without Ralph and the puppies. I continued to cry as I unpacked our suitcases and then packed another one to take to Ralph at the hospital. Deciding not to go to the hospital that night, mostly because I didn't want Ralph to see how upset I was, I called the hospital and was connected to his room.

"Hi, Donna-Girl," Ralph said, as he answered the phone, sounding like his usual, cheerful self. "I hope you're not thinking about coming to see me tonight because it looks like it's snowing outside. How are the babies?"

"I actually couldn't get them tonight because I didn't make it to the kennel before it closed," I answered, fighting back tears. I knew Ralph was waiting for an explanation, but in my present state of mind, there was no way I could explain what had happened without crying.

"Are you feeling any better?" I asked, quickly changing the subject.

"Are you sure you're all right?" he asked, obviously not falling for my diversionary tactic.

Sometimes I wondered why I bothered to talk to him out loud, since he seemed to read my mind, or intuit my body language, or listen to the tone of my voice rather than the words I spoke. He knew me so well.

"You don't have to come to the hospital tomorrow morning either. There's nothing I really need. I love you, sweetheart. Don't worry; everything will be fine."

As I hung up the phone, I wondered how I could ever live without him, if I hated being without him for one night. Although it was only eight o'clock, I decided to go to bed and get a good night's sleep, dreading going back to work after a week's vacation.

Usually I fell asleep quickly, but I started thinking about the fact Ralph might actually die from his disease. Although I didn't feel a sense of panic, because I didn't think his death was imminent, I did feel frightened at the thought of how lonely I would be if he died. It was almost impossible for me to even think about living without him. What purpose would I have to live for? I would have nothing but the puppies.

I wondered if we had given up too soon when we tried having children. When I failed to become pregnant after being married for a few years, Ralph was tested and had been diagnosed with low sperm motility, which was probably due to all the steroids and drugs he had taken over the years, along with his system's inability to absorb nutrients. Infertility treatment was on the verge of becoming mainstreamed, but it was still fairly uncommon at the time. We decided to give it a try.

I will never forget my first procedure, which was performed by a doctor to ensure that my fallopian tubes were open. Ralph was waiting for me in the clinic's waiting room.

"It will feel like medium to severe menstrual cramps," the doctor had told me.

Well, that shouldn't be too bad, I thought. I've always had rather severe period cramps, so that's nothing new.

But then, as soon as the doctor started the procedure, I felt the worst pain I had ever felt. I started screaming. The doctor didn't stop the procedure, and I didn't stop screaming. Fortunately, the procedure lasted only a few minutes.

When I followed the doctor out to the waiting room on unsteady legs, Ralph was standing at the door.

"We will never go through this again," he said vehemently. "Do you hear me? I can live without having children, but I can't bear the thought of you going through that pain again," he added in a firm voice.

It had not occurred to me during the procedure that Ralph could hear my screams.

"Her tubes must have been blocked," the doctor said to him, "but I'm sure this procedure opened them up."

Ralph, who was always the epitome of civility, didn't acknowledge the doctor. He took my arm and firmly guided me toward the door.

"It didn't last that long," I said.

"Never again. I'm serious," Ralph said. "I don't ever want you to go through anything like that again."

To make matters worse, I developed a pelvic infection after one attempt at artificial insemination and became ill with a high fever for several days.

When I went to see another fertility specialist on my own, he gave me low odds for a pregnancy. At the time, I thought perhaps we weren't meant to have children, even though I felt that Ralph would have been a wonderful father. We discussed adoption, but Ralph wasn't too enthusiastic about the idea because his favorite aunt had had many problems with her adopted sons.

As I lay in bed that night, my mind tumbled back and forth between the thought of Ralph dying, our childlessness, and having to return to work the next day. Feeling too agitated to go to sleep, I turned on the light, got out of bed, and went downstairs to the kitchen where I started pulling boxes and cans of food out of a cupboard. Activity, especially any kind of physical activity, always seemed to help me feel better when I was deeply troubled. After cleaning three cupboards, I went back to bed and fell asleep.

Although Ralph stayed in the hospital for nearly a week, nothing significant was found as a result of the many tests the doctors ordered, other than confirming Dr. Williams' suspicion of an infection. I tried to think positively about our future, but subconsciously I must have been terrified because, while Ralph spent more and more time resting in his favorite recliner chair in front of the television in the living room when he wasn't working, I became busier than ever.

Not long after Ralph's hospitalization, the wife of a close friend of his was killed in a car accident. While Ralph spent a great deal of time on the phone, consoling his friend, the young woman's death caused me to focus on how tenuous life is, whether a person is healthy or sick. Ralph was used to living day by day ever since he had been given two years to live many years ago, but it was a new experience for me. I was convinced I could handle anything as long as Ralph was well and happy; at the same time, I believed more than ever that I couldn't endure living without him.

What happens to us after we die was a total mystery to me. I had attended Catholic schools from grade school through graduate school, but I had not been in a church for a long time. Although I missed the closeness I had felt with God as a child, I had become disenchanted by what I perceived to be the superficiality of the church's teaching, the hell and damnation sermons, and the preaching that only Catholics could be saved. So where did that leave my father who refused to go to church? I wondered.

Ralph had been raised as a Lutheran but no longer went to church either. So, when challenging things happened, like Ralph's surgery or the death of his friend's wife, we had no religion to turn to for support. Whenever I became extremely troubled, however, I noticed that I always reverted to asking God for help.

Ralph's surgery, the fire in our antique store, the death of his friend's wife, and his recent hospitalization left me feeling vulnerable and on edge. Life now seemed so unpredictable. I wanted things to be like they were when we were first married. At some level, I think I actually believed in (or wanted to believe in) the "happily ever after" promise of fairy tales.

FOUR

"You're lucky you have your antique business," Lana, one of my coworkers, said over lunch one day. Lana and I were two of the highest-ranking women in our company and shared many things in common. We wore our blonde hair in a medium-length bob, dressed for work in the business pantsuit of the day, loved to shop, and enjoyed talking to each other over a glass of wine about a myriad of topics.

"Actually, I think it's about doing something together with Ralph. It's something special we've created together. I can't tell you the number of nights we sit in front of the fireplace, while Ralph researches his expanding library on antiques to find the items I've purchased, and then I label them."

"Well, I've been thinking about starting a spa business. Doesn't that sound like fun? Would you ever consider going into business with me?"

"Are you kidding? I'd love to do that. Now that the antique business is established, I have extra time on my hands. You know Ralph doesn't have much energy left when he comes home from work. Of course, I'm at the opposite end of the spectrum…I have loads of energy, even though I often think it's nervous energy. I have to keep myself busy. Otherwise, I start worrying about when his next attack will happen."

"Is he getting worse?"

"It's hard to tell. I'm not even sure he tells me about all the attacks he has at work. I only hear about them if he gets home later than usual. He knows I worry about him all the time. Once an attack is over, he quickly recovers and has an unbelievably positive attitude, acting like nothing ever happened and he hasn't a worry in the world."

"Do you think he would mind if we went into business together?"

"I'll ask him."

"I think a spa is a great idea," Ralph said, when I talked to him about it that evening. "I'd be happy to do the computer software for the business, and I offer my body for screening potential massage therapists," he said, bowing from his waist with a smile.

"I'm sure Lana and I will consider your offer," I said, with mock seriousness.

After three months of hard work, we realized our vision—our day spa, Body & Soul, was an oasis of peace, calm, and understated elegance. The rooms were ideally sized for our needs as the two-story building, which was built in the late 1800s, had originally been a doctor's office; the large reception area was a perfect space for creating a nurturing environment, and the small, former examining rooms would help a customer feel cocooned. Lana and I had done most of the decorating work ourselves, while Ralph, who had worked his way through college as an electrician, did the electrical work, and Lana's husband, Keith, helped us, too.

Although the name Body & Soul became a common one in later years, it was innovative at the time. Also, unique at the time was that we catered to men as well as women by emphasizing sports massages and basic pedicures, even hiring a man who used to be the masseur of a Russian fencing team.

Another great advantage was the location of the day spa, as it was at the opposite end of the block from my antique shop. This would enable us to have joint marketing and open house events with things such as luminaries extending from one shop to the other.

On opening day, Lana and I sat in our large reception room, which we were particularly proud of. Touches of gold sparkled throughout the mostly off-white and beige décor, while a softly tinkling waterfall and a glowing gas fireplace added to the ambience.

"I think you girls really did it," Keith said, raising his glass in a champagne toast.

"Here's to the two of you," Ralph chimed in. "Now, what's next on the agenda?"

We all laughed, knowing we had overextended ourselves financially and physically with this project. It was nice to know, however, that our husbands supported us and gave us credit for what we had accomplished.

The success of Body & Soul was short-lived. After the first year, we started losing money because of the peaks and valleys in the business and the high costs of rent, insurance, and wages.

"It might be different if one of us could be here to oversee the business," Lana said, "but we need to keep our regular jobs to pay for the spa business. The one thing we have, unlike most people, is the tenacity to never give up," Lana added, as if that was a totally positive trait.

As revenue was falling short at Body & Soul, sales at Alouette were suffering as well. Unfortunately, both businesses were in luxury categories, not businesses of necessity such as food and medicine.

In spite of my financial concerns about our two businesses, Ralph and I had promised my parents a trip to Europe, and I especially didn't want to disappoint Mom. Even Dad, who didn't get excited about most things, seemed to be looking forward to the trip. Fortunately, I worked for an airline and our airfare costs were minimal. Our plan was to fly to Amsterdam, then rent a car to tour Switzerland, and eventually drive to Paris.

Our trip didn't start out well. Fifteen minutes before the plane landed in Amsterdam, Ralph took off his seat belt and went into the restroom. Shortly afterward, the seat belt sign came on in preparation for landing.

"Everyone must be in their seats," a flight attendant said in a snarky tone as she stood beside me and looked at Ralph's empty seat.

"He's sick," I told her. "I'm sure he'll come back to his seat as soon as he can."

I hated to think of Ralph with his tall frame in the plane's small restroom. My stomach hurt, and I could feel tightness around my chest, as I was having trouble breathing normally. Just thinking about how sick he must feel made me want to cry. I glanced at my parents, sitting across the aisle; they looked upset and tense, too.

It wasn't until after the plane had landed and taxied to the gate that Ralph came out of the restroom. His tie was loosened, and he looked gray and weak.

We waited until everyone else had left the plane. "I'm okay; let's go," he finally said. We slowly walked to the baggage area; our highly anticipatory moods had vanished.

As we were driving from the airport to our downtown hotel in a taxi, Ralph asked the driver to pull over to the side of the road.

I glanced to the side of the taxi where I saw Ralph throwing up.

"Is he going to be all right?" my mother asked anxiously.

"This happens a lot," I said to my parents, who both looked as nervous and anxious as I felt. "The attack will only subside when he has nothing left in his stomach."

The sound of Ralph throwing up became louder as we sat in silence with the taxi driver.

After a few minutes we were able to resume the taxi ride and were soon checked into our hotel. Ralph laid down to rest. Although I tried to relax, too, I felt more uncomfortable and worried than usual because we were in a strange country and far away from our regular doctors.

About an hour later, Ralph was leaning over me smiling. "How are you doing, Donna-Girl?" he asked. "So, we're really in Amsterdam, huh? Why don't you call your parents and ask if they want to go out and see some sights?"

"Honey, I can never get over how sick you can be one minute and then seem fine the next."

"I know, but once an attack is over, I feel so much better."

"If it were me, I know I would be anxious about when the next attack would happen."

"I think I've learned to enjoy any time I'm feeling well. Anyway, there's very little I can do to stop an attack except to not eat much at any one time. I used to keep track of every little thing I put in my mouth, but after years of failing to find any correlation between certain foods and the attacks, I just gave up because it doesn't seem to make any difference what I eat or what I do."

"I just don't think I could help myself from feeling depressed and worried about when the next attack would happen."

"Honey, ever since I was given only two years to live and it looked as if I might not make it even that long, every day is a blessing. I don't want to waste precious time on feeling badly. C'mon! Let's get going and meet your parents."

He rarely referred to that death sentence he had been given many years ago, and I certainly didn't encourage him to talk about it.

Ralph was careful to eat only small amounts of food for the rest of the trip, but other than that he seemed to feel all right. After going to museums in Amsterdam, staying in a charming hotel in Basel, Switzerland, which had its own mineral pool of healing waters, and finally ending up in my most favorite city of all—Paris—we headed home. In spite of the good food and pleasant accommodations, however, I never totally relaxed for fear Ralph would become sick again.

Our lives over the next several years were much like that vacation in Europe, where Ralph would become violently ill and then quickly recover and feel fairly well. Over time, I became constantly anxious, always on the alert for the next attack in the middle of the night or a call from Ralph saying he would be late getting home because he couldn't drive. I began to feel our life consisted of a series of roller coaster rides.

Eventually, Ralph's attacks became more frequent, until it was not uncommon for him to have several attacks each week.

One evening after he had had a particularly severe experience, I said to Ralph, "I feel so helpless during your attacks."

"I know you do, honey, but there is nothing you can do. Just knowing that you will be there for me when it's over is all I need. You have given me everything I ever wanted in life. But lately, I've been thinking that I want to help others who have been less fortunate than me."

"You've said that before. Do you have any idea exactly what you want to do?"

"Actually, I've been talking to a newly ordained minister named Anne who has been asking for support from my company to help establish a center for victims of abuse and recovering addicts. I'd like to help her by doing the computer software for the business and some fundraising. She's also asked me to become a member of the Board of Directors. I feel like this is something I have to do. Perhaps, if my father had had a place to go when he was on a drinking binge, or my mother had had a place to take us away from him when he got abusive, things might not have been so bad for my sister and me."

Ralph's father had continued to be a heavy drinker. No matter how many times he was taken to the hospital for treatment or attended Alcohol Anonymous (AA) meetings, he went on drinking binges. When drinking, he was verbally abusive and broke many commitments. I knew that Ralph had been disappointed countless times and could understand why establishing this center was so important to him.

Ralph began devoting several nights a week to the clinic, often getting home late at night and looking exhausted.

"Ralph, please don't do this to yourself," I begged him. "I know you want to help, but can't someone else do some of the work you do?"

"Donna-Girl, I've told you I have to do this."

"I know, honey, but not at the cost of your health. Please, please don't work so late."

"It's only for a few more months," Ralph said firmly.

When the center opened, it was immediately successful in that many women and men took advantage of the classes and the counseling services offered.

"Helping with the center is the best thing I've ever done," Ralph said, as we ate dinner together one night.

I was pleased that Ralph felt so good about their accomplishment and relieved that his intensive work effort was over.

FIVE

"Ralph, you know we have to see Dr. Williams again," I said, as we lay in bed on our first night home after a week's vacation in Hawaii—a vacation I had hoped would give Ralph some much needed rest. But unfortunately, he had spent most of the trip resting on a lounge chair or throwing up in the bathroom. "You can't go on like this. Your attacks are happening so frequently now."

"I know, honey, but it seems so futile to keep seeing doctors. I'm still hearing that few people live beyond fifty years old with cases as severe as mine, and the chances of me having a colostomy bag will be very high if I have surgery again." Ralph now worked for a company that made medical equipment, and many of the salespeople, who were former nurses, kept him abreast of any news about his disease.

Although I had heard this comment before about the survival expectancy of people with severe cases of Crohn's, it had much more meaning to me now that Ralph was approaching fifty. For the most part, I had chosen to ignore that prognosis, but hearing Ralph refer to it again made me shudder. I shivered under our blanket.

"What about exploring alternative therapies?" I asked. "I've read about people who have experienced sudden healing or gone into remission through alternative treatments. In fact, my assistant's mother believes she was inexplicably cured of throat cancer through an unorthodox treatment."

"I hate to be a skeptic, but how does someone know which treatments actually work? Also, if these alternatives really are effective, don't you think more people would know about them?"

"I share your skepticism, Ralph, but your quality of life has deteriorated so much that we need to do something. Why don't we ask Dr. Williams if he has any suggestions about where we can go for help? Mexico, China, the Philippines—we could go anywhere."

"I don't know. I hate the thought of traveling all over the world and not knowing what we're getting into. It just seems so hopeless."

He didn't sound like the man I knew. Giving up was not like him, though I could certainly understand how being sick and in pain so often had worn him down.

"Let's just talk to Dr. Williams about it. We don't have to do anything."

"Okay, go ahead and schedule an appointment, but I'm not agreeing to anything yet."

A week later, Dr. Williams entered the examining room with his usual calm demeanor and welcoming smile, but his smile quickly faded when he looked at Ralph.

"You look like you've lost more weight," he said.

"Just a few pounds," Ralph responded, minimizing his weight loss.

"Ralph is getting much worse," I said, jumping into the conversation. "He has terrible attacks several times a week, and then he can't eat. That's why he's losing so much weight. I've been reading about alternative medicine."

"Ralph, let me examine you, and then we can talk about alternatives," Dr. Williams said, acknowledging my suggestion.

I stayed in the room as Dr. Williams performed the examination.

After the exam was completed and Ralph had finished dressing, Dr. Williams turned toward us with tears in his eyes. "You know I will support you and help you in any way I can. I know there are instances when people are inexplicably cured when they seek alternative therapies. And I know how much you need help. I don't know anyone else who has suffered for as many years with the kind of pain that you have had, Ralph. However, for the most part, the medical profession simply doesn't understand alternative medicine."

Ralph didn't seem surprised when he heard the doctor talk about his pain, but I was shocked. I knew Ralph had been in a lot of pain over the years, but to learn that Dr. Williams considered it worse than what any of his other patients had experienced disturbed me.

"I can put you in contact with practitioners performing alternative therapies," Dr. Williams continued. "First I would like you to consider seeing the man who originally identified Crohn's disease. He is eighty-four years old, but still does consulting for a major university hospital. From my brief examination, I think your disease is very active again. I suspect you have quite a bit of damage," he added solemnly.

As we drove home in silence after our appointment with Dr. Williams, I kept thinking about the doctor's words about Ralph's pain and remembering the tears in his eyes. When I glanced over at Ralph, who was driving, I imagined that he was probably thinking about the ordeals facing him, whether he had surgery or not.

Finally, I broke the silence. "We'll make it through this, Ralph; we have to."

"I know we will, Donna-Girl. It'll be fine."

I knew that Ralph was trying to make me feel better. He always said everything would be fine, and I always believed him, because I couldn't bear to think of things any other way.

When we arrived at the university hospital to meet the doctor who had discovered Crohn's disease, a receptionist ushered us into a large conference room with a long table and blank screens covering two walls. Five doctors were seated at the table—at least, I assumed they were doctors since they all wore white coats.

The elderly doctor whom Dr. Williams had told us about stood up to greet us. He looked much younger than his age and had a warm, inviting smile like Dr. Williams. Then he introduced the other four men: two were gastrointestinal specialists, one doctor was a surgeon, and the other was an intern.

The atmosphere in the room was solemn as we took our seats.

"We have the x-rays here that were taken earlier this week," the elderly doctor said and then motioned to the intern to illuminate the x-rays on the screen.

One entire wall lit up with pictures of Ralph's intestine. "As you can see, there are many blockages," the doctor said, using a pointer to indicate the affected areas. "Here, we have a place where your intestine was blocked and has rerouted itself," he said, pointing to a specific area on the screen. "It's amazing what the human body will do to try to correct itself, but there really is no choice. You must have surgery. It's only a matter of time before you will not be able to keep food down at all."

"What are the chances the surgery will be successful?" I asked the group of doctors.

"The surgeon looked at me calmly and responded. "I would say your husband has a good chance of coming through surgery, and I would give the operation a fifty-fifty chance of being successful. Our team of doctors is excellent; it will be a long surgery that will require several experienced surgeons. Of course, we would do a series of tests before we operate."

Fifty-fifty! How could he sit there calmly and say fifty-fifty? I wanted to scream. I kept quiet, however, and tried not to show any expression on my face, just as I had learned to do in business meetings. I didn't want to embarrass Ralph.

"Well, we'll need to discuss this," Ralph told the group of doctors, "but I suspect we will decide to go ahead with the surgery."

"You will be in the best of hands," the elderly doctor said, as he showed us to the door. "Although I am too old to operate, I will personally be there to oversee your surgery. We're learning new things every day about the disease, so don't give up hope. In fact, after the surgery, I'd like to recommend an experimental drug that has been showing some promise.

We can talk about that later."

"What do you think, honey?" Ralph asked, as we drove home from the university hospital.

"It's really up to you," I replied. "Although I don't like the odds, we don't know how successful alternative medicine might be either."

"I'm leaning toward giving it a try," Ralph said. "Fifty-fifty is not so bad, considering I was given only two years to live many years ago."

"Let's go ahead then," I said, trying to give him the support I thought he needed. I found it hard to understand how he could be so calm.

The soonest he could be scheduled for the surgery was in six weeks.

"This empowerment class I'm supposed to take for the next two weeks sounds really interesting," Ralph said, when he came home from work one night. "During the introduction to the course today, a woman who took the class last year spoke to us about her experience. She had cancer and believes she went into remission because of practicing the principles taught in the class. Even though she had undergone traditional cancer treatment, she believes that her positive thinking played a major role in her recovery."

"What did the doctors say about her going into remission?"

"I guess the doctors were surprised and didn't know what to make of it. They thought her traditional medical treatment might have slowed the growth of her cancer but not eliminate it all together."

"That's the kind of thing I was talking about with alternative therapies—miracles like that."

Before I knew it, I was packing suitcases for the hospital.

"Don't forget to pack my tape recorder and the tapes I received from the class," Ralph said, as I packed his bag. "I want you to play the tapes when I come out of surgery. Even if you think I'm sleeping, keep changing the tapes and play them in order. The tapes are numbered from one to ten."

"I promise I will do that," I assured him. We had requested a private room at the hospital so the sound of the tapes wouldn't disturb another patient.

When the time came for us to leave for the hospital, Ralph bent down to say good-bye to our youngest dog, Cupcake, who had been diagnosed six months earlier with an advanced case of cancer. We had taken her to the veterinarian when we noticed the first tumor on her belly. Sadly, the doctor told us she was beyond the stage where surgery, radiation, or chemotherapy would help. During the past several months, we had watched as tumor after tumor grew on her body. Cupcake had a special place in Ralph's heart ever since he first found her curled up inside an empty pork-and-bean can when she was just a few weeks old. He nursed her back to health like a baby.

"You be a good girl, sweetheart," Ralph told the dog as tears rolled down his face. "I'm counting on you to be here when I get back."

Ralph and I were both crying when we left Cupcake and our two other dogs in their pen.

When we walked into the hospital, it felt like yesterday that Ralph had had his last surgery, not ten years ago. The subdued noises, the solemn looks on visitors' faces, and the medicinal odors assaulted my senses. Suddenly, I remembered the young man who had died in the room next to Ralph's. Then, in spite of my resistance again, Ralph signed a form, indicating he did not want to be kept alive on life support systems or to be resuscitated.

That night, before his surgery the following morning, we listened to Ralph's tapes for several hours.

"I just know you're going to be fine," I told him, although I felt very uneasy.

"I think so, too, Donna-Girl. I'm not afraid, and I have a very good feeling about this surgery. Remember, keep the tapes playing when I get back to the room."

I lay on a cot next to Ralph's bed that night, but hardly slept.

Early the next morning, when the staff wheeled him on a gurney to the operating room, I didn't make it as far down the hall as I did for his last surgery before I began crying out loud. I was so overwhelmed with emotion that I couldn't talk, as Ralph lifted his head off the gurney, smiled at me, and said "I love you", before the doors to the operating room closed.

Having slept so little the night before and expecting Ralph to be in surgery for a long time, I decided to go back to his room to rest for a while, since he was expected to be in surgery for at least four hours. Just lying on the rumpled sheets and pillows where he had slept the night before comforted me.

I must have fallen asleep. Several hours later, a nurse in scrub clothes came into the room and woke me up. I looked at the clock and was surprised several hours had passed. She was called a coordinating nurse whose job included keeping the patient's family informed during surgery through interim reports.

"He's doing remarkably well," she said. "His heart rate and all his vital signs are perfect, but the doctors think the operation will take much longer than they originally thought. It will be at least another five or six hours before he's taken to the recovery room."

"Why is that?" I asked, wondering if doctors always underestimated the length of their operations.

"They have found more diseased places than they expected to see. The doctors will be able to explain everything to you when the surgery is completed. I'll find you and give you another update in a couple of hours."

Her update frightened me. I walked over to the waiting room and sat there for the next six hours, with my heart pounding and my fists clenched, almost afraid to move or breathe. The next update from the nurse was similar to her first report in that Ralph was doing well. Finally, about seven that evening, one of the weary-looking surgeons came to talk to me.

"Your husband is being taken to the recovery room right now," he said. "Everything went well, but we performed a new procedure after we saw how extensive the damage was in his intestines. Normally, we would have cut out the entire diseased section with only two cuts at each end. But in your husband's case, this would have meant taking out most of his intestine. So, we removed many smaller pieces of the diseased tissue, which required us to cut and stitch his intestine in sixteen places. This means that more of his intestine remains, but it also means there are sixteen places that could become infected or not hold together. Just one break at any of the juncture points could be fatal. We will watch him very carefully over the next few days."

What the doctor had said made sense to me. I believed he was doing his best to prolong Ralph's life. What I didn't know, however, until many years later, was that not only was the surgery experimental, it was the first surgery of its kind.

On the second day after his surgery, Ralph developed a fever. Based on what the doctor had said, I assumed it was caused by an infection. Naturally, I was worried, though I tried to conceal it from Ralph while I sat there with him.

"Don't worry, Donna-Girl. I'm going to be fine," Ralph said, seemingly unconcerned. "Go home and take care of the puppies. Cupcake needs you more than I do right now."

Even though the doctors had talked with us about the possibility of a second surgery, Ralph seemed unworried. I sensed no crabbiness or irritability in him after this surgery, unlike what I had experienced the previous time. In fact, he kept the nurses smiling and amused with jokes.

The next day, Ralph's fever subsided almost as quickly as it had started.

"The real test will come when he begins to eat," the head surgeon said. "If the stitches hold together while food passes through his system, the surgery will be considered successful."

Everyone but Ralph seemed to be anxious about what would happen when he started eating. Five days later, he began drinking liquids, and then shortly afterward, he started eating solids. Much to the doctors' amazement, he recovered so quickly that he was released from the hospital eight days after the surgery.

As with his last surgery, Ralph's three childhood buddies had driven many miles and were waiting to see him when he got home.

"I'll go out and get the puppies from their pen," I said, after his friends had all given him a bear hug.

"No," Ralph said. "I'll go out and get them."

"But you're not supposed to be walking too much," I reminded him.

"It's okay. I'll be right back. Maybe you could get something for the guys to drink."

I decided not to argue with him; he seemed so happy, and it really wasn't that far to the puppies' pen.

A few minutes later, Ralph walked back into the house, carrying Cupcake in his arms. I was just about to scold him for lifting her so soon after his surgery, when I saw the tears in his eyes and the solemn look on his face as he walked through the back door.

"She died in my arms almost immediately after I picked her up," he said, gently laying her down on the floor. His friends walked out from the family room to see what was happening when they heard us talking.

"I really think she waited for me to come home before she died. She must have been in a lot of pain," he said, as tears streamed down his face. "Can you guys give me a hand burying her out back? I dug a hole for her several months ago. Donna, can you get a blanket to wrap her in?" he asked, turning toward me.

I found a blanket and handed it to Ralph. Feeling numb, I watched as he wrapped her snugly in the blanket, and then carefully raised her in his arms and held her against his chest. While the four men took Cupcake to the back of our property to bury her, I climbed the stairs to our bedroom and began slowly unpacking Ralph's suitcase from the hospital. After I finished, I sat down on our bed and wept—tears of relief that Ralph had made it through surgery and tears of sadness for Cupcake.

SIX

Sometimes, I felt as if Ralph had recovered from his surgery better than I had. I felt tired and tense most of the time now, whether it was from worrying about Ralph's health, working long hours at my corporate job with the airline, making sure Alouette had enough quality antiques for sale, or spending time with Lana, trying to figure out how to increase revenue at Body & Soul.

"I think you need a vacation, Donna-Girl," Ralph said one night. "How about spending a week in Kona, Hawaii? I know that's your favorite place, and I'll make all the plans."

The minute we stepped off the plane, I felt my body relax. That's the effect Hawaii always had on me—almost as if I had taken a tranquilizer. After we arrived at the resort where we would be staying, which was fashioned after the Hawaiian open-air tradition, we put on our bathing suits and walked down to the beach. Feeling exhausted from the long trip, I spread a towel on the sand and lay down on my stomach. The warm sun caressed my body, as I watched Ralph walk alongside the ocean in search of seashells. Before long, I drifted off to sleep.

I awoke to a sensation that felt as if a feather or a butterfly was fluttering on my neck. I moved my head from side to side to chase away whatever was tickling me, so I could get back to sleep, but the fluttering continued—this time, it moved up my body from my ankles to my neck. Finally, I opened my eyes to see what was causing the sensation and looked up.

Ralph was sitting down next to me smiling, and I realized he had been the one tickling me. "You better cover up, Donna-Girl, before you get sunburned," he said. "Let's go in and take a short nap before the sun sets." When he leaned over and gently kissed my lips, I knew we would be doing more than taking a nap."

As he caressed my body, his lovemaking reminded me of the first time we had made love. Just like the first time, he slipped inside me with seemingly no effort at all, and a loving, peaceful feeling spread throughout my body, making me feel whole and complete, as if I had returned home once again to the most comfortable place in the world. I drifted off to sleep in Ralph's arms.

A little while later, I awoke to Ralph's fingertips gently massaging my body. "Wake up, sweetheart. We don't want to miss the sunset," Ralph said, giving me a gentle tap on my bottom.

We sat on the lounge chairs on our balcony, holding hands and watching the sun make its final descent over the ocean, spreading its red and orange hues over the water.

"I always hate to see the sun disappear," I said. "It makes me sad, even though it's beautiful. It's like having to say good-bye to a friend."

"Well, I have some good news to share with you, Donna-Girl," Ralph said in a quiet voice, and then paused a moment to be sure I was listening. "I think I'm in remission."

"What!" I exclaimed, turning my head sharply to look at him. "How do you know?"

"I just know," he said calmly with conviction. "I've actually thought so for a while, but I didn't want to say anything to you until I talked to the doctors. When I had my appointment the other day, the doctor agreed with me. To confirm his opinion, he even talked with the Crohn's expert we consulted before my last surgery. They both agree that my disease was so active before my surgery that I would have had symptoms by now if I weren't in remission. It's funny, because they didn't want to say anything to me until I told them myself that I thought I was in remission."

"Oh, my God!" I exclaimed, jumping up from my chair and throwing my arms around him. "I can't believe it! What wonderful news! How could you wait this long to tell me?"

"It was hard, but since it's only been a few days since I saw the doctors, I figured I could wait and tell you at a special moment. But I couldn't wait any longer; I can't believe it either. It's now been almost twenty-five years since they gave me two years to live."

"I'm so happy for you—for us!" I exclaimed, hugging him and kissing him all over his face. "Do you think you went into remission because of the experimental drug?" I asked, but then suddenly remembered the positive-thinking class he had taken and the tapes he had listened to.

"I'm not sure. It's possible, because some other patients taking the drug have gone into remission as well."

"But, you think it might have been the class, don't you?"

"Honestly, I don't know…and I'll probably never know. Maybe, it was a combination of the drug and my attitude. All I know," he said, pausing to give me a lingering kiss, "is that this is going to be a wonderful vacation, and I can eat for once without worrying about pain or throwing up. Let's get dressed and go out and celebrate, and not worry about money on this vacation."

And, it was a wonderful vacation. I truly relaxed for the first time in a long time. We swam in the ocean most days, as I floated aimlessly on my back and looked up at the sky, thanking God for our good fortune. We made love every afternoon, after strolling hand in hand on the beach.

"Now we can truly start planning for retirement," Ralph said one evening. "You know, I was always afraid I wouldn't live long enough for us to retire, but now I can't wait. Maybe we could look for a small farmhouse in the countryside in France, like you've always talked about."

Now that Ralph was in remission, I thought our lives could finally return to the carefree times we experienced when we were first married. How I longed for those simple, happy days before I knew about disease and pain.

When we returned home and picked up our two dogs at the kennel, we learned Cookie had been having seizures.

Why can't things be as they used to be? I wondered. I was so looking forward to coming home and not having to worry about Ralph being sick. And now I was worried about Cookie. But I was still grateful for Ralph's new lease on life.

Cookie died one evening when we were both home. We watched in horror as she had a seizure and then quickly expired. Although she was fifteen years old, Ralph had not prepared for her death by digging a hole in the backyard as he had done for Cupcake. I was afraid the ground would be too frozen to dig a grave for her.

"Don't worry, Donna-Girl," Ralph said. "We can put her in the freezer downstairs until next spring when the ground thaws."

"You can't be serious," I protested. "I couldn't sleep in this house, knowing she was in the freezer downstairs."

"Why not? It's only a body now; she's not really there. Her body's not much different than the beef and chicken in the freezer."

"Well, I can't help it. I still think of her body as who she is."

"People are cremated all the time and their ashes are scattered on land or water. Does that bother you?"

"Yes, that bothers me, too. Remember how you asked me for a blanket to wrap around Cupcake when she died? Why would you have done that if you didn't still have some feelings for her body?"

"Okay," he acquiesced. "I'll go see if I can dig a hole."

It was unusual for Ralph and me to have conflicting views on anything of importance. Our feelings about how we viewed bodies after death was one of the first major differences I recall us ever having.

Fortunately, the ground was not as frozen as Ralph had originally thought, and he was able to dig a shallow grave for Cookie.

Shortly after Cookie's death, our other dog Chip, who was also fifteen years old, started frequently peeing all over the house. Knowing we would never put him to sleep simply because he was a nuisance, I spent the better part of a weekend, trying to find a disposable diaper that fit him. Although Ralph or I usually had to get up at least once during the night to change his diaper, it was certainly better than having him pee all over the house.

Then came the day that Ralph thought he might never see—he turned fifty. And, not only did he turn fifty, he felt good. Although he couldn't eat a lot, particularly at one sitting, he was pain free, and with the help of vitamins, he had more energy than since he was a teenager. We celebrated with just the two of us going out for a quiet, romantic dinner.

I think turning fifty was such a milestone for Ralph that he almost believed he was indestructible. He had survived several complex operations, battled with a terminal illness for many years, and reached an age the doctors thought he might not achieve.

SEVEN

Less than a month after Ralph's fiftieth birthday, my father was scheduled for a relatively minor surgery to replace a small vein in his leg that was not allowing enough blood to flow to one of his feet. Although my brother Bill and I, as well as Mom, had been at the hospitals during his other more major surgeries, this one seemed so minor that neither my brother nor I planned to be there. The surgery was scheduled to be done in a small hospital in a remote town in Wisconsin where my parents had moved after leaving Florida. Although Mom had resisted the move, Dad had said he was tired of the bugs and heat in Florida, and wanted to live near a freshwater lake for fishing.

"Well, I guess this is just something I have to do," my dad said to Ralph and I, who were on separate telephone receivers the night before his surgery. "How are your jobs going?"

My dad took such pride in our executive jobs and wanted to hear about every promotion so he could brag to his friends about how successful we were. "I could never work for anyone else," he used to say, and I agreed with him because he thought his way was the only way. That's why he had had a variety of entrepreneurial businesses.

Recently though, he had become even more critical and intolerant than usual. Although we were all used to my dad being difficult to please, his behavior had become increasingly bizarre. One afternoon at a family gathering, he stood up and said he was going home because he didn't like how the dogs were playing together. We never knew what to expect from him. So, it was refreshing to hear him talk so normally again that night before his surgery. I could almost feel his love for us across the phone lines.

"Have Mom call us as soon as the surgery is over," I said before we hung up the phone.

"Don't worry, I'll talk to you tomorrow," he said in a confident voice.

Since he had seemed so calm, I was surprised to hear my mother's version of what happened the next day.

"After parking the car in front of the hospital," she said, "he hesitated getting out of the car. Then he acted like he was having a panic attack—his breathing became labored and his chest began heaving up and down. He assured me he was all right and that he just needed a little time. Finally, after quite a while passed, he slowly walked into the hospital. Although I thought his behavior was a bit unusual, I figured he had had an anxious moment about the surgery."

"How's he doing now, Mom?"

"There seems to be some complication," she said. "He's not coming out of the anesthetic like he should."

"What do you mean? What exactly did the doctor say?"

"Well, that's what the nurse said—that he's not coming out of the anesthetic like he should."

"What are they going to do?"

"Well, I don't know, honey."

I immediately stopped asking questions, knowing my mother was telling me all she knew. She wouldn't have asked too many questions of the doctors, believing they knew what they were doing and would tell her what she needed to know.

I arrived at the hospital the next morning to find my mother sitting in a waiting room in a bewildered state. "He's awake," she said, "but he looks like he doesn't see me. He just stares at the wall."

"Can he talk?"

"I don't know; he hasn't said anything. Like I said, it's as if he is awake but doesn't see anything."

"Have you talked to the doctor this morning?"

"No, he hasn't been around yet."

When I walked into my father's room, I found him sitting up in bed, staring at the wall. I greeted him in a perky voice as I approached his bed. "Hi Dad, how are you feeling?"

Mom was right. He looked fine, but he just stared into space. I put my hand on his arm, trying to get his attention. "Dad, how are you feeling?" I asked again, putting a little pressure on his arm. There was no reaction.

"Mom, we've got to talk to the doctor. He should be coherent by now; the anesthetic from surgery should have worn off."

I walked outside of the room and found a nurse in the hallway. "Will you have my father's doctor paged?" I asked her.

"I'm sorry, but the doctor won't be back until this afternoon."

"Well, could you have another doctor paged? There's something terribly wrong with my father."

"What's wrong?"

"He just stares into space. He doesn't seem to hear us when we talk to him."

"Is your father a heavy drinker?"

"What?"

"How much alcohol does he drink every day?"

I looked at my mother, who had followed me, to get a clue as to how she wanted me to answer. We both knew that my father drank far more alcohol every day than either of us thought he should.

"I already told the doctor he drinks too much," my mother replied.

"Well, that's probably why he's having trouble coming out of the anesthetic," the nurse said with a tinge of disgust in her voice. "We see this all the time."

Sensing the nurse was not sympathetic to my father's situation, I decided to discontinue the conversation. "Will you please have the doctor on call paged?" I asked her.

"It won't do any good. His regular doctor will be here before the doctor on call can get here."

I found her answer disturbing, as most of my experiences had been at large university-affiliated hospitals where there were often hundreds of doctors in residence. Realizing that it wouldn't do any good to argue with her, I decided to wait for the doctor to come that afternoon. In the meantime, I would start making plans to have my father moved to another hospital.

"Mom, let's go get a cup of coffee," I said, turning toward my mother. As we walked through the hallways to the cafeteria, I was surprised at the number of offices we passed.

"How can there be so many patient rooms and offices without there being more doctors on site?" I wondered aloud. "This place doesn't make any sense to me."

"Mom, I think we should investigate having Dad moved to a bigger hospital with more doctors," I said, as we sat down.

"Oh, I don't know, honey. I think it's too soon to talk about anything like that. He might just take a little longer to recover from the anesthetic. Let's wait and see what your brother has to say. He said he'll be here this afternoon."

Late that afternoon, the doctor who had performed the operation on my father came into his room. "This is very puzzling," he said, after examining my father. "The surgery was successful because the blood is flowing strongly into his foot. And all of his vital signs are good. I just don't understand why he isn't more responsive."

"What do you think the problem is?" I asked.

"At this stage, I don't know. We'll have to run some further tests on him, which I will order tomorrow."

"Wouldn't it be better if you started running the tests today?" I asked, trying to keep my voice polite and respectful, even though I was irritated with his laid-back approach.

"Well, we won't have technicians here until tomorrow," he answered. "I will have the nurses watch him carefully tonight." With that, he went over to check on the patient who was sharing the room with my father.

It was all I could do to control my impatience and aggravation with the doctor. I wanted to speak frankly, but I decided to wait and discuss the subject of moving my father with my mom at dinner. I hoped my brother would support me.

I waited until our entrees had been served. "I think it's very important that we have Dad moved," I began. "A larger hospital would have up-to-date equipment and many more doctors and specialists".

"The doctor seems nice," my mother replied. "Maybe we should wait for the tests to be done. I hate to have him moved if they can help him here."

"Mom, they move people all the time. Did you see the helicopter landing on top of the hospital? That's what it's for." I knew my voice sounded perturbed and that I was barely controlling my anger.

"Maybe Mom is right," my brother said in support of my mother. "Maybe we should wait for the tests to be done here."

I began to feel that my arguments were futile; the more I tried to persuade my mother and brother, the more they resisted me. I was much more familiar with hospitals and doctors—and, most important, with the things that could go wrong—than either my mother or brother. I still vividly remembered the young black man who died in the room next door to Ralph's. I just didn't have the same respect for the medical community that my mother and brother seemed to have. To my mind, there were good doctors and bad doctors, just like there were good managers and bad managers, good technicians and bad technicians, and it was up to the patient and their families to figure out the difference. It seemed hopeless to pursue the argument any further with them.

I headed home the next morning, so I could be at work on Monday, feeling frustrated and defeated.

When I talked to Mom every day during the week, Dad's condition seemed to be the same.

The following Saturday a frightening thing happened to me. When I stepped out of my rental car that I had parked in front of the hospital, my vision became unfocused and my eyes started pulsating. Streaks of jagged light flashed in front of my eyes like lightning bolts. Nothing like that had ever happened to me before. Feeling frightened, I slowly walked into the hospital lobby and sat down on a chair.

After about ten minutes, the jagged light faded and my normal vision returned, but I felt exhausted, as if I had just run a long race. I knew that my body was telling me it couldn't tolerate any more stress and that I needed to slow down.

In addition to worrying about my father, my job had become extremely stressful, because I had recently been named acting Chief Information Officer (CIO) of United Airlines. I was put in charge of the technology that the company depended upon for most of its operation. Often, in the middle of the night, I would receive phone calls about a critical system that couldn't be fixed: an overseas flight having problems with the flight planning system; a baggage system flinging bags haphazardly underground; an employee payroll system unable to produce checks; or a reservation system that was malfunctioning. All of these problems could obviously cost the company millions and needed immediate attention. Ralph seemed truly proud of me, boasting to his friends and coworkers about my position. But to receive this "dream job" during my father's illness couldn't have been worse timing, and it only added to my stress.

The more stressful my life became, the less emotion I showed, though I seethed inwardly. I was so angry over my father's inept treatment and the doctors' inability to diagnose his problem that I literally couldn't see straight. And that's exactly what happened: my body reacted by distorting my vision and giving me the classic symptoms of migraine.

Moving slowly and cautiously after my migraine attack, I walked down the hall to my father's hospital room. As I walked into Dad's room, I saw Mom standing next to his bed. I walked up to her and hugged her; she seemed so small and frail.

"Hi, Dad. How are you doing today?" I asked. Although my mother had told me there had been little change during the week, I still hoped he would show some sign of recognizing my voice. He didn't move—he just kept staring into space. Tears welled up in my eyes as I looked at him, while my mother gave me another hug.

"The doctor told me this morning that he thinks your dad has an infection," my mother said.

"What kind of infection?"

"They don't know. They have to do some more tests."

"Has he eaten anything?"

"No. They're still feeding him through the IV."

Mom and I sat next to his bed for several hours, watching him stare into space at the wall. His eyes were open, but he showed no emotion. Finally, it was time to pick Ralph up at the airport.

Ralph was quiet on the ride to the hospital. With tears in his eyes, he walked into my father's room and stood next to his bed. "How are you doing, Dad?" he asked. Ralph had started calling my father "Dad" many years ago, and I believed he thought of him as the father he had always wanted. He held my father's hand for a while, as he talked to him softly about the things going on at home and at work.

"You will be so proud of Donna," Ralph told him. "She has been named Chief Information Officer and has thousands of employees reporting to her."

Again, Dad showed no reaction. If anything would have gotten his attention, news of my success in the corporate world should have done it.

After a while, Mom, Ralph, and I walked into the hallway.

"I agree with Donna that Dad should be moved to a larger medical facility," Ralph said to my mother.

"I hear what you're saying, Ralph, but Bill and I both think Dad is better off here. We don't want to put him through the strain of moving."

"I understand. Yet, the doctors here would sedate him so that he would hardly be aware that he's being moved."

"I just don't know," she sighed, looking so pathetic that Ralph didn't push the issue any further.

As angry as I was at my mother and brother for not agreeing to move my father, I ceased arguing with them, as I knew it was only upsetting all of us.

The migraine headaches during which my eyes pulsated and distorted my vision began happening frequently, often two or three times a week. I always knew about five minutes before an episode that it was going to happen, usually because I was extremely agitated about something, but there was nothing I could do to prevent it. When a migraine attack happened at work, I would pretend that nothing unusual was occurring, even though I could barely see who or what was in front of me.

"These migraine headaches you're experiencing are probably stress induced," Dr. Williams told me when I went to see him.

"You know, what's interesting is that I know exactly why I'm having these headaches. My frustration level is so high with my father's doctors that I'm often in a rage. Between the doctors doing so little for him and the pressures of my job, I want to scream much of the time. But, of course, I can't. I have to remain calm. And then, sometimes my body just can't take anymore, and that's when I lose my vision."

"It sounds as if you understand what's happening to you pretty well. Deep breathing and meditation are probably the best medicine I can suggest. At least Ralph is doing better so you don't have to worry about him all the time."

"I know. I've waited so long for him to be well, and now all of this happens. Sometimes I wonder if God just wants to keep us on our toes by throwing one challenge after another at us."

The doctors never identified the type of infection that my father had contracted during or after his surgery. After waiting two weeks for a culture to mature, the results were inconclusive. Then his kidneys began failing, and his heart became weak.

Before walking into my father's hospital room the following Saturday evening, I tried to cover up my feelings of helplessness and hopelessness by putting a positive look on my face.

"I don't know how he gets his hair so messed up," my mother said softly, as she combed my father's hair. Watching her tenderly stroke my father's brow, I had no doubt that any differences they may have had in the past had been reconciled. I also realized that I had forgiven my father for his often harsh, angry behavior and the undo strain he had placed on the entire family for many years.

Mom walked out of the room. "What do you think is wrong, Dad?" I asked him, fully expecting a response.

He slowly shook his head from side to side, as if to say he didn't know. For the first time in two months, I felt he tried communicating with me, even though he had not spoken a word.

The following Monday morning, I had no sooner sat down in my office than my assistant told me Ralph was on the line.

"He's gone, Donna," Ralph said, choking back tears. "He died peacefully early this morning. You're all set to fly there in two hours. Someone needs to be there with your mother."

There was nothing more to say. One of my staff drove me home to get a change of clothes and then took me to the airport

Unsure of what funeral arrangements my mother would want to make, I had grabbed a new pantsuit that needed hemming along with a needle and matching thread. The fact I had the presence of mind to do such a mundane thing amazed me. Although I cried during most of the flight, focusing on the needle going in and out as I sewed helped me stay calm.

I never saw my father's dead body. By the time I arrived at the hospital, it had already been taken away to be cremated. That was okay with me; I didn't want to see his dead body.

Death had always held such terror for me. I couldn't go to a funeral parlor without feeling sick to my stomach. The mere thought of walking up to a casket and looking at a lifeless body scared me. Where did the person go? I wondered. What kind of experiences were they having now…if any? What were their lasts moments like?

Mom had decided to spread Dad's ashes in their lake at some future date; she said she wasn't ready to do it yet. After spending several days helping Mom sort through Dad's belongings, my brother and I went back to our respective homes and jobs.

Ralph greeted me with a hug at our front door, holding me tightly as if he didn't want to let me go. "I have some more sad news," he said. Immediately, I feared something was wrong with his health.

"Not your Crohn's again?" I asked fearfully.

"No," he said. "It's Chip. I took him to the animal hospital after he had several seizures. The veterinarian assured me it was his time, so I gave the okay to put him down. I really felt it was the right thing to do, and I didn't want to call you and upset you even more."

"I know you did the right thing, Ralph. I trust your judgment."

As Ralph continued to hug me, I felt something wet on my ankle. I looked down and saw a little puppy nuzzling my leg.

"Her foster parents said her name is Matilda, or Mattie for short."

"What would I ever do without you?" I said, looking at Ralph who had tears in his eyes. "You always make me feel better."

That night as I snuggled in bed with Ralph and Mattie, I thought about my Dad and Chip, both dying at about the same time. How similar the two deaths seemed; both of them had bodies that occupied this earth, and then they were gone. Both had experienced joy and sadness, pleasure and pain.

I also thought about the role alcohol may have played in my father's death. Could his nurse have been right about my father's excessive drinking being the reason he didn't recover from the anaesthetic? If that's true, why don't surgeons warn patients about the potentially harmful effects of alcohol before performing surgery? And, what about that supposed panic attack he had before entering the hospital? Did he have a premonition he was going to die?

For me, there were many unanswered questions surrounding my father's death.

EIGHT

Ralph seemed to have a harder time getting over my father's death than I did. Although I had been extremely upset when Dad was in the hospital, once he died, I accepted the fact that his life was over, while Ralph continued to struggle.

"I wish we had tried harder to have your dad moved to another hospital," Ralph said.

"We did try, honey. You know we couldn't do it without Mom's consent. And she thought she was doing the best thing for him by not having him moved."

"I know, but I really miss him. I just can't believe we'll never hear his two cents about every project I do; I think I miss his criticism as much as his praise."

"You never did take his disapproval much to heart," I remarked, thinking about how I had strongly reacted to every one of my dad's criticisms. I guessed that was the difference between being his daughter rather than his friend, although Ralph never let criticism of any kind affect him much anyway.

"If only he had recovered enough to hear about your promotion," Ralph said wistfully.

Then Ralph lost his job.

"Earlier today," Ralph said, when he called me late on a Friday afternoon, "one of my managers asked me if I was sure I was part of the new organization. When I asked my old boss, he admitted my job had been eliminated and there was no position for me in the new organization."

I was shocked. Ralph had never played business politics very well, but he was so technically talented that I had never considered he might lose his job.

"Remember a couple of weeks ago when I mentioned a new vice-president had come in from the outside to head up our division?" he asked me.

"Sure, I remember when you told me about him."

"Well, he and I have very different opinions about the overall direction the division should take. He wants to throw out most of the computer systems we've spent years developing and spend a tremendous amount of money on developing new ones, while I would rather see the company invest in human resource development. I guess I was pretty vocal about my opinions."

Knowing how opinionated and stubborn Ralph could be over principles, I imagined the new vice-president didn't want anyone in his division who was so diametrically opposed to his plans. "I'm sorry, Ralph," I said, feeling badly for him. "I know how difficult this must be after all the time and energy you've put into the company. Why don't we go out to dinner tonight and talk about this? I'll cancel my plans for tonight."

"No, don't do that," he quickly responded. "I'm fine…I really am. We have plenty of time to talk about this. I've looked into my options, and I'm going to continue working for a few more months and leave at the end of the year."

Much as I wanted to be with Ralph and support him, this was the first time in several years that a group of my peers had planned to meet after work for a drink and some frank conversation about things going on in our company.

"Then, I think I'll stop for just a short while," I said. "I'll be home by seven."

Looking back, I wished I had immediately gone home to be with Ralph. Although he hadn't sounded upset, I think he was hurt. After having one drink with my colleagues, I went home to find Ralph lying in his favorite recliner chair engrossed in a television show, seemingly as if nothing had happened.

Ralph immediately got up from his chair when he saw me. Then he walked toward me and put his arms around me. "You know, I'm almost glad this happened," he said. "I was getting bored with my job, and I think this is what I needed. I'm looking at this as an opportunity."

"I think you're right, Ralph," I said encouragingly. "You've been at the same company almost ten years now and something different might be more challenging and interesting."

Although I didn't say anything at the time, I was concerned about the financial implications from the loss of his job, because we had expected the majority of our retirement funds to come from his profit sharing.

"I'm sure you'll find another job soon," I said, wanting to be supportive. "There aren't many people who are as knowledgeable as you are in computer technology."

"And, the company will provide outplacement services for me with an executive search firm."

Nonetheless, some things were not in his favor. It was the era of major corporate downsizing. Middle management had been hit hard and a lot of fifty-something men were looking for jobs. Ralph had received a good salary and expected something similar. Yet more important, I think, Ralph had never had to work very hard to achieve most things. Except for the battle with his illness, everything since he was a child had come easily to him—excellent grades, basketball scholarships, friends, good jobs, promotions—a lot of positive things with very little effort. Given his age and his salary expectation, and the competition in the marketplace, I feared that finding a comparable job would not be as easy as he thought.

"Since I'm being paid for several months before I retire at the end of the year, I think I'll wait until the first of the year to start looking for a job in earnest," he told me.

"Don't you think you should start contacting people you used to work with to let them know you're looking for a job?"

"Not yet. I think I'll start by seeing what jobs are available in the ads in the Sunday papers."

"You don't think you might have more luck if you called a few people who know you and your work?" I asked, trying not to appear too pushy.

"Maybe later if something doesn't turn up."

Weeks passed, and nothing turned up that looked suitable for him in the newspaper. I was surprised (and somewhat dismayed) that he didn't regularly use the outplacement services he had been provided. He only went a few times to the outplacement agency and then stopped going there altogether.

"I don't want you to buy any Christmas gifts for my family this year," Ralph said one night after Thanksgiving while we were watching television together.

"Why not?" I asked, surprised by his statement. Ralph's mother had died several years earlier, actually waiting for Ralph's visit before she finally let go after months of being close to death…much like Cupcake had waited for him. Since then, he talked to his father when he wasn't drinking excessively and spoke almost weekly to his sister.

"No gifts. Nothing. I mean it," he said emphatically without any further explanation.

"It's not worth hurting them. You know I'm a thrifty shopper and can find nice gifts without spending a lot of money. I know I always complain about the last-minute shopping and mailing, but I really don't mind."

His comments were so uncharacteristic that I was truly bewildered. Normally he wouldn't do anything to hurt anyone, especially members of either of our families.

It was the first seriously unkind thing I had ever known Ralph to say or do. I ignored his request and bought Christmas gifts for his family as

I had always done. I was certain he saw me wrapping and addressing the gifts that I had bought, but he didn't say anything to me about it.

As the year drew to an end, Ralph had made no progress in finding a job, and I became more worried. Both the spa and antique businesses were consistently losing money. Though I received a decent salary, it was not covering our losses, and we were forced to start using our savings.

Ralph and I had decided to get another puppy, as a playmate for Mattie, from a breeder who lived near Ralph's best friend Mack, and we were excited to learn we could pick up the new puppy the week before Christmas. That would give us the opportunity to visit Mack and his wife Doreen, as well. I always looked forward to these visits, listening to the non-stop, back and forth banter between the two boyhood friends as they recalled their childhood pranks.

Ralph seemed in good spirits during our five-hour drive, but as soon as we arrived at Mack and Doreen's house, something seemed different about him; he acted more reserved than usual, and somewhat bored and restless.

"Ralph, is something wrong?" I asked as we lay down on a sofa bed that night. "You just don't seem like yourself. Did I say or do something to upset you?"

"Mack is so phony; I'm tired of it," he replied.

Nothing could have surprised me more than this response. I felt as if a stranger was lying next to me—that's how uncharacteristic his words sounded to me. For a minute, I thought about how he had reacted about buying Christmas gifts for his family. The two incidents were similar in my mind, because they were both so unlike Ralph's normal behavior. That was the first time I had ever heard him say anything remotely negative about Mack.

"What do you mean by phony?" I asked.

"You know, just fake."

Ralph continued to act somewhat bored and detached the next day.

After lunch, we picked up our new puppy that we named Buffy. She cried continuously until Ralph tied her up with his shirttails and held her in a pouch against his stomach.

The next few weeks were busy ones for us with holiday parties and end of the year events, and I didn't give any more thought to Ralph's comment about Mack or his strange behavior that weekend. Later on, I would look back on it and criticize myself for not realizing he was in some kind of trouble emotionally or psychologically

By the first of the year, I felt more certain that Ralph wasn't looking for a job in the most productive way.

"You need to use your contacts," I told him. "I don't think just looking in the Sunday papers is the right approach."

"I see a lot of jobs that look right for me," he insisted. "I just need a little more time. If I don't find something my way, I can always call people I know later."

I knew he spent much of his day watching the O.J. Simpson trial on television because of the details he told me about when I came home. Several entrepreneurial opportunities surfaced that could have afforded him some easy money, but he said he wanted to hold out for a job in a large corporation.

I became busier than ever, taking frequent trips for my airline job, attending auctions to buy inventory for Alouette, and even doing the laundry for Body & Soul to save money. Over time, I became more frustrated with what I perceived to be Ralph's lack of aggressiveness in looking for a job, and more worried about our financial situation that continued to deteriorate. My migraine headaches continued, because I felt frustrated and worried much of the time.

"Why don't I start cleaning the house and do some of the other things we usually contract out?" Ralph suggested, knowing how concerned I was about using our savings.

"That would help. Will you be upset if I give you a list of things I'd like to have done?"

"No, not at all."

"Well, on the top of my list is fixing the ceiling light fixture in our entryway. I hate coming home to a dark house."

The light hadn't worked for over six months. Whenever I forgot it was broken and turned on the light switch without thinking, one part of the house lost power. I was especially annoyed, because I knew fixing the light would have been an easy task for Ralph, since he had earned extra money as an electrician when he was in college. He just didn't seem interested in doing much around the house since he lost his job, so I was pleased he had volunteered his services.

One night when I came home from work, Ralph began talking to me before I even set down my briefcase.

"I have an opportunity to buy into a food franchise," he said enthusiastically. "My friend Shelley was thinking about doing it, but decided she didn't have enough time to devote to the business. There is minimal capital investment required, and we have the perfect location for the business in our antique store. Twice a week, fresh meals are delivered, and all we have to do is refrigerate them until the customers pick them up, or we can deliver them to their home or workplace. The meals are great for people with all kinds of medical problems, including diabetes and heart disease."

I didn't want to dampen his enthusiasm, but I couldn't see how something like this was going to help us much financially. Also, I knew I had a tendency to be somewhat on the defensive whenever Shelley's name came up, because she had been one of Ralph's girlfriends in grade school. They had maintained their friendship over the many years since then, mainly through telephone calls and now email, as she lived across the country.

"Have you figured out how much money you could make doing this?" I asked, trying to maintain a neutral tone of voice and not sound too critical.

"Sure, I expect to make a profit in a little over a year."

"Are you sure you want to spend your time doing this when it will take time away from finding a real job?"

"I can do both," he said confidently. "I'll hire someone else to work during the nights when we don't already have coverage for the antique shop."

I elected not to oppose the idea since Ralph seemed so enthusiastic about it, even though I definitely did not think the food franchise was a wise decision.

Ralph continued to look at employment ads in the Sunday papers and sent out several resumes each week, but he received few calls for interviews. When he did have an interview, the job wasn't a right match for his experience, the salary was too low, or, in most cases, he didn't get an offer even though he was given a lot of encouragement in the interview. I decided that if Ralph didn't get a job soon, we would need to change our lifestyle and sell or shut down Alouette and Body & Soul.

What bothered me most was that Ralph seemed content with things as they were, while I was constantly worried about our finances. In my view, he seemed to be spending an inordinate amount of time working on advertising and promotions for the food franchise, time that could have been invested in a serious job search.

Late one Sunday afternoon, I decided to confront Ralph more insistently than usual about my concerns. "We need to talk about our finances," I said. "We're spending our retirement funds on our businesses. Maybe, we should stay home and not go out to dinner tonight so we can save some money."

"You worry too much, Donna-Girl. Everything will be all right as soon as I get a job."

"We can't go on spending our savings like this. Maybe we should sell Alouette. I'm so worried about our finances that I almost wouldn't care if we got rid of it."

"I just need a little more time to find a job," he said. "Let's not talk about it now. There's plenty of time to make a decision."

As I walked into the kitchen before getting ready to go out to eat, I noticed a lot of empty beer cans in the wastebasket. For some reason, I decided to count them. I was shocked: twelve cans.

"It seems like you're drinking more than usual," I said, as I walked into the living room where he sat watching a football game on television. Although I had tried to keep my voice calm, I know I must have sounded accusatory.

"Leave…me…alone," he said, enunciating each word in a loud voice. "I don't need any more suggestions from you."

Ralph had never spoken to me in such a harsh tone of voice. I felt my entire world was falling apart, but instead of continuing the conversation, I decided to let things go for a while. If he had had that much to drink in one day, I didn't think his thoughts could be clear. Also, I thought he would only get angry, if I said anything further.

As I walked upstairs to get ready for dinner, my stomach was in knots. While I fixed my hair and put on makeup, my inner turmoil was playing itself out inside my head. Since I had emptied the wastebasket that morning, I reasoned, Ralph must have drunk all that beer today. How could he drink a dozen cans of beer in one day and act normal? I tried to quiet my mind and finish getting ready for dinner.

We drove to the restaurant in silence. Then, as we walked from the parking lot to the restaurant, Ralph walked several paces behind me. Since we usually walked side-by-side holding hands, his behavior further upset me.

The restaurant, a local hangout, was crowded, and we were told there would be an hour's wait for a table. We sat down at the large bar area and ordered a drink.

"Ralph, I need you to tell me what's wrong. What's really bothering you?"

"Well, maybe I should just leave and be alone for a while," he said. "I'm tired of your constant nagging at me about finding a job."

I breathed in sharply and felt nauseated. Then I started to cry.

"Why don't we just enjoy this dinner together?" he said, in a kinder and gentler voice.

Neither of us talked or ate much of our food. When we returned home, Ralph fell asleep quickly, while I lay sleepless most of the night, trying to figure out what was wrong with him and our relationship.

When I walked into the house after work the next evening, I heard the answering machine beeping in the kitchen. One of the messages was in regard to a job offer, which Ralph accepted the next day after negotiating his pay. He would be a consultant for a large technology company.

I wished he had told me about the opportunity earlier. But then I realized that even if he had felt fairly certain about getting an offer, he had been turned down so many times that he probably didn't have the confidence to tell me about it. And, even if had told me about it, I would have been skeptical. So much in life is all about timing, I decided. If he had received the offer one week earlier, I may never have known how upset he was with me for nagging him to find a job.

"I think it's a great opportunity," Ralph said, the night after accepting the position, "but I'm not sure it's what I really want to do. I find helping people to become healthier through the food franchise more satisfying than my last technology job. And, of course, setting up the clinic with Anne was the most rewarding thing I've ever done."

I didn't respond, because I was thinking that the food business and the clinic didn't bring in money. It made me realize that Ralph and I now had differing opinions and goals: I was still focused on making money and climbing the corporate ladder; Ralph was no longer focused on money, power, and position, but rather on helping others.

"Once we retire, Ralph, we'll have lots of time to devote to charitable activities," I said.

"Maybe so. I hope we get there."

"Of course, we will. Now that you're in remission, we don't have to worry all the time."

He didn't respond.

I didn't feel good about our conversation. Something was missing between us. Whenever I thought about his comment about leaving and being alone for a while, I felt a chill throughout my body. We never talked about that night again.

NINE

One night, when Ralph was working late, I stopped into the antique shop to meet Bunko, the man Ralph had hired to help him with his food business.

"Well, how's the little woman?" Bunko asked, as soon as I walked into the shop.

"What?" I stammered and took a step back, unable to believe how he had addressed me.

"I asked how you were."

"Please don't ever call me that again," I said angrily. "I think it's demeaning."

"Aw shucks, ma'am. You know that's just an expression."

"I know, but I don't like it."

Besides, I didn't think he presented a good image for a food business that catered to health. He was overweight with what appeared to be a large beer belly. The thought of this rather rough-looking character greeting customers in our antique shop made me shudder. Entering our antique shop was like walking into a beautifully furnished museum to have high tea. I didn't want to think about the shock on the ladies' faces when Bunko greeted them with, "How's the little woman?"

Then one night when I walked into the antique shop, he popped open a can of beer.

That does it, I said to myself. I was hoping Ralph would realize for himself the unsuitability of Bunko for the job, but after this incident, I knew I would have to talk to him about it.

"That's just his way," Ralph said when I approached him about Bunko. "He means well. Actually, I think the women kind of like him. I've heard him joking around with them on several occasions."

"Maybe there are some customers who like him, but I think he's totally out of place."

"He really cares about the job and the food business, and I think he feels good about having this kind of responsibility after the hard, physical labor he did all his life in construction."

"Even so, you seem to spend so much time showing him how to fill the orders and package the meals for customers that I don't see how he's saving you much time. I even saw him drink a beer while he was working."

"Sometimes I stop in and have a beer with him at the shop. It's no big deal, Donna. He's a nice man, and we've become friends."

"Okay, but tell him to knock off the 'little woman' comments," I said, ending the conversation on a strained note and feeling uncharitable. How Ralph could make derogatory remarks about his wonderful friend Mack being phony, while praising this man who seemed to patronize him, was beyond my comprehension.

Then it occurred to me that Bunko might be serving as a substitute for my father. But still, I asked myself, how could Ralph and I see things so differently now? And why do I feel like a snob? Have I become one of those bitchy women who constantly complain and harp about something to their husbands?

As the weeks went by, I saw Ralph less and less because he had started working nights as a consultant for a telecom company that was developing a new system. Usually, we saw each other briefly in the evening before he left for work when I was just getting home. To make matters worse, since his work schedule now extended into the weekends, we hadn't gone out to eat or done anything fun together in months.

"How's Ralph's new job going?" Lana asked one evening, as we sat together in the reception room of Body & Soul to review the results of the week's business.

"I don't know, Lana. I am so worried about him. He works such long hours, and every time I see him he looks more tired. I just don't feel we communicate anymore."

Just then Ralph walked in on our conversation.

"I just stopped by to pick up the laundry," he said, with a slight nod in our direction. "I forgot you were meeting here tonight."

Since Lana and I had started doing the laundry ourselves to save money, every night one of us had to pick up the dirty sheets and towels from the day and take them home to wash.

"He does look exhausted," Lana said, after Ralph had gone into a back room. "And, thinner," she added.

"You know, a year ago he would have sat down with us and had us laughing over our terrible financial results. Sometimes I feel I don't know him anymore," I said, as tears sprang into my eyes.

"I bet he's just working too hard, trying to prove himself at this new job," Lana said, patting my arm.

As Ralph walked across the room with a bundle of laundry in his arms, he stumbled and lost his balance. For a second, I thought he was going to fall. I jumped up from the sofa where I had been sitting and ran across the room to him.

"Ralph, are you sick?" I blurted out, grabbing his arm to help steady him.

"No, I'm just exhausted," he said.

His face looked drawn, and his hair looked as if he hadn't washed it in several days.

There's got to be something terribly wrong with him, I thought.

"I'm not working tonight," he said as he opened the door. "I'll see you at home."

About a month later, right before Thanksgiving, Ralph walked into our bedroom where I was undressing and sat down on the bed. He looked dejected and exhausted.

"You know," he said, "I remember the picture over the bed because I've seen it before, but it's blurry now. Also, my whole side has felt numb all day."

"What!" I exclaimed, horrified by his admission, especially since I had been begging him to see the doctor for months. "Ralph, you have to go to the doctor right away!" I shouted. "This sounds serious!"

The next day, Ralph was admitted to the hospital for tests after Dr. Williams examined him.

"I told Dr. Williams I would stay in the hospital for only one day," Ralph said, as I stood next to his bed in the hospital. "I have to get back to work."

"Ralph, you look terrible. You've got to stay here until they figure out what's wrong with you," I said, furious with him about the time constraint he had given the doctors. "How can you even work when you can't see well?"

He turned away from me without any comment.

His boss and several of his coworkers came to see him in the hospital that evening. At least he seems to have made some new friends at his job, I thought.

After testing Ralph for many diseases, the only problem the doctors could find was a severe vitamin deficiency, which they said could have contributed to his vision problem and fatigue.

As soon as I heard the diagnosis, I remembered something I was supposed to have done a long time ago and felt immediately guilty for not having accomplished it.

"Oh, Ralph, do you remember when you asked me to get your prescription renewed for vitamin shots? Oh, my God! That was over a year ago. I remember asking the doctor's receptionist to request a refill, but I forgot all about it after that."

Suddenly, many of his symptoms and the way he looked made sense to me. Extreme vitamin deficiency may have not only caused his physical deterioration but might also account for his change in attitude toward Mack, his family, and me.

"Oh, Ralph, I'm so happy they found something," I said, feeling grateful the problem had finally been identified, even if it was partially my fault. "I feel terrible I didn't follow up on getting your prescription renewed. Did you forget about it, too?"

"I just didn't think the vitamins were all that important."

"It's been a terrible year, honey. Maybe, things will get back to normal now. I desperately need you to be your old self again. I miss seeing you and being with you all the time."

"Don't worry, Donna-Girl. Everything's going to be fine," he said, just as he used to say when I was anxious about anything.

He rested during the weekend after his release from the hospital. But the following Monday, he went back to work, and quickly returned to his routine of working every night. Although he was giving himself vitamin shots, it didn't look to me as if they were doing much good. His hair still looked limp and lacked its usual shine, and his skin looked sallow.

One night before he went to work, I sat down next to him. "Ralph, you still look like you're not feeling well. I think this job is killing you. We've worked so hard all of our lives, but it's not worth it if we don't have our health. You can't keep working like this!"

"This might be my last project," he said, sounding dejected and holding his head in his hands.

"What do you mean?" I asked, alarmed by his matter-of-fact tone.

"I don't know," he said, shrugging his shoulders.

"Ralph, what's happening to us? After almost thirty years of being sick and in pain, you're finally in remission, but we both seem unhappier than we've ever been."

"It's just because I feel so exhausted," he said, "and my eyesight is so bad, even with the vitamin shots. I've scheduled cataract surgery for right after I finish this project. In the meantime, I use a magnifying glass at work so I can see."

The deadline for the completion of his project had slipped several times, and it was now scheduled for February of the following year. "Please take some time off of work, honey," I pleaded with him. "Even just a weekend. What about Christmas? I hope you can at least take a few days off then."

"I'm afraid I can only take off Christmas Day. I scheduled myself to work over the holiday, because I want the staff to have some time to spend with their families and kids."

"What about us?" I asked, feeling abandoned.

"I'll cook a turkey dinner for you and your mother on Christmas Day. Why don't you take a few days off and go somewhere with her during the holidays? It would be good for the two of you to get away together."

"I really want to be with you."

"I know; I want to be with you, too. As soon as this job is over I'll have more time. Maybe I can even go with you on some of your business trips. I've never been to Hong Kong or Singapore, and you seem to enjoy those places."

"Sure. Maybe I will talk to Mom about getting away after Christmas," I said with little enthusiasm. "I would like her to take advantage of the inexpensive flights, while I'm still working for the airline."

As promised, Ralph made a delicious turkey dinner with all the trimmings on Christmas Day, but no one talked much during dinner. Ralph, who had always kept us entertained with his good humor and jokes, barely said a word and hardly ate any of his food. Near the end of the meal, his head suddenly dropped toward his plate, as if he was falling asleep, and then snapped back up before actually hitting the plate.

"Ralph, you're scaring me!" my mother cried out.

"I'm okay, Mom. Just a little tired...."

As hard as I tried to convince myself there wasn't anything seriously wrong with Ralph or with our relationship, I didn't succeed. I hated to leave home at that time, but I wanted to keep my commitment to Mom, so the day after Christmas, we left for our brief trip to the Gulf Coast of Florida where Mom used to live.

Although Mom was a wonderful traveling companion, flexible and ready to do almost anything, everything she said and did on the trip irritated me for no apparent reason. I found it hard to be civil to her or anyone else. I felt restless and impatient and just wanted to go home to be with Ralph.

It wasn't until we got back home several days later and I walked through our front door, greeted ecstatically by Mattie and Buffy, that I felt better.

"Mom, I know I wasn't much fun on this trip," I said, as I watched her get ready to drive home.

"Don't worry, honey. I know you've got a lot on your mind. Just take care of yourself and Ralph."

Ralph and I had been talking over the past couple of years about selling our home and buying one with an adjacent house for my mother to live in when she became too old to live alone. After our trip to Florida, our realtor showed me a house I liked that also had a second, smaller house on the property.

"Maybe we can rent the smaller house until Mom is ready to move," I said to Ralph.

"I think that's a good idea. Did you know Bunko doesn't live that far from there? Maybe he knows someone we could rent it to."

I stiffened at the mention of Bunko's name, but kept quiet. More than anything, I was hoping a change would be good for Ralph and our relationship.

We quickly negotiated a contract and put our house up for sale. The closing on the new house was scheduled for February, whether our house was sold by then or not. Financially, we knew this was risky; yet in spite of his comments about this job being his last, Ralph planned to start another one after he finished his project in February. In fact, his company had already started talking to him about what his next job might be.

Although Mom wasn't ready to move yet, she came to see where she might eventually live. "Are you sure Ralph feels up to moving right now?" Mom asked. "He looks so tired. Actually, I've been worried this past year that maybe something was wrong with your marriage, but then I watch Ralph's eyes follow you whenever you walk out of a room, and when you're not around, he asks where you're at and when you're coming home. So, I've concluded there's something else wrong with him. Maybe he's just working too hard."

"I know, Mom. I'm very worried about him. I've tried to tell him not to work so hard, but it doesn't do any good. At least I've gotten him to agree to go on a vacation to Maui for ten days before he starts his next project. Maybe if he gets some rest, he'll feel better."

We closed on our new house, but decided to wait until after our vacation to move in.

On one of the rare nights when Ralph was home, we decided to watch the news on television together. It was almost like old times, when we used to watch the news together most nights. During a commercial break, Ralph got up to go to the bathroom, and I used the opportunity to take a sip from his glass of orange juice. I immediately tasted liquor—vodka, I thought, although I often got gin and vodka mixed up.

"Ralph, are you drinking?" I asked when he returned from the bathroom.

"I can't believe you're checking up on me," he yelled back at me. "Can't

I even have a drink once in a while without hearing about it from you? Why can't you leave me alone?"

"Remember how we both agreed when we got married that we would only drink wine and beer, not any hard liquor because of our fathers' drinking histories?"

"Well, don't tell me you've never had a Screwdriver."

"Only on vacation. Ralph, I can't believe we're arguing about this. All I want is for us to be happy and feel close like we used to be."

He didn't reply, but the next morning he hugged me tightly and kissed me tenderly after putting my luggage into my car. I was leaving on a trip to Taipei that afternoon. Although he didn't say anything about our disagreement the previous night, I could sense his remorse.

"Please be very careful over there, Donna-Girl," he said as he kissed me good-bye. "I wish I could go with you; I don't like you traveling so far alone."

"I'll be fine," I told him. "I'll be back before you miss me." I could see him waving at me in the rearview mirror of my car as I drove down our long driveway.

The trip to Taipei was the worst travel experience I had ever had. After flying for over twenty hours, the pilot announced that the Taipei airport was covered in fog and that we would land in Okinawa. Since the small Okinawa airport was closed for the night when we arrived, everyone except the flight crew was asked to stay in the plane.

Before long, the toilets became clogged, and there was no more food or water. For a while, everyone remained calm, but then several people got off the plane in order to smoke a cigarette. Armed guards were stationed at the foot of the aircraft stairway, where shouting erupted.

All of a sudden, I jumped out of my seat, hurried down the aisle, and descended the steps of the plane. Three guards motioned me back as I marched toward the terminal, but I ignored them and kept walking.

Wouldn't Lana be proud of me? I thought. She was always telling me I was too nice and not forceful enough. Instinctively, I knew that the guards wouldn't shoot an unarmed woman who looked to be American. When I walked into the empty terminal, I saw a row of pay phones, and much to my surprise, I was able to quickly get through to Ralph at his office.

"I contacted the airline when I didn't hear from you," he said, "and they're well aware of the situation. I just wish you didn't have to travel so far by yourself. But, you'll be fine, sweetheart. Please be careful. I love you."

I hung up the phone and walked back to the plane, thinking how different I was now from the shy, timid girl Ralph had married. Back then, I was afraid to stand up for myself and demand anything of others. Now, I felt I had to defend myself and fight for my rights all the time. I wondered if all the years of climbing the corporate ladder had hardened me. Could this be why my relationship with Ralph has changed so much? Is it because I've changed so much? Is this why he no longer wants to be with me and do things together? I hoped that wasn't true.

One thing I knew for sure was that I couldn't go back and pretend to be that shy, reticent girl who had once had panic attacks. I hoped that, during our upcoming vacation, I would have the courage to explore some of these concerns with Ralph.

TEN

The week before we were supposed to leave for Maui, I came home from work to find Ralph at home, apparently sick with the flu and looking even paler than usual.

"Do you know anyone else who has the flu?" I asked, as I sat down next to him.

"No, but I'm pretty sure that's what it is. I've been throwing up all day."

"You're sure it's not your old disease?"

"No, this feels different…more like the flu."

He stayed home for two more days and then went back to work for the final two days of his project. Although he had been scheduled on his last day to meet with the manager who was in charge of placing him on his next assignment, the man didn't show up for the meeting. Ralph was understandably disappointed and now wouldn't know what his next assignment would be before we left on vacation.

Finally, the day for leaving on our long-awaited trip arrived.

"Would you mind driving to the airport?" Ralph asked before I got into the passenger side of the car.

"No, of course not. Are you sure you're feeling all right?"

"I'm okay. I'm just a little tired.

This was the first time Ralph had ever asked me to drive anywhere except after his surgeries, because he liked to drive and I enjoyed having him drive. Although I was surprised by his request, I thought he must have been tired after staying up late to finish some paperwork.

When we arrived in Honolulu, we boarded a Wiki-Wiki tram that would take us to a different airport terminal for our flight to Maui. After sitting down next to each other, Ralph placed his hand on my leg, just above my knee. As he caressed my leg, I felt the warmth and caring in his touch.

"Let's have a good time on this vacation, Donna-Girl," he said in a wistful voice.

"I hope we do, too," I responded, trying to match his positive mood. Somehow, the soft touch of his hand and his few simple words communicated more than any conversation could have done; I believed he wanted to regain the closeness we had always had as much as I did.

We planned to stay for a week in a condo that had been recommended by an acquaintance, and then move to a resort for the remainder of our stay. When we arrived at the condo, the building looked neglected on the outside, with peeling paint and loose boards; I hoped it would be better maintained inside.

As soon as we walked into the condo, I knew we had made a mistake. The one large room, which included a kitchen and a bed, looked rundown and dirty, just like the outside. But since we had already paid for the week, I decided not to make a big deal out of how much I disliked the place.

When we returned to the condo after buying groceries for the week, I noticed that Ralph had hung up the clothes he had worn on the plane in the closet. Usually, he just threw his clothes on a chair, leaving me with a choice of hanging them up myself or asking him to do it. I took the fact he had hung up his clothes without any nagging on my part as another sign that he was trying to start out the vacation on a positive note. How easy it is, I thought, to do some small thing that either triggers a positive or negative reaction in a close relationship.

"Remember the last time we were in Hawaii when you told me you were in remission?" I asked, as we sat watching the sunset. "That seems like so long ago."

"I know. It's hard to believe that was only five years ago. I feel so much older now."

"I do, too. Maybe that's a sign we're getting ready for retirement."

Ralph didn't move off the couch that night. He tried to eat a little bit but said he wasn't very hungry. As I lay in bed alone, I realized this was the first night that Ralph and I hadn't slept in the same bed on a vacation. Even at times when a hotel didn't have a larger bed available, I would insist that two twin beds be pushed together.

The next day, he continued to lie on the couch, dozing on and off, but mostly staring at the floor or ceiling. He didn't bathe or shave.

Although I tried not to become overly concerned about Ralph's lethargy, I became more worried when the same behavior continued into the third day of our vacation. He hadn't left the room, only occasionally walking out onto the balcony, and had hardly eaten any food.

When I sat down next to him on the couch, I noticed his stomach was extended and swollen. "Ralph, what's wrong with your stomach?" I exclaimed, sounding more concerned than I intended.

As his eyes met mine, I saw what looked like fear in his gaze, which caused me to be even more concerned.

"I don't know," he answered. "I guess I'm a little poofy." That was the term he had always used when he used to have a flare up of Crohn's disease.

"Your stomach has never been this extended. Maybe you're having a flare-up of Crohn's. Remember how you were sick before we left? I didn't hear of anyone else having the flu."

"No, I don't think so. This is different. I think maybe I just need a little more rest. I'm sure I'll be fine."

"Ralph, I think we should see a doctor. I'm sure there are some excellent clinics and doctors here."

"I don't want to go to a doctor I don't know. I told you...I'll be fine."

I felt it was futile to keep arguing with him because he sounded so insistent. I left the room to go down to the beach to collect my thoughts. Although I was always soothed by walking on the beach, I couldn't relax and take my mind off of Ralph's stomach, which looked as swollen as the belly of a woman in her ninth month of pregnancy.

For the rest of the day, I alternated between walking on the beach and returning to our room to see Ralph. He usually kept his eyes closed when I walked into the room, although I often wondered if he was sleeping.

I could feel myself falling into a state of panic and returned to the room to try reasoning with him again. "Ralph, we have to see a doctor," I said, as I tried to control my hysteria.

"No," he said, shaking his head, as if uttering that one word was the most effort he could make.

"Please, Ralph; I don't understand why you won't go. You don't have to do anything but just talk to a doctor."

He turned over on his side and faced the back of the sofa without responding to my plea.

Waves of hysteria rose up within me as I walked down to the beach. I felt as if a tidal wave could wash over me at any moment. I have to stay calm, I kept telling myself. I can't lose my mind. Just breathe slowly.

Sitting down on a rock alongside the beach, I forced myself to focus on my breathing. After several minutes of watching my inhalation and exhalation, I felt my body relax. Thank God for the meditation classes I had taken at a women's health club. I may have had a nervous breakdown if I hadn't known about meditation.

During the next several days, I could only stay in the room with Ralph for a few minutes before becoming anxious. I became focused on my own survival by trying to stay mentally and physically calm. I meditated, swam in the ocean, and read a book by the popular spiritual teacher Deepak Chopra, *The Seven Spiritual Laws of Success*. It was the first inspirational book I had ever read and interested me because I initially thought it was about being successful in business. Little did I know that I had found an author who would help me through many trying times in the future.

Fortunately, after our week in the condo was over, Ralph seemed to have a little more strength the next day, as I drove us to the resort where we would be staying for the rest of our trip. At least, he sat up straight in the car and held his head up.

As soon as we walked into the resort, which was much more like the places we were used to staying, I felt much better. Our room was bright and cheery with a king size bed, and everything looked clean. After unpacking, we both lay down on the bed to rest.

Suddenly, I felt inspired. "You know what, Ralph—I bet you have an acute case of indigestion. I think you didn't have time to recover after you had the flu and that your stomach filled up with gas because you hadn't eaten enough food. I have some of the medication with me that I use when I have a bout with my reflux problem. Why don't you take one of my pills? I really think this might be the problem."

Ralph took the glass of water and pill from my outstretched hands. I felt so much better for having come up with a possible diagnosis and solution to his problem. Not having any productive activity to throw myself into during the previous week had been difficult for me, since I had always found my refuge in work. At least now, I thought I was doing something to help solve his problem.

The next morning, I awoke to the sound of the telephone ringing.

"Good morning, Donna-Girl. Would you like to join me for breakfast this morning?" Ralph asked in an upbeat voice. "I'm at a restaurant with a veranda that has a spectacular view."

"I'll be right there," I said, hanging up the phone. I was elated. He sounded like his old self—warm, inviting, and loving. Just hearing those few words, I sensed the person I had always known. This was the turn-a-round I had been hoping for—Ralph sounding and acting like his old self. I felt it was almost too good to be true.

I rushed to get dressed and almost ran down the stairs to the veranda where he said he would meet me. My spirits were somewhat dampened when I saw him, however, because even though he had sounded better on the phone, he still looked awful in person. Trying not to let his appearance discourage me too much, I sat down at the table with Ralph and gazed at the beautiful ocean view in front of us.

"Why don't we take a boat trip and do some snorkeling?" Ralph asked, as we ate breakfast. "You know, I think you may have been right about the indigestion. I'm feeling much better since I took that pill you gave me yesterday."

"I bet if we went to any doctor here, he could give us some more pills," I said, hoping Ralph didn't think I was just trying to get him to a doctor but, of course, that was still what I wanted him to do.

"It's only a few more days 'til we go back home," he said. "Let's go snorkeling."

After we paid for the 4-hour snorkeling cruise and boarded the boat, Ralph surprised me by asking for snorkeling fins and a mask. Initially, I thought he had only suggested we go on the cruise because he knew I enjoyed snorkeling. He must be feeling much better, I told myself.

We managed to find two empty seats near a bar where free Mai Tai drinks were being served. Ralph had been drinking very little on this vacation, but he helped himself to a Mai Tai. I took one, too, and sat down next to him while we watched the deck hands prepare fishing lines.

As we pushed off from shore, I turned to look at Ralph and noticed he looked a little woozy. Within minutes, he was laying down on a bench next to the men's washroom. Worried about him, I walked over to where he was resting.

"Ralph, what's wrong?" I asked.

"Leave me alone," he snapped.

I was startled and hurt by the tone of his voice and the abrupt change in his behavior. I walked to the back of the boat to watch the fishermen and soothe my wounded feelings.

The next time I glanced back at Ralph, he was sitting up with a drink in one hand and a cigarette in the other. I was enraged when I saw the cigarette. Feeling the strain of the last week wash over me, I walked quickly to where he was sitting.

"How could you do this?" I yelled at him, fighting back tears. "How could you start smoking again? Don't you have enough problems?"

Bursting into tears, I turned away from him and walked back to the rear of the boat. After all the effort that he had put into quitting smoking, I couldn't believe he had started again. I glared at him with tears in my eyes, and he defiantly stared right back at me.

Suddenly, one of the young fishermen reeled in a big fish and threw it down at my feet. Blood gushed from the fish's mouth. I felt trapped in the back of the boat with the gruesome, flailing fish. I knew then that I also felt trapped in my relationship with Ralph. I wondered what had happened to the man I used to know—the beautiful hair, the charismatic smile, the happy-go-lucky charm, the thoughtfulness, the sexual appeal—everything was gone.

Ralph and I remained apart for the rest of the cruise, and neither of us went snorkeling. I couldn't wait for the cruise to be over.

When the boat was docked, Ralph came to my side, and we walked down the exit ramp together. Neither of us spoke as I drove back to the resort.

As soon as we got back to our room, I put on my swimsuit and went down to the beach. I alternated between swimming and meditating for several hours. Later, I saw Ralph standing on the far side of the beach. Through the distance, I could feel his dejection; he seemed to be trying to take in as much of the view as he could. For me, it was just one more painful sight. I even imagined he was saying good-bye to the ocean.

I returned to our room and left him standing outside.

"Will you go to the store and buy some breath spray for me?" Ralph asked when he came back to the room. I took his request as his way of saying he was sorry for having smoked a cigarette. When Ralph had quit smoking several years earlier, his only crutch had been a breath spray that he used every time he had an urge to smoke.

"I ran out of the spray yesterday," he said. "It's no big deal if you're not going out anyway. I just thought if you were, you could pick some up for me."

I got dressed and immediately left for the nearest grocery store. The store was out of his brand of spray, so I continued fighting the traffic, and stopped at store after store to look for his particular brand, until I found it. As angry as I had been with him earlier in the day, I still desperately wanted to do anything to help him. The search for the breath spray also gave me something to focus on—something other than my fearful, depressing thoughts.

When I got back to our room, Ralph was sitting on a chair with his shirt open. I knew beyond any doubt there was something seriously wrong with him.

Both of us looked dejected as we left for our long trip home the next morning. If anyone had asked me why we hadn't ended our trip early and gone home, I don't know what I would have said. The thought of leaving early had never entered my mind, and, even if I had suggested it, I doubt that Ralph would have agreed to leave. I think we were both just hanging onto the hope that time and rest would make him feel better.

The meditation and time spent alone on the trip had given me a chance to do some introspection. I realized I had always been an optimist— sometimes to the point of being unrealistic. As a child, I used to wait every night for my dad to arrive home, hoping he would act pleasant and be kind to my mother and praise her for the dinner she had made. That never happened. As an adult, I had hoped my parents would learn how to get along better, but things had only seemed to get worse. So, I guess it wasn't too out of character for me to think Ralph would get better, despite every indication to the contrary.

And then I asked myself why I hadn't just called a doctor and asked him to come to our room? That thought hadn't occurred to me either. What is wrong with me, I wondered? Am I just not thinking, or am I afraid to go against Ralph's wishes?

As I walked into our house, the darkness in our front hallway added to the bleakness of my mood. "I wish you would fix this light fixture," I said, as Ralph walked into the house behind me. "I hate walking into a dark house."

Ralph didn't respond. I actually didn't blame him because I sounded pretty crabby and bitchy even to myself.

We both went to bed, not even bothering to check the mail or unpack our bags. I had made an appointment for Ralph to see Dr. Williams the first thing the next morning.

ELEVEN

"You'd better pack a bag for me," Ralph said, acting disgruntled as soon as he woke up the next morning. "You know they will put me in the hospital, don't you?"

I didn't respond but got ready to leave.

We drove in silence to Dr. Williams' office. Although we were angry with each other, I knew that our anger was a response to an intense fear about Ralph's condition.

Dr. Williams' eyebrows rose sharply when he walked into the room and glanced at Ralph.

"I'm not really sure what's going on here," Dr. Williams said after examining Ralph, "but you're in pretty bad shape by the look of your skin and abdomen. Tell me again why you don't think this is a Crohn's episode?"

"I don't know," Ralph answered, shrugging his shoulders with his head hanging down. "It just feels different."

"I'm sure you know you need to be in the hospital," the doctor said.

Ralph glanced over his shoulder and gave me an angry I-told-you-so look, as if to say it was my fault he had to go into the hospital.

"I want Donna to drive you over to the hospital…right now."

Although he seemed to be looking at Ralph for some kind of response, none was forthcoming.

"Let's go, Ralph," I said, interrupting the silence.

There was little else I could do for Ralph after dropping him off at the hospital, and apparently he didn't want to talk to me anyway, so I decided to leave in spite of how sad and forlorn he looked. When I leaned over to give him a hug and a kiss, he responded warmly and gave me a hug in return. I did hate leaving him alone, but I felt I needed to get back to work.

When I returned to the hospital that evening, Ralph seemed in better spirits. For one thing, he had been on an IV of fluids all day, which usually made him feel immediately better.

"They've scheduled tests over the next several days," he said. "I might as well get it over with."

I was relieved he seemed resigned to staying in the hospital this time.

Although Ralph's first tests revealed extensive prior damage due to Crohn's disease, the disease did not appear to be active again.

"The remaining tests are exploratory in nature," Dr. Williams explained. "The specialists aren't sure what they're looking for."

When I arrived at the hospital after Ralph's third day of tests, a nurse pointed me in the direction of the lab where he had been taken for a colonoscopy. It was a quiet day in that area of the hospital, and I sat down to read the newspaper with no one around to disturb me.

I must have been sitting there for over an hour, when a tall, handsome doctor came out of the lab and sat down opposite me. "I'm Dr. Noyes," he said. "I'd like to ask you some questions about your husband."

"Surely," I nodded. He made me uncomfortable, as he looked at me with a piercing gaze, almost as if he was assessing me in some way. Actually, he looked remarkably like Ralph…or how Ralph used to look.

"How much does your husband drink?" he asked.

"Usually, just a couple of beers a day."

"That's what your husband said when I asked him the same question before I started the colonoscopy procedure. You know," he continued in a matter-of-fact tone, "I have seen a lot of livers damaged by drinking. Are you sure your husband only drinks moderately?"

I nodded affirmatively.

He leaned toward me, looking directly into my eyes with a probing stare. "You know, the wife is often the last to know."

"Well, you're wrong in this case," I said firmly and then stood up abruptly and walked away from him.

I went to find Dr. Williams to ask that Dr. Noyes be removed from Ralph's case because I believed he had tried to trap me into saying Ralph had a drinking problem. I was incensed.

Suddenly, I felt my legs shaking. Reaching for the nearest chair, I sat down to wait for Ralph to come out of the recovery room. Dr. Noyes' words haunted me. Of course, I knew there were times in the past when Ralph had too much to drink, but usually only on vacation. If he drank some beers while working outside at home on the weekends, he didn't drink at night, and he always drove home when we went out for the evening—except recently, because of his cataracts. A person who isn't sober can't do those things well, can they? I asked myself. Yet, a nagging feeling of doubt persisted in my mind.

All of a sudden I thought about Bunko, with whom I had had an irritating conversation shortly after Ralph had been admitted to the hospital. When I had called Bunko to tell him he would need to take care of the food business by himself, he asked me what I thought was an inappropriate question under the circumstances.

"Did he happen to mention the money he owes me for last week's pay?" he had asked, before inquiring about Ralph or the reason for his hospitalization.

"No, he didn't," I answered with obvious annoyance. "Do you need it tonight?" I asked sarcastically.

"Well, I'd kinda like to have it."

"How much does he owe you?" I asked him curtly.

"One hundred twenty-five dollars."

"It'll be at the shop sometime tomorrow," I said, and then slammed down the phone.

Though I hated the thought of talking to Bunko again, if anyone knew whether Ralph had been drinking too much, it would probably be him. After all, as far as I knew, Ralph saw him in the shop several times a week.

Before I allowed myself to think any more about it, I walked out to the pay phone in the hall and dialed Bunko's number, actually hoping he wouldn't be home. He answered on the second ring.

"I want you to listen to me carefully, Bunko," I said, fighting off the anger and other strong emotions that were cutting off my windpipe. "This is a life or death situation, and if Ralph dies, and you don't tell me the truth, I will hold you responsible. Do you understand?"

There was silence at the other end of the phone. "Do…you… understand?" I said, as strongly as I could.

I heard Bunko emit a deep sigh. "You know I've really been worried about him. He's my best buddy."

"Was…Ralph…drinking…a…lot?" I asked, slowly enunciating each word.

"He would really be upset if I told you, Donna. That's why I haven't said anything. Yes, it was like he was trying to kill himself."

"When did it start?" I spat out the question as an interrogating lawyer might do.

"Sometime after Thanksgiving, when he got out of the hospital. I would meet him at a bar in the morning after he got off of work. I tried to tell him. Everyone did," he whined.

"How much did he drink?"

"Oh, I'd say four to six double Screwdrivers. I usually followed him home to see that he got there okay," Bunko said in a childish voice.

I bet you did, you son-of-a-bitch, I thought to myself. I'm sure he was good for a lot of free drinks.

"Do you know why he was drinking? Did he ever say anything about me?" I asked in spite of myself. I wanted to know, even if it came from

Bunko.

"No, he worships you. You're all he talks about. It was the job. It was killing him. He said he couldn't just go home after working all night and fall sleep."

"You're sure he never said anything about me?" I asked again, feeling foolish for wanting to know so badly.

"No, if anything, I think he might of felt less—you know—less of a man because of your success in your job."

I was grateful to Bunko for the insight. Even though I didn't like him, I knew he was telling the truth to the best of his ability. I hung up the phone, walked back to the nurse's station, and asked for Dr. Noyes to be paged.

Within minutes, Dr. Noyes was sitting down next to me.

"You were right," I told him, with no emotion in my voice. "He's been drinking heavily at least since last Thanksgiving, maybe before that. I don't know."

"Thank you for finding out that information," he said quietly.

I burst into tears. The first thing I did then was to call Mack and Doreen.

Doreen answered the phone.

"This Dr. Noyes said Ralph has cirrhosis of the liver," I told her. "He told me that sometimes the liver can heal itself, but I guess it either has to regenerate itself or be transplanted with a donated liver, because a functioning liver is necessary for anyone to lead a healthy life."

"Well, in one way I'm relieved, because it sounds like something that can be treated," Doreen said. "I can almost understand why he drank too much after all he's been through. Maybe he really thought he was dying when he was in the hospital last fall."

"But he was finally in remission," I said, still shocked that he would do something so stupid as to drink excessively.

"Maybe he thought something else was seriously wrong with him and began drinking to numb the fear. I know he kept talking about a brain tumor, but I just dismissed his concern as unfounded."

Next, I called my mom.

"Well, honey, you knew something was wrong with him," she said. It was too early for me to realize how differently I would handle Ralph's illness than how she had handled the situation with my father's tragic death.

After talking to my mom and Doreen, I went to see Ralph. I could barely look at him. He had turned sullen. Somehow, he knew that I knew.

"I can't believe you did this," I said angrily, trying not to yell at him so others nearby could hear me. "For the first time in almost thirty years you were in remission; a few more years of working and we could have had a great life together. How could you do this to us? How could you?" I repeated in a state of disbelief.

Dr. Williams walked into the room and beckoned me into the hallway.

"Dr. Noyes just told me," he said. "I should have noticed something last fall when he was in the hospital, but I always asked him how much he drank, and he always told me a couple of beers. I can't imagine how you must feel if I feel so betrayed. You know, I consider myself to be Ralph's friend as well as his physician." Dr. Williams paused briefly and shook his head. "He is one of the most intelligent men I have ever known. How could a man of his intelligence do such a thing?"

I would ask myself the same question over and over again during the coming months. And, just as Dr. Williams felt guilty for not diagnosing the problem sooner, I felt guilty for not having been a better wife. I thought surely I had something to do with Ralph's problem. Why hadn't I seen signs of his drinking? I wondered. And then, when I did see things, like all those beer cans in the wastebasket, why didn't I do something about it? Why didn't I know that my successful career made him feel inferior? Maybe if I had spent more time at home after he lost his job, this wouldn't have happened. Maybe I should have tried harder to make him happy.

That night I went directly to Lana's house after work. She opened the door, handed me a glass of wine, and led me into their living room. I had given her a brief synopsis about what had happened, so she would have some time to think before we got together.

"It was the loss of his job," she said matter-of-factly as soon as I sat down.

"How can you say that? He's too confident in himself to let something like that bother him that much. Of course, losing his job must have been a blow to his ego, but that alone wouldn't have done it."

"I don't know. Keith and I had a short time to talk before you arrived and that was his first reaction, too. Guys react differently to losing a job than we would. It's a big part of their identity. Remember how devastated Keith was when he lost his job?"

"I know, but after everything we've been through…he finally had a chance to lead a normal life. How could he do this? He had seemed so certain that it was a good thing he lost his job and that he would find a better one quickly."

"He probably didn't think much about drinking during the day, as he sat around for a year, waiting for job opportunities," Lana added.

"But he should have known better with his father being an alcoholic."

"You know, we may never fully understand why this happened, but we need to do everything we can to focus on how he can get better."

"I know you're right, Lana, but I am so angry at him and his stupidity that I can't think straight."

"I don't blame you. I'd feel the same way."

"I'm kind of surprised that four to six drinks a day would get him into this bad of a condition. I know that's more than he should have been drinking, but it's hard to believe that would be enough to make him this sick."

"I'm sure it was a combination of alcohol, a body weakened by all his surgeries, his inability to absorb nutrients, and probably a host of other things. You told me he hadn't been sleeping much or eating well. What about the time last year when he was in the hospital because he forgot to take his vitamin shots?"

"I know…I know. I feel if I had paid more attention to him and what was going on instead of spending so much time at work, he wouldn't be in this situation."

"You know better than that, Donna. This is not your fault."

"Well, I can't help but feel I'm partially responsible. Bunko told me today that he thought Ralph felt somewhat less of a man because I was so successful in my career."

"Oh, c'mon, Donna. Are you going to listen to someone like him? You know how proud Ralph is of you."

"I don't particularly like him, but I do think he was trying to be honest with me today. I also think this has something to do with the fact Ralph believed he would never live to be fifty years old. I don't really understand how that affected him, but I think he became careless with his health when he went into remission and turned fifty…you know, like forgetting to take his vitamin shots. I don't think he knew how to handle being well. Even before he was diagnosed with Crohn's disease in his early twenties, he had a variety of physical ailments as a child. I wonder if people get used to thinking of themselves as being sick, and then if they go into remission, they don't know how to act and feel well, and so they make themselves sick again."

"That could be."

"Or, remember when he was in the hospital last November and he thought he had a brain tumor? He said he didn't believe his problem was a lack of vitamins. Perhaps, he didn't want to live through another illness. He always said he didn't want to live a life of poor quality. Maybe, Bunko is right. Maybe he really has been trying to kill himself. Dr. Williams is right, too. Ralph is too smart not to know that drinking a lot, with his weakened body, was suicide."

Lana and I talked for hours. I desperately wanted to understand and make sense out of what had happened to Ralph. When I left Lana's house that night, I didn't feel like I had a firm grasp on what had happened to Ralph or why, but I did have a better understanding of the contributing factors. Nevertheless, I didn't think I would ever be able to accept what had happened.

Two weeks went by as Ralph's doctors tried to balance the chemicals in his body. Dr. Williams explained to me that when the liver isn't functioning properly, confusion, mood swings, and abnormal behavior often occur.

"So that explains why he would become angry with me and why he started smoking again after he had a few sips of liquor," I said.

"Yes. We all have the same emotions, and when a person's system becomes chemically unbalanced, the resulting behavior is often abnormal, and usually it is the darker side of a person we see."

"I think the hardest thing for me to deal with is Ralph's surliness. He has always been such a kind, loving, and happy man. It's as if a different person now inhabits his body."

Ralph and I had not had a collaborative, honest conversation since he had been diagnosed with a liver problem. I knew I was being cold and distant toward him, but I couldn't help myself. As far as I was concerned, he had ruined both of our lives.

I was impressed by the way his sister Sarah handled him when she came to visit during his third week in the hospital. He seemed to respond well to her take-charge, no-bull-shit manner.

"You let me know, Ralph, when you're ready to be civil," I overheard Sarah say in a firm voice one day. "Otherwise, I'll just go home."

I knew I needed to start dealing with our financial situation. Wherever I went, I carried two large paper bags of bills and tax material, which I worked on in the morning before seeing Dr. Williams and every evening when I visited Ralph. We now owned five houses and three businesses; the mortgages on the houses were a huge financial drain, and the businesses were all in trouble.

Although I wanted to shut down the food business immediately and get rid of Bunko, I refrained from doing so in deference to Ralph. I thought if Ralph recovered, it should be his decision because it was his business. I did make Bunko accountable, however, for every hour he worked and every screw-up he made.

Perhaps the biggest shock, other than finding out that Ralph had been drinking too much, was the realization that most of our business and personal bills had not been paid since last November. It was now March. Sales and employee taxes had not been paid. Each house we owned had electric, telephone, and water bills past due.

Ralph had computerized everything for our businesses as well as our personal finances, but he had written the software himself, and his menus were like a secret code. He scoffed at people like me who used standard software. Even if I had been able to figure out his software, I wasn't home enough to spend time on the computer.

I felt consumed by rage, especially since Ralph had always been meticulous with all of our bookwork and finances. Raccoons had strewn litter over our lawn, because garbage pickup had been discontinued. Fines on overdue payments had accumulated. We had sold two houses five years ago, for which we still carried the financing, and I realized the buyer was never going to get a mortgage and had let the places get terribly run down. I took the house we were living in off the market and let the one we were going to move into remain vacant. I seemed to discover a new financial problem every day, and I couldn't see a way out of the mess we were in, even if Ralph did recover and could help me deal with everything.

Something must have happened in November to cause all of this, I thought. Ralph had been in the hospital for one day that month. Bunko said he thought Ralph had started drinking in November, and, the last time Ralph had paid our bills was last November. Yet, as hard as I tried, I couldn't figure out what had actually happened in November.

One morning, as I sat in a lounge near Ralph's room, with my papers spread out on two sofas and several tables, Dr. Williams came into the room and sat down across from me. He looked tired.

"Donna, I know you and Ralph can get through this. All marriages have their bad times."

"Bad times? Are you kidding?" I asked, almost screaming at him. "This is a disaster. I don't know how we'll get out of this financial mess. He's not even the same person anymore. How could this happen?"

"I know both of you well, Donna," he persisted. "I know you can get through this. Just remember that we all have the same emotions. The chemical imbalance in Ralph's body is causing him to react much differently than he normally would. Once we are able to get his system balanced, you will hopefully see the old Ralph again."

"That's so hard for me to believe. I can't imagine ever feeling good about him again. There's just no way. I feel like I've thrown twenty years of my life away."

"I know you feel that way now, but give it some time. You are both very strong people."

As much as I admired Dr. Williams, I thought he must not understand the depth of my negative feelings and anger toward Ralph. There was no way I could ever see us in a loving relationship again. Never! As far as I was concerned, Ralph had ruined our lives forever.

After three weeks in the hospital, the doctors thought Ralph was stable enough to go home. On the night before he was released, Dr. Williams had asked to talk to both of us.

"First and foremost, Ralph, it is imperative that you never have another drink. Never! Not one drop! Do you think that is going to be a problem for you?"

"I really don't think so, because I haven't missed it while I've been in here."

"Donna, when you go home tonight, you may want to throw out any liquor in the house so there won't be any temptation."

I nodded.

"Now, let's go over the options facing you. The first option, and this is certainly the most preferable one, is that your liver renews itself. The liver is an organ that has remarkable regenerative capabilities, and if you never have another drink again and maintain proper nutrition, your liver may recover. The other option, a liver transplant, is a much more difficult path. First, you would need to be put on a list with other patients waiting for a liver transplant. The list is long, and there are many more patients than donors. Moreover, a liver transplant is a very difficult operation in that organ rejection is high, and there is a lengthy recovery period. Many patients do not recover. So again, let's hope that with good nutrition and no drinking your liver will regenerate itself."

"What do you think my chances are for getting a donated liver?" Ralph asked.

"I'm not sure. This is not my specialty. I know your chances are better if you're recommended by a well-respected physician. In your case, Dr. Noyes would be an excellent choice, since he used to work with a team of doctors that performed liver transplants."

Dr. Williams sent us home with the hope that Ralph's liver would recover.

TWELVE

Although I had been civil to Ralph in the hospital, I think that was largely because I didn't want to embarrass myself by acting out my anger. At first when he came home, I was cold and distant. Then when I realized that he was ignoring me, I became even angrier.

"How could you do this to us?" I screamed. "We had everything to live for and now our lives are ruined. Ruined!"

Ralph just sat in his recliner chair and didn't respond.

"I'm asking you to tell me why you did this," I said, yelling even louder.

Ralph got up out of his chair as if to leave the room, and I grabbed his arm. "I want you to tell me why," I said angrily, trying to keep him from walking away without answering my question. My nails dug into his arm and blood seeped from my nail imprints.

"Look what you've done to me! I'm going to tell the doctors," Ralph said, almost gleefully.

Even though I thought his comment was childish, I was appalled that I could have done something like that to him. I didn't realize how thin his skin had become now that his liver wasn't functioning properly.

I went upstairs and sat down on the landing at the top of the steps, crying and calling him every foul name I could think of. "Worm shit! Weakling! Low-life," I yelled, loud enough for him to hear me. I couldn't think of words horrible enough to hurt him.

Our puppies knew something was wrong. They had scampered up the stairs after me, Mattie looking at me with forlorn eyes and Buffy softly whining as she sat next to me. From the minute Ralph came home from the hospital, they had left him alone, and he left them alone.

To my knowledge, Ralph had never broken down and cried since he had become so critically ill. He maintained a tough, defensive demeanor, and love and affection from his beloved puppies would have been too much for him to bear. It was probably easier for him to listen to my ranting, raving, and name-calling.

Ever since Ralph had come home from the hospital, he had chosen to sleep downstairs in his recliner chair in the living room, because he said his back hurt too much in bed. I got used to hearing a thumping sound whenever Ralph raised or lowered the footrest, but one night after he had been home for about a week, I heard a scraping noise and then some muted banging sounds. I wasn't frightened because I figured Ralph must be doing something. I quietly walked downstairs where I found him turning knobs on the television set.

"It's broken," he said, when he saw me walk in the room. "So is the phone. Neither work."

"We'll fix them in the morning, Ralph. Don't worry about it." He looked so forlorn and pathetic that I could feel myself starting to soften toward him. I was still upset with him, but I seemed to have gotten a lot of my anger out of my system by yelling at him that past week.

The next morning when I examined the phone's handset, I saw that the batteries had been taken out of it. I put them back inside and immediately heard a dial tone.

Then I looked at the television. The front panel was open, and I remembered seeing Ralph turning some knobs the night before. On a hunch, I looked in the back of the set and saw it was not plugged in; I plugged it back in, readjusted the knobs, and it worked fine, too.

I stood up and looked at Ralph who had been watching me. "Ralph, do you remember fooling around with the phone and TV?"

"Not really. I know neither of them was working last night."

I called Dr. Williams to tell him about Ralph's bizarre behavior.

"I wouldn't worry too much about minor incidents," he said. "This just means his liver is still malfunctioning and that he has some chemical imbalance. Just be sure he doesn't hurt himself and his confusion doesn't become more frequent or severe."

"How am I going to do that and keep working?"

"Just do the best you can. Let's hope his liver renews itself soon."

I thanked Dr. Williams, and added the need to keep a close watch on Ralph's behavior to my list of worries.

A few days later, I checked on Ralph before taking the dogs out.

"Where is my knee?" he asked with a beseeching, confused look on his face that tore at my heart.

"What did you say?"

He shrugged.

Later, I went to tell him good-bye before leaving for work.

"Where's my elbow?" he asked this time.

I can't leave him like this, I told myself, as I phoned Dr. Williams.

"I think you'd better bring him into the hospital," Dr. Williams said, after I told him about Ralph's episodes of confusion, which seemed to be increasing.

The doctors quickly determined that Ralph was dehydrated again, and severely chemically unbalanced.

"I don't know why I'm in the hospital," Ralph complained.

I ignored him because I didn't want to fight with him.

"I feel fine. I want to go home," he whined. "When are they going to let me go home?"

"As soon as they can balance your system, Ralph," I said, in a voice I would use talking to a young child.

"Well, if I have to stay here, then I need some things. Get me a paper and pen so I can write them down. I know you won't remember everything if I don't write things down for you."

I could have smacked him, but I gave him a pen and paper.

Ralph slowly printed out the list of items, carefully folded the paper, and handed it to me. "Now, I want everything on that list," he said, insinuating that I might pick and choose what I brought to him.

I shook my head and swallowed hard, trying to control my irritation with him. Then, I opened the paper to be sure I could read everything on it. His printing was very neat: "CANDY, SLIPPERS, COKE, PIANO, RAZOR."

"Why would you need a piano, Ralph?" I couldn't resist asking him, grateful for once to have proof of his bizarre behavior.

Ralph looked surprised when I pointed to the word PIANO on the piece of paper. "There must be some reason I put it down," he said, smiling for the first time in many months.

He acts like this is a game, I thought. He's smiling because he's been caught. Perhaps I should have found some humor in the situation, but I couldn't. The pressure of trying to handle everything myself, including Ralph, was overwhelming to me. I felt exhausted and was relieved to have him back in the hospital.

"I won't release him, Donna, until you think you can handle him," Dr. Williams said. "We are less hopeful now that his liver is going to repair itself. He needs a transplant, and Dr. Noyes is our best hope for a recommendation. For some reason, however, Dr. Noyes doesn't think Ralph wants to live badly enough, and he doesn't think it is right to give him the opportunity for a transplant over someone who wants to live and has a better chance of surviving the operation. Also, Dr. Noyes may struggle with the idea of giving someone whose condition has been brought about by drinking alcohol a chance for a liver when many others will die through no fault of their own. I'm not sure what his view is on that. We know what a wonderful person Ralph is, but Ralph needs to convince Dr. Noyes that he really wants a chance to live."

I detected a sense of urgency in Dr. Williams' voice that I hadn't noticed before.

"Dr. Williams told me he thinks Ralph needs a transplant…that his liver won't rejuvenate on his own," I said to Dr. Noyes at my first opportunity when I saw him making his rounds at the hospital.

"Actually, I think he may be too far gone for that."

"What? What do you mean? He's not that bad!" Although I knew Ralph's condition was serious, none of the doctors had hinted thus far that he might die.

"I've seen many cases of liver failure. A liver transplant is a difficult operation. Do you have any idea what kind of life you would have for at least a year after surgery—if he lived? Anyway, I don't believe your husband wants to live badly enough or that he really wants a transplant."

"How can you say that? You don't know him. This isn't how he usually acts. He's a wonderful person! Did Dr. Williams tell you about the clinic he helped establish?"

"It doesn't really matter. I'll show you what I mean," he said, beckoning me to follow him into Ralph's room. Then, he laid down a piece of paper in front of Ralph and randomly printed the numbers from one to twenty on it.

"Ralph, I want you to connect the dots next to the numbers from lowest to highest," he said, handing him a pen.

Ralph began connecting the dots and looked up proudly at Dr. Noyes when he had finished.

"See," I said, looking at Dr. Noyes.

"It was nowhere near the speed at which it should have been done," he said, looking back at me.

"So what!" I said. "At least he can do it. There's nothing wrong with his mind."

"I've heard Dr. Williams say many times what a wonderful person your husband is, but I don't think he's ready for the fight he would have to go through to survive a liver transplant."

Then he walked away, as I stood there alone, feeling helpless. Without his sponsorship, I thought, there is little hope for Ralph.

The next night after work, I walked into Ralph's hospital room and was horrified when I saw him. His dinner was on a hospital tray, which had been placed over his legs, and his head was hanging down until his face rested in the mashed potatoes. I was immediately irritated that the nurses would allow that to happen, but I also knew that even in the best of hospitals, only patients in the greatest need at the moment were taken care of, especially on a floor like this one where most everyone was critically ill.

I didn't know whether Ralph was sleeping, or if he was just too weak to hold his head up. I walked over to the side of his bed and gently lifted his head up. My emotions had come full circle. I didn't care what he had done or not done. I loved him and wanted him to live.

His body should have been fairly well balanced by then, because Ralph had been in the hospital for several days. He was hydrated and was receiving good nourishment, although he wouldn't eat unless I spoon-fed him like a child. As I stood there, a strong feeling of fear washed over me. Somehow, I knew he was ready to die. I didn't know how I knew... I just knew he had given up hope. Maybe this is why Dr. Noyes doesn't want to give him a chance for a liver, I thought to myself.

I decided to stay with him overnight; I wasn't going to let him die, and no one was going to make me leave him.

After dinnertime, when the lights in the hospital were turned down, I slipped into bed beside Ralph and held him in my arms. It was uncomfortable with the two of us lying in his single bed; I had to lie close to the edge because Ralph was unable to move over much with all the tubes attached to his body.

We lay quietly together, listening to the sounds of the hospital. Since the patient in the adjacent bed had been a former officer at my company, I was somewhat self-conscious about having him listening to our conversation, especially since his wife had been probing earlier that evening for information about Ralph's condition. Nothing else is important but keeping Ralph alive, I told myself.

I heard one of the nurses walk into the room. "It's okay for you to stay as long as you're out of the bed before the doctors make their rounds in the morning," she whispered. "It's against the rules to be in bed with a patient."

I silently mouthed the words "thank you" and nodded my head.

Ralph's roommate was now snoring, but I knew Ralph wasn't sleeping.

Finally, Ralph broke the silence. "Please…let…me…exit," he said slowly, pronouncing each word carefully.

I felt my body tense, knowing exactly what he meant. "Exit" was a strange word to use, but I figured it was part of his language confusion. Then I felt a surge of strength and enormous energy race through my body, feeling as if I could tackle any job.

"There's no way I'm going to let you go, Ralph. No…way…do you understand? I couldn't live without you. We've worked our whole lives to enjoy retirement, and I won't enjoy anything without you. You don't have to work. I'll work three more years and then retire."

"I don't think I can wait that long," he said solemnly. "Can't you quit work now?"

"No, honey. We need the health insurance from my job, and we have many unpaid bills." As I talked, I wondered if I was wrong to disappoint him, but since this was the first time in a long time we were having a meaningful conversation, I wanted to be honest with him.

"You and the puppies can stay with Mom over the summer," I said. "She'll love to have you. You can recuperate, and I'll visit on weekends. The puppies will love it too."

Ralph's eyes lit up with the mention of my mother and the puppies. I knew the idea of spending a summer with my mother would appeal to him. Now that I had his attention, I ventured forth with the discussion I knew we had to have.

"You have to convince Dr. Noyes that you want a liver transplant," I said. "Really want one," I added.

"Okay, can we sleep now?" he asked, as if he was a sweet child.

I kissed him gently on his forehead, and he closed his eyes. At least that's a start, I thought. But, he has no idea what a long way we have to go and how tough it's going to be. It doesn't make any difference though, because everything's all right between us. I didn't think I could ever feel this way about him again.

I dozed on and off as Ralph slept through the rest of the night.

The next morning, we patiently waited for Dr. Noyes to make his rounds.

"Dr. Williams tells me you want to have a liver transplant. Are you sure you want to fight for this transplant, Ralph?" Dr. Noyes asked him.

"I'm sure," Ralph said.

"Are you sure you will never drink again?"

"I'm sure; I don't miss it at all."

I believed he was telling the truth. Ralph had never shown any signs of withdrawal, contrary to what the doctors had anticipated, and he wanted anything with even a minor amount of alcohol in it removed from the house.

The two men's eyes locked in a fixed gaze for several seconds.

"I'll see what I can do," Dr. Noyes said brusquely. Then he handed me a business card with the name and number of a doctor at another hospital. "Call her and make an appointment as soon as possible."

He began walking out of the room, but then turned around abruptly. "And, Mrs. Fridrych, will you stop eating his food?" he asked, with an admonishing look. "We're trying to measure his food intake."

I didn't respond, though I was irritated by his scolding. As if eating a little bit of Ralph's food could hurt anything, I thought to myself. I turned and smiled at Ralph. He looked a little better. We had made it through the crisis of the previous night when he had wanted to die; he was still alive.

Every day I thanked God for my boss and Lana. They were my emotional and analytical support as well as my sanity check. I still worked every day, but certainly not the kind of hours I had worked my whole life. I told myself this was the time to pay myself back for all the unpaid overtime I had worked almost every day for the past twenty years.

"Actually, work is a blessing for me right now," I told my boss, Randy. "When I'm here, I can temporarily focus on something other than my worry about Ralph."

"Just so you know you can take whatever time you need."

"I haven't mentioned this to you, probably because I'm embarrassed, but the doctors think Ralph's current condition was caused by drinking alcohol."

There…I had said it. No one at work but Lana knew how seriously ill Ralph was or what was wrong with him. Lana told me she was vague when anyone asked questions.

"Things we're not proud of happen in all of our families," Randy said.

"I can't tell you what your understanding and support means to me."

Less than a week after his release from the hospital, Ralph became disoriented again. Fortunately, he didn't resist as I drove him to Dr. Noyes' clinic.

After a brief examination, Dr. Noyes turned to me. "He needs to be in the hospital again," he said with a sigh, while Ralph lay on an examining table with his shirt unbuttoned. "Do you have an appointment with the doctor I told you to call?" he asked, as he slowly buttoned Ralph's shirt.

"Yes, but not for another two weeks; she's on vacation."

Dr. Noyes didn't look up as he finished buttoning Ralph's shirt.

No wonder he is so brusque, I thought. Underneath his gruff manner is a very caring and sensitive man.

Then, showing no emotion, Dr. Noyes walked over to where I was sitting and looked at me. "Don't you realize how serious this is?" he asked in a stern voice, as if talking to a lackadaisical child. "I told you to make the appointment right away. He can't wait two weeks."

"But, you gave me her name," I said, shocked by his words and his harsh tone of voice, and began to cry. "That was the first time she was available."

He left the room without another word. When he returned a few minutes later, he handed me a card with another doctor's name and telephone number.

"Call him immediately and mention my name. You should be able to get Ralph in within a week. I will also call him myself. And, when Ralph is released from the hospital this time, I want you to get a fulltime caregiver who can watch his every move. I've told you how important it is to monitor his fluid intake. Ralph craves liquid like a parched man in the desert. I've known patients in his condition who drank water from a toilet. You need to make sure he drinks a minimal amount of any kind of liquid. I want the caregiver to measure and record every ounce of liquid he puts in his body. The nurses in the hospital can provide you with a list of agencies. Do you understand?"

How dare he talk to me like that! I thought. I wanted to lash out at him, but nodded affirmatively. As much as Dr. Noyes had upset me, I knew in my heart that I would do anything to keep Ralph alive.

THIRTEEN

"He has entered into a difficult stage," Dr. Williams said to me, as Ralph was being released from the hospital. "He will be a handful for anyone. Be sure he doesn't choose a caregiver he thinks he can manipulate."

Ralph had only been in the hospital over the weekend, and driving back home, I wondered if he had been released too soon. He seemed cantankerous, especially after I told him I had contacted three caregiver agencies that we would be interviewing.

"I don't want and I don't need a caregiver," Ralph said stubbornly.

"Dr. Noyes says we have to do this. Maybe you will find someone you like."

When we arrived home, the first group of caregivers was waiting for us at our front door. Ralph walked into the house and immediately went to the refrigerator. I followed him.

"Ralph, you can only have a few more ounces of fluid today," I told him firmly, as he took a can of soda from the refrigerator.

Ignoring me, he popped open the can and started guzzling the soda.

"Let's go into the dining room so you can interview the caregivers," I said, while trying to snatch the can out of his hand. He turned away from me sharply, pulled the can protectively to his chest, and looked at me over his shoulder with a defiant glare.

"Okay, let's go," I said, realizing I wasn't going to get the soda away from him without a fight.

Ralph hunched his shoulders and hung down his head, as he followed me into the dining room where an agency representative and three caregivers were seated.

He sneered at them and continued drinking his soda. The agency representative politely refused the job. They know, just by looking at him, how difficult he would be, I thought. I'll bet they're hoping to take care of a docile, senile patient.

The people from the second agency never showed up, so Ralph and I went to wait on our screened-in porch for the third group. Ralph seemed to have settled down by the time the next set of candidates arrived.

"Could you tell us a little about your backgrounds and experience?" I asked, addressing the four caregivers after inviting them to sit down.

"I love my patients," said one of the caregivers, who had identified herself as Janice. "Praise the Lord! I takes good care of all them."

Ralph kept his head lowered, so I wasn't sure if he was listening.

"I from Belize," Janice continued. "I can do everything—clean house, take care of baby, all the work. Praise the Lord!"

Each time Janice said 'Praise the Lord', she raised her eyes upward with a radiant smile and lifted her arms in the air.

"I no drive car. Praise the Lord!"

"I want Janice," Ralph said quietly when the four candidates had finished their recitals.

Janice was a very large woman, with light brown skin and a broad smile. For some reason, Ralph was drawn to her, as she was the only one he seemed to have listened to.

Grateful that Ralph seemed agreeable to having a caregiver, I told the agency representative that I would like to hire Janice and agreed to pick her up at the train station the following afternoon.

Ralph and I woke up early the next morning. For the first time in many months, we had slept in our bed together.

"I'd like to go visit Lana and Keith at their new hot dog stand," he said, as we lay together in bed talking quietly.

It was the first time he had expressed the desire to do anything since the time he had asked to go on that awful boat ride in Maui. I was encouraged by all Ralph's signs of normalcy and got ready to go out.

Although we didn't stay long, I thought the visit with Lana and Keith went pretty well. Ralph's attempt to be friendly was encouraging, because I knew any exertion was an effort for him.

Then we went to meet Janice at the train station. As she stepped off the train, wearing a bright floral dress and a large straw hat, I noticed how she towered over Ralph's 6'4" frame. She must have weighed twice as much as he did.

"Have you had any lunch yet?" I asked her.

"No, ma'am," she said in her singsong voice; her speech had a charming lilt to it.

"Well, let's go across the street. Do you like Chinese food?"

"Surely, ma'am. I likes all the food. Praise the Lord."

Her melodic voice with its Caribbean-sounding accent fascinated me, and I wondered if that was what had attracted Ralph to her. She also projected a motherly demeanor, which made me hopeful that she would take good care of Ralph.

We walked into the small Chinese restaurant and ordered two meals for the three of us to share. As soon as our food arrived, Janice started urging Ralph to eat, placing a spoonful of food in front of his mouth.

"One more bite," she insisted, when he shook his head that he was finished after taking only a few mouthfuls.

I was pleased at how Janice was handling Ralph; she seemed to have a strong will that matched my own. My biggest concerns were how she would handle dispensing his numerous medications and restraining his fluid intake.

It was touch and go from the beginning.

When I came home after the first day she took care of him by herself, Janice was waiting at our front door. "He trick me to give him more drink," she said, with her hands on her hips.

"I'll talk to him," I assured her.

The next night when I came home, Janice and Ralph were sitting together on the living room couch, both looking tired.

"Bunko came over today and drove us to the hardware store so I could find some parts for the light fixture in the entryway," Ralph said. "But I didn't find them. I think I have to go to an electrical supply store."

"How could you even think of doing something like that now, Ralph?" I asked in disbelief. "Even if you found the right parts, how could you climb on a ladder and fix it?"

"You said it was your number one priority," he said, looking dejected.

"I know, honey, but that was before all this happened. Janice, please don't let him go anywhere with Bunko, and don't let him touch anything with electricity," I said, although I wasn't sure she could prevent him from doing anything.

Two days later I got a call from Janice at work.

"You come home," she said, obviously distraught and crying. "I leave here before I do him harm. I don't want do anybody harm. Praise the Lord!"

I understood how Janice felt, having felt the same way many times in recent months because of Ralph's obstinacy.

"Let me talk to Ralph," I said.

"She doesn't know what she's doing," he said belligerently. "She's not giving me what I need."

I felt as if I was dealing with two five-year-olds.

"Stay in your room until I get there," I ordered both of them.

By the time I got home, all was well.

"I want Janice to stay," Ralph said, as I sat down with the two of them.

"I hope you're not just saying that because you think you don't have to listen to her."

"No, I know I have to be careful of what I eat and drink."

So, it was settled, and Janice stayed.

With Ralph's permission, I called Anne, the minister at the clinic that Ralph had helped establish, and asked her if she could arrange to have Ralph inducted into AA. I wasn't concerned about Ralph drinking any alcohol, because I knew he really had no opportunity to do so, but I thought his enrollment might help convince the doctors he was serious about never drinking again.

On Saturday evening, Anne and three members of AA came to our house. When they had finished their meeting and were ready to leave, Anne threw her arms around me and hugged me.

"Call me if there's anything I can do," she said, with tears in her eyes.

"Look at my book and medal," Ralph said proudly. "They gave me a book with large print so I can read it better."

I was pleased that he seemed to have taken the meeting seriously.

We made it through the weekend and got up early on Monday morning to get ready to meet with the transplant doctors. I wanted to be sure we made a good impression on the doctors, so I planned to dress Ralph in his best, casual business clothes and to pay particular attention to his grooming. After he had taken his shower and shaved, I began blow-drying his hair with a wire brush and a little mousse.

"Ow, that hurts!" he yelled.

I thought he was kidding because I had hardly touched him. I started to brush his hair again.

"You're trying to hurt me," he howled. I tried to ignore him and did the best I could to get his hair dry. It wasn't until weeks later that I would learn that along with dehydration, his skin had become sensitive to the slightest touch.

When Ralph, Janice, and I arrived at the university hospital, we were ushered into the office of Dr. Landmeier, the head of a team of gastrointestinal specialists.

As soon as the doctor walked into his office, Janice jumped up from her chair. "I'm his nurse," she announced. "I'm here learn how take care of him. Praise the Lord!"

She sat down as abruptly as she had stood up. Ralph grimaced at her and shook his head with a disgusted look on his face.

Dr. Landmeier took Ralph's medical history and examined him. "He needs to be admitted to the hospital," he said after his examination, "but we don't have any rooms available today. I expect to have some available within the next several days. Do you understand the process for receiving a transplant?"

"No, we haven't been briefed on the details."

"First, you need to understand that we have many patients waiting for a liver transplant, and many of them will die before receiving one. Then, of those who are selected to undergo the transplant surgery, many die within a year after the operation."

"I understand. But, how do you decide who actually receives a liver and who doesn't?"

"We have a point system that determines the order candidates can receive a transplant. The longer a patient is on the list, the more points he or she accumulates. Moreover, a patient in a regular hospital room waiting for a transplant receives more points than say a patient who is waiting at home. In order to be admitted to the hospital, however, a patient must meet certain criteria that qualify him or her to be here; usually that criteria involve some medical equipment that is only available in the hospital. When patients enter the Intensive Care Unit, the ICU, their points accumulate even more quickly."

He paused and looked at me intently before he continued.

"We have many patients who have been waiting in this hospital for over a year to receive a transplant. From my examination, your husband won't be able to wait that long. I'm not sure he has more than a few weeks."

I was horrified at how impersonal he sounded. How could this man sit in front of us and practically give Ralph a death sentence? I wondered. He talked in a nonchalant manner as if Ralph wasn't even in the room.

"Well, what do you think his chances are of getting a transplant in the next few weeks?" I asked, trying to swallow the panic threatening to rise inside of me.

"I really can't answer that," he said. "I can only tell you that our list is very long. I understand from Dr. Noyes that your husband developed his condition from drinking alcohol."

"He did drink excessively for a very short period of time, but I think this happened because his body was in such bad shape from the Crohn's disease he suffered from for so many years. He had forgotten to take his vitamins for several months, and I think he was depressed because he lost his job." I knew I was rambling, but I didn't want Dr. Landmeier to think he was an ordinary drunk.

"Weren't you told that alcohol was bad for someone in his condition?"

"I don't ever remember that being talked about specifically," I answered, feeling I was on the defensive.

"Well, wouldn't you suppose someone with your husband's medical condition needed to be careful about how much he drank?"

This conversation is terrible, I said to myself, but I don't know how to stop it. How can I make him think well of Ralph? "Ralph is a member of AA, and I know he will never have another drink," was all I could think of to say.

"Well, before being put on the transplant list, he would be examined by a psychiatrist who would determine the likelihood of him drinking again. I suggest you go home and do everything possible to keep his fluid intake to a minimum. We will call you as soon as a bed opens up. You should be prepared to bring him in at a moment's notice."

"Thank you for your help, Doctor," I said, forcing myself to be polite. "We will be anxiously waiting for your call." I wanted to get out of his office and the hospital as fast as we could. All of my instincts told me this wasn't a good place for Ralph and that Dr. Landmeier wasn't sympathetic to our situation.

On the way to the car, Ralph pulled me aside. "Can't you control Janice?" he asked. "She makes me look like a fool."

I didn't say a word. It was true that Janice was always jumping up and announcing her status as his nurse and adding a few "Praise the Lords" to what anyone said, but I couldn't believe that Ralph, who had never cared about what anyone thought, would be bothered by her at a time like this. It was as if he had no idea how close he was to dying. I wanted to scream.

On the way home, Ralph asked me to stop the car so he could throw up. "My eyes hurt so much," he complained.

As much as Ralph had been through, he rarely complained about being in pain, but Dr. Noyes had warned me that the pain behind his eyes would become progressively worse.

"Can we stop at the spa?" Ralph asked. "Maybe a massage would help my pain."

Janice and I practically carried Ralph into the spa, where we were greeted by a young massage therapist who was working that night. I had been out of touch with our spa business and had not met the young man previously.

"I'll be happy to give him a massage," he said, looking at Ralph with a worried expression.

"I think if you could concentrate on his neck and head, that would be best," I told him.

"I think I'm going to throw up again," Ralph said.

Janice rushed to place a bucket in front of him.

"Janice, maybe you should stay in the room in case Ralph needs you," I said.

I joined Lana and our manager, who were meeting in our reception room, going over the results of the week. Shortly, the young massage therapist walked out of his room and beckoned to me.

"Have you said your good-byes?" he asked in a concerned voice.

"No, and I'm not going to," I answered angrily. I was not about to take any advice from some overly sensitive kid. The nerve of him to upset me by saying something like that, I thought. How much more can I take? I paid him for his services and said good-bye to Lana and our manager.

Janice and I helped Ralph stumble into our house and put him downstairs in his favorite recliner in the living room. He was so weak that he could barely walk.

I couldn't remember ever feeling so tired. As I reflected on the day, I knew my problem was much more than fatigue. Between the comments made by Dr. Landmeier and the massage therapist, I was beginning to feel like our situation was hopeless. I could almost see a tidal wave coming towards us with nowhere to go. I also knew that now, more than ever, I needed to stay calm and strong for Ralph. I tried to push all negative thoughts out of my head, as I forced myself to relax and try to asleep.

Early in the morning, I was awakened by a loud noise. I jumped out of bed and ran downstairs. Ralph was lying on the floor near the kitchen. I tried to help him stand up, but I couldn't lift him off of the floor by myself.

"Janice, come help me!" I screamed. "Janice! Janice!" I couldn't believe she didn't hear me, since she was sleeping in the family room next to the kitchen. I tried to scream louder.

"Janice, get in here. I need your help. Janice!"

Finally, I heard the door to the family room open, and a bleary-eyed Janice walked into the kitchen.

"Praise the Lord! Praise the Lord! What is my baby doing on the floor?" she asked, sounding surprised.

"Let's put him in your bed," I said. Together we dragged him onto the bed where Janice had been sleeping, while Ralph moaned loudly.

"It's my head. My head hurts so much," he said between moans.

"Do you want me to call Dr. Williams?" I asked.

"No hospital," he said.

Janice went to get him a cold cloth and placed it on his forehead. I rubbed his arm and within a few minutes he fell asleep.

"I'll watch him, honey," Janice said to me. "Why don't you get some sleep?"

Clients had already flown in from Europe and South America for an important meeting with me later that day. I had postponed the meeting previously because of Ralph's health and hated to do so again after they had made the long trip. I decided to go back to bed and make a decision in the morning.

As I finished dressing early the next morning, Janice walked into our bedroom. "Don't go work today," she said. "He's very bad."

Janice had never sounded this solemn, and I respected her opinion. I called my office and told my assistant to communicate my regrets and that I would conference in later to the meeting by phone.

When I went downstairs, Ralph was still moaning. Then he started repeating, "Donna, god damn it," as he thrashed on the bed in the family room.

Janice tried to calm him, while I phoned Dr. Williams.

"Dr. Williams wants you to bring him to the emergency room," the receptionist said.

"I don't think I can handle him this time," I said, barely able to talk through my sobs. "I'm not sure…we can carry him."

"Call an ambulance. It will be better if someone else drives."

The paramedics arrived within ten minutes after my call.

"We've seen worse, ma'am," one of the paramedics said, after he took Ralph's vital signs. "We will be leaving for Artesian Hospital shortly if you would like to ride along in the ambulance, or you can follow us there."

"No," I said. "He needs to go to Meridian Hospital; that's where his doctors are. They're waiting for him there."

"I'm sorry, ma'am, but our orders are to take him to the nearest hospital, and that's Artesian. It's two miles closer than Meridian."

"But he has to go to Meridian. His doctors are there."

"Once we get to Artesian, you can have him transferred to Meridian later if you want to."

"Please, can't you see how sick he is?"

"Those are our orders, ma'am."

"Could you please let me talk to your supervisor?" I asked, realizing I wasn't making any progress with them. I couldn't believe the absurdity of the situation. Were these people trying to make me lose my mind? I wondered. First, there were no rooms in the hospital yesterday. Now they're trying to take us to the wrong hospital. They won't bend the rules for two miles. Are they crazy? Calm down, I told myself. Calm down.

One of the paramedics handed me the phone. "We're sorry, ma'am," a woman's voice said, "but our instructions are to take him to Artesian Hospital. You can call a private ambulance service, but your insurance probably won't pay for it."

I slammed the phone down and turned to one of the paramedics. "Give me the number of a private ambulance company," I said.

"We'll stay with you until the other ambulance arrives and monitor his vital signs," the younger of the two paramedics said.

It took about fifteen agonizing minutes before the next ambulance arrived. Ralph continued to moan and say, "Donna, god damn it." I felt badly that he used my name like that and didn't understand why he was upset with me. They put him on a stretcher, carried him outside, and then lifted him into the ambulance. I followed the ambulance to the hospital in my car.

When I walked into the emergency room where Ralph had been taken, I saw two nurses and a doctor leaning over his body.

"He lapsed into a coma," one of the nurses said, as I approached the bed.

An unearthly, cold feeling came over me. It was the first time in over twenty years that I felt disconnected from Ralph. Whether I felt love, anger, respect, or irritation, I had always felt connected to him since the first time we had made love. It is difficult to describe the void I felt; the silence was deafening. I felt as if I had been in a hurricane with the wind howling and suddenly the air became still.

Lana had quietly entered the room. She reached out to touch Ralph's forehead and gently stroked his brow. "We need you, Ralph," she said. "You can't leave us now. I know you can hear me."

Just then, Dr. Williams entered the room. He looked at Ralph and then motioned for me to follow him into the hallway. For the first time in my life, my knees buckled. By the solemn look on Dr. Williams' face, I knew that whatever he had to say would be difficult for him to say and difficult for me to hear. Not trusting my legs to hold me upright, I backed up against a wall for support.

Then I envisioned myself slipping under a glass cover—the kind of dome-shaped, glass cover that dolls are displayed under so that no one can touch them or get them dirty. I felt protected by the glass cover and knew that nothing Dr. Williams could say would penetrate this barrier.

"You know I've been the most optimistic of all the doctors," Dr. Williams began, "but given the current circumstances, I'm forced to change my mind. You need to start thinking about the decision you may have to make, Donna, and we both know Ralph's wishes."

Now I knew why my knees had buckled and why I needed to be protected. Subconsciously, I must have known what Dr. Williams was going to say. Suddenly, I felt a surge of rebellious strength course through my body, as I stepped out from under my glass cover. There was no way I was going to make such a decision. Ralph had rallied before and confirmed his desire to live, and he could do it again.

Rather than enter into a discussion with Dr. Williams, however, I turned and introduced Lana, who had followed us into the hallway.

"We're going to move Ralph into the ICU," he said, after acknowledging the introduction. "It will probably be an hour or so before he's settled in there, so why don't you two get something to eat? I'm worried about how much weight you've lost, Donna."

Lana and I walked into another room so we could talk. Unknowingly, we must have wandered into the doctors' library because the room was filled with shelves of medical books. Lana began pulling books from the shelves.

Exhausted, I sat down on a chair to wait for Lana to finish her perusal of the books. I doubted whether she was going to find anything in the hundreds of books in the room, but I knew it wouldn't do any good to try to dissuade her. She had such an inquisitive mind, and she believed that, between the two of us, we could figure out anything. For one of the few times in my life, however, I was devoid of energy and had no desire to participate in her search.

"From what I can tell from this medical book," Lana said, "Ralph is in a pattern of renal failure, which is a pattern where one major bodily function fails, followed by a progressive failure of all the major functions of the body."

"That sounds a lot like what happened to my father. But, I refuse to accept that Ralph is going to die."

In fact, at some level, I knew that I had gotten into the habit of refusing to believe the worst would happen whenever a crisis occurred, particularly during the many health crises I had faced with Ralph. Since the worst never seemed to happen and Ralph had always survived, my denial mechanism had been reinforced. My calm, optimistic approach had also served me well in business, as I was presented with many crises each day. A psychiatrist might consider this to be an unhealthy state of denial. A student of positive thinking might think of it as a healthy affirmation. For me, at the time, it was simply a survival technique.

FOURTEEN

"Ralph is awake," Dr. Williams said, after gently touching my shoulder to awaken me.

I sat up slowly on a sofa in a waiting room across from the ICU where I had fallen asleep.

"Did you hear me?" the doctor repeated. "He's awake and alert."

I wasn't surprised to hear the news, as the doctor seemed to be, but I refrained from telling him that I knew Ralph would come out of the coma.

When I walked into the ICU, I was shocked by Ralph's appearance; his eyes and mouth were caked with dried blood.

"I couldn't stand being without you, honey," I said, trying to ignore the way he looked.

He smiled weakly. "I'm glad to be here," he said, looking somewhat bewildered.

Just then, Lana walked into the room and stood next to Ralph's bed. In spite of his appearance, she placed her hand on his forehead and gently stroked his brow.

"Nice Lana," Ralph said with a small smile.

I would never forget Ralph saying that about Lana. No matter what differences or little spats Lana and I would have in the future, I would think of that moment.

During the next hour, Ralph's mood seemed to change dramatically. He resisted the nurse's efforts to clean him up and barely said another word to Lana or me.

Then Mack and Doreen walked into the room—Mack, with his customary grin, and Doreen, quietly following a few paces behind him.

"Fuck you," Ralph said, as soon as Mack walked up to his bed.

Mack's friendly smile quickly changed to a look of surprise, and a heavy silence filled the room.

"I'm sorry, Mack," Ralph said, breaking the silence after a few seconds. "I didn't mean it," he added meekly.

Then Mack began crying. I didn't know whether he was upset about how Ralph looked, or shocked at the obscenity directed toward him, or both. Doreen left the room.

I couldn't help but reflect on how differently people react to crises and distasteful situations. First, there was Lana, who acted calmly and compassionately no matter what was going on. Then there was Doreen, who could barely handle the situation at all. And then there was Mack and I, who were somewhere in between; we were very emotional, but forced ourselves to remain calm and support Ralph. Temperament and personality must determine how people react, I decided, because Lana certainly didn't have any prior experience with extreme illness.

As I was walking back from the restroom to the waiting room, where I had left Mack, Doreen, and Lana, I overheard them speaking.

"Do you remember what they did for Chip during his last years?" Doreen asked.

"Who could forget how they kept the dog in diapers and got up every night to change him for almost two years?" Mack said.

"That dog was extremely senile," Lana added.

"Well, you can imagine what she's going to do for Ralph, if she would do all that for a dog," Doreen concluded.

"Of course, I'm going to do everything possible to help Ralph," I said as I walked into the room. "And, I know he's going to make it," I added with more confidence than I felt. "Look at all he's survived so far. I know that everyone thought he was going to be in a coma for a long time."

"And we'll all be there to support you," Doreen said, looking somewhat embarrassed.

Although I believed Doreen was just trying to help Mack and Lana realize what was ahead of them, overhearing that conversation reinforced my desire to keep everyone except Lana at a distance. Above all, I didn't want anyone second guessing my fight for Ralph's life, worrying about my emotional and physical well-being, or trying to take my mind off of Ralph. Lana was the one person whom I trusted to do everything she could to help me save Ralph.

The next morning, Ralph seemed to be in a much better mood and more coherent than he had been in days. "I really want the operation so I can go home," he said. "I don't think I've told you how sorry I am that you've had to go through all of this, Donna-Girl."

"We're in this together, baby, and all I care about is that you get well."

"I'll see a psychiatrist or do anything you think will help."

"Let's not worry about that now. I know you will never drink again."

"I don't understand how this happened to me."

"I don't either, but I'm sure it's both our fault. I was so busy climbing the corporate ladder and working on the antique shop and day spa that I lost track of what's really important. I'm sorry, too, baby, but I know we can get through this now. I love you."

"I love you, too, Donna-Girl. There could never be anyone else but you."

I started crying, knowing he truly loved me as I loved him. What a change from when we first found out about his liver failure, I thought. "I'm so grateful for this moment," I said out loud, as tears rolled down my face.

Dr. Noyes entered the room as paramedics from an ambulance service were preparing to take Ralph to a hospital about fifty miles from where we lived—the hospital affiliated with the clinic where we had met Dr. Landmeier.

"Are you sure you're ready for this fight for your life?" Dr. Noyes asked Ralph. "This will be more difficult than anything you've ever done."

"I'm ready," Ralph answered in a strong voice, squeezing my hand tightly and giving Dr. Noyes a brief smile.

I felt ready, too, to put my full attention on helping Ralph get the liver transplant he so desperately needed. I planned to move into a hotel one block away from the hospital, so I could spend as much time as possible with Ralph. Janice would stay at our house and watch the puppies. Greg, a young handyman that Lana had recommended, would maintain all of our properties. There was no need to ask the managers of Alouette and Body & Soul to assume more responsibility; they were as close to Ralph as they were to me and were willing to do anything to help us.

Ralph reluctantly let go of my hand as the paramedics lifted him onto the stretcher.

When I arrived at the university hospital downtown, I learned that Ralph had been placed in their ICU because there weren't any regular patient rooms available. I remembered how Dr. Landmeier had hoped to put Ralph in a regular room, but that was before he went into a coma and was placed in the previous hospital's ICU. As I sat in the ICU's waiting room, a short, scholarly-looking doctor with large, black-rimmed glasses walked briskly out of the ICU and stood in front of me.

"My name is Dr. Koster," he said, offering his hand for me to shake and then sitting down next to me. "I am one of three head surgeons responsible for performing the many operations each week in this hospital, including transplants. We alternate so that each of us is in charge every third week. This is my week to head up the surgeries."

Then he jumped up from his chair and started nervously wringing his hands.

What is wrong with him? I wondered.

"I understand your husband is in desperate need of a liver transplant," he said. "I briefly talked to Dr. Noyes, and he indicated he may have only weeks…if that long."

I tried not to react. Tears and anger would not help Ralph or me, but I didn't think I could ever get used to these kinds of insensitive statements from various doctors.

"We never know for sure," he said. "It's hard to pinpoint how much time these patients have, but I'm a pretty good judge. It's more of an art than a science. I'll let you know what I think after I examine him."

Then, without another word he hurried back into the ICU.

My first impression of Dr. Koster was that he seemed like a mad scientist on the edge of instability, or perhaps slightly over the edge. He also seemed arrogant and highly emotional—very different from most of the other doctors I knew who were generally more reserved in demeanor.

"Please follow me," a nurse said a short time later.

As I walked through the imposing ICU wing of the hospital, I counted six large rooms, each one about ten times the size of a normal hospital room and holding only four beds. Even though I had spent a lot of time in hospitals, I had never seen anything quite like this. I concluded that the large room size was necessary to accommodate all the machines in those rooms.

In Ralph's room, there were three other people, and all of them were hooked up to respirators and other machines. I was feeling a little overwhelmed by all of this when Dr. Koster rushed into the room and came right up to my face, much closer than normal protocol dictated. I backed away from him.

"This place is the last hope for most of these patients," he said. "Mayo Clinic and the other university hospitals in the country wouldn't touch your husband. He's too far gone. They want to give transplants to people with better odds. Unfortunately, he needs a liver transplant right now."

"What are his chances of receiving a transplant soon?" I asked, trying to ignore the implication of his last statements.

"He'll be lucky if he gets a chance at all," Dr. Koster said, looking at me as if to say what a stupid question I had asked. "Do you have any idea how many points a patient needs to get to be a Priority 1? And believe me, Priority 1 patients are the only ones who get a chance for a liver transplant these days. We have patients who have been in the hospital for a year who are still a Priority 3."

"And this is all because there is such a shortage of organ donors," I said to him as much as to myself. "I probably should have known how important it is to be an organ donor, but I honestly hadn't given it much thought when I gave my assent on my driver's license. Imagine how awful I would feel today if I hadn't done that, now that Ralph is in this position."

"You would be surprised how many people don't give much thought to becoming a donor or have some fear about doing so…like thinking a doctor might let them die to get their organs."

"Could you explain this priority system to me? I understand that patients accumulate points depending upon how long they've been on the list and whether they're at home or in the hospital."

"As I said, a patient needs a lot of points to get to be a Priority 1. It was sheer luck that we didn't have any regular rooms available today and that your husband was placed directly into the ICU. He would never live long enough to become a Priority 1 if we had had a regular room available. He needs a transplant now, and this is where he belongs—in ICU. He's failing quickly."

"How can you tell he's failing quickly?" I asked, bracing myself for his answer.

"All the typical signs of terminal renal failure are evident. Normally, in his condition, I wouldn't expect him to last more than a couple of weeks."

Even though I had heard similar words before, I still felt shocked, but I didn't say anything, as I had to put all my effort into controlling my tears.

"Oh, and here's the tricky part," he said almost gleefully. "This is why

I call this business an art instead of a science. We surgeons need to pick the exact time when we think a patient can successfully survive a liver transplant. I mentioned that a patient is usually near death by the time he has enough points to be a Priority 1. Since organ rejection is high, particularly during the first year, we need to pick the patients who can hopefully recover from the operation in spite of being near death."

"These operations sound so risky."

"Oh, you have no idea how dangerous they really are. Furthermore, the risk of infection after surgery is also high, and many patients die before or after surgery because their immune systems cannot fight common infections. We will never operate on someone who has an infection because the antirejection drugs administered during surgery actually augment any kind of infection a patient may have."

Oh, Lord, this is awful, I said to myself. How much has Ralph heard of this conversation? I wondered. I'm afraid he's heard too much. But, maybe Dr. Koster's enthusiasm is a good thing. It bothers me that he talks as if his profession is a challenging game, but if he wins, his patient wins.

"There's one other thing I haven't mentioned," he said, interrupting my thoughts, "although I consider this to be a lesser challenge; the patient's blood type and other general, physical characteristics must be a match with the donor. Your husband has the most common blood type, so I don't see that as being a problem."

"Thank you for explaining the system to me," I said, not wanting to hear anymore.

"Well, I'll be here and in charge all week, so don't hesitate to ask me any questions. Let's hope for the best." With that, he almost ran out of the room, his gait reminding me of a small dog.

I turned toward Ralph, who was lying only a few feet from us, and wondered again how much of the conversation he had heard.

"You're going to make it," I told him firmly. "That doctor is overly dramatic. Remember that he said your chances for a transplant are much greater because you're here in ICU."

Ralph looked at me somewhat skeptically.

"I'm going to check into the hotel," I told him, "and then I'll come back to see you."

"Don't be gone long, Donna-girl," he said, in a voice that sounded like a little boy eager for his mother to return. "I'll be waiting for you."

More than anything, I wanted to get away for a while to calm my turbulent emotions. With his sense of urgency, Dr. Koster had caused me to fear that Ralph may not have long to live.

The spring day was warm, as I walked through a park on my way to the hotel and reflected on my conversation with Dr. Koster. I had never really thought about the transplant system, I guess because it had never directly affected me or anyone I knew. Although I had given my consent to be an organ donor on my driver's license, I had no idea at the time how many desperate patients were waiting to receive organ transplants. But I knew it wasn't right to focus on hoping someone would die so Ralph would be given a chance for a liver. Rather, I had to believe that if it was someone's time to die, their gift of an organ was a gift of love.

As I walked into my hotel room, I forced myself to forget how afraid I was and think only positive thoughts about how Ralph would get a transplant and get well. After all, I told myself, he has met every medical challenge up to now. My job is to make sure that he believes he will survive the operation and that he wants to fight to live. Just remember how well he recovered after his last surgery. By the time I walked back to the ICU, I had talked myself back into a positive state of mind.

A nurse, who was taking Ralph's temperature, looked up as I entered the room. "I don't know if anyone told you about our experimental visitation schedule that has just begun," she said. "Normally, visiting hours are very restricted here in ICU. But, as of this week, family members can check in with the head nurse and be given approval for visitation almost anytime.

Unfortunately, this is one of those few times when visitors can't be in the room, but you can come back in about twenty minutes."

I walked out to the waiting room and sat down next to a man I had seen visiting a patient in Ralph's room.

"My wife just got her second liver transplant," he said. "She waited almost three years for the first one, but it failed after six months."

"Do the doctors know why it failed?"

"The doctors don't know much around here, or at least they don't say much. Everyone is afraid of lawsuits."

"I understand the hospital has lost a lot of patients recently," said another woman, who joined in on our conversation. "I've also heard the hospital has been served with quite a few lawsuits and is under intense pressure to improve its performance."

"How did you hear that?" I asked.

"You spend enough time here, and you'll hear the nurses talking."

I wondered if the woman had heard facts or was just listening to idle gossip. After waiting a few polite seconds, I stood up to leave, because I could feel myself becoming anxious again. Above all, I was determined to stay in a positive state of mind.

The flexible visitation schedule gave me the opportunity to visit Ralph frequently and stay abreast of his condition. I settled into a routine where I went to work after talking to the doctors during their morning rounds, and then returned in the late afternoon as they made their final rounds of the day. My boss Randy continued to be supportive and encouraged me to spend as much time as possible at the hospital.

Without knowing why, I felt it was extremely important to stay abreast of Ralph's treatment and to be aware of what went on in the ICU. To that end, I took copious, detailed notes every day. Furthermore, the mere act of note-taking seemed to calm me.

Dr. Koster looked more concerned than usual when he approached me one Monday morning after Ralph had been in the ICU for several weeks.

"Your husband has developed a lung infection," he said. "According to standard procedure, he has to be on antibiotics for ten days, and during that time he cannot be a candidate for a transplant."

Naturally I was disappointed, but I accepted the news as a temporary setback. "I thought someone else is in charge of surgery this week," I said.

"That's true, but I like to continue visiting patients who are waiting for a transplant or who have recently undergone surgery. That way, I can be in tune with the patients' progress when it is my week to be in charge again."

For all his odd ways, he truly is a committed doctor, I thought, as he turned to examine the woman across from Ralph's bed.

On the seventh day after Ralph had started taking antibiotics, Dr. Koster examined him again.

"His lungs are as clear as they could possibly be," he said, "and if I were in charge, I would put him as a Priority 1 on the active list again. Unfortunately, the head surgeon this week plays by the rule book and wouldn't take a chance if it was his own mother. Now is the time your husband should be operated on; I know in my gut this is his chance."

"Isn't there anything you can do about it?" I asked, feeling myself getting upset as he talked.

"I can try, but officially I'm just an observer this week. We have our weekly meeting in a few days when the transplant surgeons and gastroenterologists get together to discuss each patient waiting in the hospital for a transplant. By that time, however, three more days will have passed, and, technically, Ralph will have completed his ten days of antibiotics and can be considered to be active again on the transplant list. It will be very important that he maintain an active Priority 1 status after that meeting. Time is running out. My biggest concern is Dr. Landmeier, who is the head of the gastroenterologists."

I felt a chill run through my body at the mention of Dr. Landmeier's name.

"I don't think he liked Ralph when we met with him many weeks ago before coming into the ICU," I said, hoping Dr. Koster would deny my suspicion.

"You're probably right…for both moral and technical reasons. From a moral standpoint, Dr. Landmeier favors patients who need a transplant through no fault of their own. For example, the woman who is in the bed opposite Ralph, and who supposedly never drank any alcohol, recently underwent her second liver transplant after her body rejected the first one."

"I know. I've talked to her husband on several occasions."

"Medical doctors and surgeons are supposed to ignore the reasons for a patient's condition and leave that up to the psychiatrists," Dr. Koster continued, "but, I sometimes think they pass judgment on patients. For example, Ralph wouldn't have a chance if the psychiatrists hadn't already determined he would stop drinking. But, I think some doctors think they have the right to play God."

Dr. Koster was on a roll, and I could feel him working himself into a frenzy.

"As for the technical aspects…this is the part that really bothers me. Historically, it has been both the responsibility and the prerogative of surgeons to decide when and if a patient is ready for a transplant. After all, it's we who have to bring the patient through surgery. Remember when I told you this is an art, not a science? There is usually a small window of time when a patient is strong enough and free of infection to successfully undergo a transplant. The karma has to be just right, and, I assure you, surgeons are best able to determine that time. These theoretically-minded gastroenterologists don't have a clue, but they think they do…especially Dr. Landmeier."

By now Dr. Koster was almost shouting, and I felt a sharp pain in my stomach as I braced myself. His talk of "karma" sounded so unscientific, and it made me extremely uncomfortable. How does anyone stand a chance in this system? I wondered. It's not surprising there are so many deaths and lawsuits. I forced myself to take a deep breath.

"Don't you think special consideration should be given to the fact Ralph had a severe case of Crohn's disease, which may have weakened his body to the effects of alcohol?"

"At this point, no one cares why he drank. What is on his record is that his cirrhosis of the liver was caused by alcohol abuse. The fact that he had Crohn's for so many years only weakens his chance of survival after surgery and, therefore, is a negative factor."

I cringed at the doctor's words. "He has a lot of things against him, doesn't he?"

"Yes, but don't forget…he is in ICU and accumulating points quickly."

"I'll be here after your meeting tomorrow."

"Yes, you seem to be here all the time, even though we've discontinued the experimental visitor program, you know," he said with an amused glance at me.

I couldn't tell whether he disapproved of my presence or not. Noticing that most of the other family members who had been visiting during the experiment were now gone, I was hoping no one would pay attention to me in the frantic world of the ICU. I didn't check in before entering the ICU, tried to be as unobtrusive as possible, and kept out of the way of the nurses.

"In fact, I don't think I've known anyone who has spent as much time in this ICU as you have," Dr. Koster said.

"Well, don't you think that's because normally Ralph would have been placed in a regular hospital room and most patients are in and out of ICU in days or a week at most?"

"You're probably right."

FIFTEEN

Lana, who tried to come to the hospital at least once a week, was there on the afternoon that Ralph completed his ten days of antibiotics.

"You aren't going to believe this, Lana," I said, "but I was able to look at one of the hospital's computer terminals when no one else was around and was surprised when I saw that Ralph has been designated as a Priority1."

"Wow! That's great!" Lana said.

"I know. I used to read the handwritten notes that doctors wrote during Ralph's previous hospital stays, so I don't think looking at the computer is much different. I do feel a bit guilty, but I'm not doing any harm. I should have a right to know his status."

Just as Lana was about to respond, Dr. Koster entered the room. He seemed anxious and nervous.

"What is Ralph's current status?" Lana asked, after exchanging greetings, in spite of what I told her.

"Oh, he's a Priority 1 because that's how I put him into the system. If the right donor became available now, he's near the top of the list nationwide."

"Can anything change his status?" Lana asked in a sweet voice unlike her normal tone.

"As of today, only we surgeons have the right to change the priority of a patient who is in ICU. Unfortunately, a new system is under consideration that would allow the gastroenterologists to become a collaborative part of the decision-making process. Of course, they have no idea which patients could actually survive a transplant. As for now, the new system is still being discussed and hopefully will never take effect."

This was the first time I had heard anything about the transplant system possibly changing.

"So, I want to be sure where that leaves Ralph," Lana said.

"He came into this hospital under the old system, and he will be grandfathered under the old system, even if it changes in the future," Dr. Koster said in an overly confident voice that made me think this might just be his opinion, not a fact.

"Cowboys," Lana said, as Dr. Koster disappeared down the hallway. "You can practically feel the testosterone in the air whenever any of the surgeons are around."

"Maybe his fervor is a good thing," I said. "There's no doubt he's going to fight to keep Ralph a Priority 1 in the meeting tomorrow."

Lana said goodbye and left the hospital, while I sat down next to Ralph's bed.

"My back hurts so much from lying in bed for so long," Ralph said. "Could you swab my mouth with ice chips, Donna-Girl?"

I found it disturbing to be around Ralph now and see his discomfort. There were at least six tubes attached to various parts of his body. He could neither eat food nor drink fluids and had lost all interest in watching television. The only thing he ever asked me to do now was to hold up his AA book for him to read or swab his mouth with ice chips.

"Please, God," I prayed quietly. "Don't let him get another infection or go into a coma before he has a chance for a transplant. I've seen that happen to so many patients here."

An hour or so later, one of the junior surgeons came into the waiting room where I was seated after leaving Ralph's room.

"Mrs. Fridrych," she said, "I have some consent papers I would like you to sign for a potential transplant on your husband tonight."

"You must be mistaken. I saw Dr. Koster only about an hour ago, and he didn't mention anything about a transplant tonight." Besides, I knew that the head surgeon on duty had a kidney transplant scheduled that evening.

"We just found out about this. Two doctors from our surgical team are already on their way to Florida to remove the liver from the donor's body. It will be many hours before we are ready to begin the operation, but I suggest you sign the papers now."

Even though I had been hoping and praying for weeks for this very thing, now that it was happening, I couldn't believe it.

"Of course," I said, as my hand shook while I signed the papers. "I'm surprised two doctors from here have to fly all the way down to Florida."

"We want to remove the donor's liver ourselves so we can be sure it's done properly and so we can assess the deceased's overall physical condition. The final testing as to the suitability of the liver won't be done until they return here. So, it's going to be a long night. I suggest you go back to your hotel and get some rest. We have your number if we need to get a hold of you."

I immediately called Lana on her cell, knowing she wouldn't be home yet.

"I'll call Keith and tell him I will be staying with you tonight," Lana said, after hearing the news.

"Thank you. You are such a good friend. This is one night I don't want to be alone."

Now my challenge was to be sure Ralph was in the best possible frame of mind before the operation. I could feel the excitement in the ICU as I walked toward his room; the hospital had not received a liver in many days.

"Hi, baby," I said, as I stood by Ralph's bedside. "I have such good news for you. You're going to get a transplant tomorrow morning, then you're going to get well, and we can go home."

Ralph didn't say anything, but he nodded his head and seemed relieved. There was no doubt in my mind that if he received the transplant, he would survive. He knew that I needed him to live for me—and for us. If Ralph didn't survive, then I didn't want to live either. I had the wherewithal to support myself, but for what purpose? So this fight for Ralph's life was as much about my life as it was about his.

Ralph fell asleep while we were waiting for news of when the transplant operation would begin, so I returned to my hotel. Lana was still there resting in my room.

About three in the morning, the phone rang.

"I'm sorry, Donna, but we've cancelled the surgery," Dr. Koster said. "After we performed tests on the donor's liver, I decided it wasn't healthy enough to take a chance with. From the very beginning I knew it was a long shot because all of the other hospitals in the country had turned down the liver, even the other university hospital here in town, but I wanted to be sure there wasn't a chance. I figured it was Ralph's best shot before the meeting today. Anyway, the karma seemed right to me."

"At least, we know Ralph is at the top of the priority list," I told Lana. "Otherwise, he wouldn't have been given this chance."

"Someone should have told us the other hospitals had turned down the liver," Lana said. "If we had known that, we might not have gotten our hopes up so high and be so disappointed now."

Lana continued complaining while she freshened up to go to work. I was only half listening because I was thinking about what I would say to Ralph.

"You'll get another healthy liver," I said, after telling him the disappointing news. I wished I felt as positive as I sounded. Like Dr. Koster, I feared we had missed one of those rare windows of opportunity.

"When?" Ralph asked, with a pleading look that tore at my heart.

"Soon, baby, soon," I said, kissing his forehead as tears rolled down my face. I cried much of the time now. Will there ever be an end to this sadness? I wondered.

"I am not going to be able to attend the meeting today," Dr. Koster told me before I left for work, but, my boss, Dr. Wyman, will attend and argue vigorously for keeping Ralph as a Priority 1. I need to rest today because I am supposed to assist this evening with another transplant operation on the woman across from Ralph's bed. This will be her third liver transplant, but she won't live more than twenty-four hours without it. That's why she has been moved to the top of the list."

"Why would you or your boss have to argue to keep Ralph as a Priority 1 if you surgeons have the final authority for patients in ICU?"

"As I've told you before, this is a complicated system," Dr. Koster replied, sounding slightly irritated.

I had to admit that I could see valid reasoning for opposing arguments regarding which patients should be given highest priority for a liver transplant. Since at the time, only about fifty percent of those patients needing a liver were given the opportunity to receive one, I could understand the argument for giving the highest priority to patients most likely to survive after the operation. I could also understand the argument for giving the opportunity to patients closest to death, if they had a reasonable chance of surviving afterward. In either case, subjectivity was involved in determining those patients most likely to survive, as well as those who were closest to death.

From my discussions with various doctors, it was obvious to me that the opinions among the gastroenterologists and the surgeons weren't even consistent. The one thing the doctors were clearly divided on, however, was who should have the final authority to decide which patient received a liver. Understandably, the surgeons were up in arms because their long-standing authority was being challenged by the gastroenterologists. Unfortunately, Ralph was there in the heat of the conflict. The potential changeover to a new system had escalated the controversy between the two groups of doctors and created an extremely adversarial environment.

I tried querying several doctors about the outcome of the Thursday meeting, but was consistently told to wait to talk to Dr. Koster.

"My prayers are with you and your family," I told the daughter of the woman who had been across from Ralph's bed. "She's been in surgery an awfully long time, hasn't she?"

"Yes, we fear the worst, but are still hoping this transplant takes," she said, as she started crying. "We know it's her last chance."

I put my arms around her and held her as she cried. Under the trying circumstances, I had become close to several of the other families that were waiting for transplants for their loved ones. I was never jealous when someone else received the opportunity for a transplant; I just hoped Ralph's chance would be next.

I left the hospital late Friday afternoon without having talked to Dr. Koster in order to attend a wake for an employee's brother who had committed suicide.

Shortly after arriving at the funeral home, I was able to spend a few minutes alone with my colleague who had lost his brother.

"Please don't mention to anyone that my brother's death was a suicide," he said.

"You don't think your brother's suicide is a bad reflection on you, do you?"

Giving me a surprised look, he nodded his head affirmatively, and I noticed his body relax. "I should have known how depressed he was."

"I'm sure there was no way for you to know he was contemplating suicide. You need all the support you can get right now, and I know your coworkers will have even more empathy for you if they know what happened. Let them help you. Don't go through this alone. Your brother's suicide is not a bad reflection on you."

Although our circumstances were different, I could identify with how he felt, because I felt ashamed about Ralph's drinking, just as he was ashamed of his brother's suicide.

After spending some time at the funeral home, I returned to my hotel, feeling more depressed than usual. I decided to wait until the next morning to see Ralph, hoping I would be in a more positive mood.

When I walked into the ICU the next morning, Dr. Koster immediately approached me. "I tried calling you last night at your home," he said. "I have some bad news."

Surely someone would have gotten in touch with me at the hotel if he died, I thought, as a wave of panic rushed through my body.

"Ralph has been taken off of Priority 1 status and is no longer a ready-now candidate for a transplant. All I can think is that your insurance company must be cutting money off or questioning our treatment. That's the only possible answer. The problem is that he needs to be on the list now. He needs the transplant right now," he shouted in frustration.

I started crying loudly and gulping for air. "Put him back as Priority 1," I demanded. "I'll pay…I'll sell everything!"

Dr. Koster looked at me as if I was crazy. "You have no idea how much this can cost. Another half a million at least. And, there's no assurance Ralph would make it even if he received a transplant."

I was panic-stricken. "I'll pay!" I screamed at him, as I began frantically rummaging through the paper bags that I always carried with me. "Here's a bank statement. Here's a mortgage statement. Here's another one," I said, as I flung pieces of paper at him. Go! Make a copy of these statements. Get him back on Priority 1!"

"And, you go and get a grip on yourself," he said firmly. "Call your company. Call an attorney. Find out what's happening."

He's right, I said to myself. I absolutely have to get control of my emotions. I have to stay strong for Ralph. What would he do without me? He would surely die quickly if I weren't here to plead his case. Oh, my God, what will I do if he dies? Okay, that does it, Donna. Stop! You've got a job to do, I told myself firmly.

I bought a cup of coffee and walked to the pay phones because my cell didn't work in the hospital. Although I hated to call my boss on a Saturday morning for something personal, I felt I had nowhere else to turn.

When Randy's wife answered the phone, I was so overwhelmed with emotion that I could barely talk. "I need…to talk…to Randy," I said between sobs.

Randy called back on his car phone within minutes. As soon as I heard his voice, I started sobbing again. Although I knew crying was the worst thing a woman could do in corporate America no matter what the circumstances, I was beyond being able to control my emotions. I felt it was now or never for Ralph.

"If Ralph doesn't get a transplant soon, he will die," I said between sobs. "I told Dr. Koster I would pay for everything and gave him all of our personal financial papers."

"That was the right thing to do," Randy said soothingly, obviously trying to calm me and understand why I was calling.

"How could the insurance company cut off payment? Why didn't they notify me? You don't think all of a sudden they found out about Ralph drinking, do you?" I asked, again feeling on the verge of hysteria.

"I don't know. Let me check into it. You know I'll do what I can," Randy assured me.

I knew if anyone could help us, Randy could; he was one of the top-ranking executives in my company.

Randy called back promptly at one o'clock, as I stood by a pay phone waiting for his call. "I am absolutely certain the insurance company did not make any waves. Dr. Koster must have jumped to the wrong conclusion."

"How could he do that?"

"I don't know, but I think hospital politics are at play here. You need to get to the bottom of it, Donna."

I had Dr. Koster paged. "My insurance company is not the problem," I told him angrily.

"I know that now," he said, sounding angry as well. "One of Ralph's tests came back indicating he may have tuberculosis."

"What! After all the testing he's been through, now he has TB. Are you kidding?"

"I know what you're thinking, Donna. It's hard for me to believe too, but I saw the results myself. We will have to wait seven days or potentially longer for the culture that was taken to mature. My challenge now is to keep him in ICU and not let him be released to the gastroenterologist team. I've already ordered one of the rooms to be taken over in ICU where he can be quarantined."

A nurse sitting at a desk behind us said in a loud voice: "They want him off the list."

I ignored her and turned my attention back to Dr. Koster. "When did they take him off of Priority 1?" I asked.

"At the Thursday meeting," Dr. Koster admitted. "I was not aware that the change in status was determined at the meeting. This is the first time in twelve years that a priority has been changed without consulting me. My boss has threatened to resign over this unless he is given back the final authority to decide who is or is not a Priority 1 in ICU. Everyone at the meeting agreed that Ralph has less than a fifty-fifty chance of survival, even with a transplant. Livers have been more scarce than usual, and Dr. Landmeier and several other doctors want to see someone higher on the list with better odds of surviving."

"And now we're trapped by the TB threat," I said, knowing they couldn't operate if there was a chance of infection because the antirejection drugs administered during transplant surgery could augment the infection.

"Still, the timing of what happened isn't right," I said, as I tried to figure out the sequence of events during the past few days. "He was grandfathered under the old system, right? How could they change his status on Thursday? The TB test result only came in today, Saturday, right?"

"Maybe it's time for you to talk to the Dean or the President of the hospital," Dr. Koster said, not directly answering my question.

"What?"

"I've been thinking about this. You're the first outsider who has spent enough time here to see what's going on. I think it was wrong that Ralph was taken off of Priority 1, and I think they might listen to you."

"Yeah…right," I said sarcastically, shaking my head from side to side. "Do you honestly think the President or Dean is going to listen to a half-crazed woman who is hysterical about losing her husband?"

A gastroenterologist whom I had never met made the rounds later that morning. She was a woman of East Indian descent with kind, intelligent-looking eyes.

"Your husband is confused about the month, the year, and the name of the hospital he is in," she said softly, after talking to Ralph.

"I'm not surprised by that," I said defensively. "He's been in and out of so many hospitals; no wonder he's confused."

"I understand how distraught you must feel. You were given false information the other night. Your husband would not have been given the liver transplant on Wednesday night. Dr. Koster acted irresponsibly."

"How can you say that? I signed the consent papers that night."

"You will figure this all out because you are very intelligent. You have been lied to on multiple occasions. Don't you need to question the character of someone who lies to you?"

"I'm tired of being caught up in the politics of this hospital," I said. I felt anything but intelligent and doubted I would ever figure out what was really going on.

"I do agree with Dr. Koster on a couple of things," she continued. "This battle between the internist and the surgical teams has been going on far too long. I encourage you to meet with hospital management to raise their awareness of this conflict that is hurting everyone."

"Did Dr. Koster tell you he told me to do the same thing?"

"Not exactly, but let's just say these hospital walls hold few secrets."

"My focus should be on helping my husband, not on resolving this hospital's internal politics."

"That's probably true, but right now the only way you can help your husband is by dealing with the situation as it is."

On Monday, I called a lawyer to discuss our options.

"You could contact the American Medical Association and file a complaint regarding how your husband has been treated," the lawyer said. "Another alternative would be to file a lawsuit against the hospital and doctors. Or, you could demand a meeting between the surgeons and the gastroenterologists with counsel present."

"All of those options would take time, and my husband doesn't have that kind of time. His condition is deteriorating rapidly, and his kidneys are now barely functioning."

"Well, all of the options I can think of will take some time. I don't think there's any way around it. Maybe you should plead your case to the hospital's management. I don't think you have much to lose."

As his physical condition deteriorated, Ralph became less restless, less talkative, and less interested in what was going on in the outside world. So I was surprised when he asked to see a newspaper one afternoon.

I walked out into the waiting room and picked up a sports section, knowing Ralph had always liked sports.

"Look, Ralph, you'll like this story about Michael Jordan," I said. I started to read the article out loud to him.

"I told you to get the paper…the whole paper," he said, sounding extremely upset.

"Why, honey? What do you want to read?"

"The obituaries. There's a whole conspiracy going on around here. These doctors…these very same doctors," he said, lowering his voice to a whisper, "are killing babies in the basement. You've got to believe me. You can see their names in the paper."

He seemed so intense and so certain that for a second I stepped back and thought about what he was saying. Everything else seemed so absurd and crazy, why couldn't this be true?

Then I shook my head vigorously, unable to believe I could even contemplate such a thing. I can't stand anymore, I said to myself. Now I'm going crazy, too. What is wrong with me?

I turned back toward Ralph. "I'll try to find out what I can," I said calmly. "Don't worry, honey, I'll take care of it."

He looked relieved that I seemed to believe him.

Later that day, I described the incident to the psychologist who had been assigned to check up on me and other family members of patients in ICU.

"This often happens to people who have been confined in ICU for a long time," the psychologist said. "It's a form of hallucination we see frequently."

Ralph did not mention the murders again. But then, he started calling out to his deceased grandfather.

"Is your grandfather in the room, Ralph?" I asked.

"He's right here. Can't you see him?"

Then he started singing "Old McDonald" in a sweet voice that sounded like a little boy. He smiled, and I cried as we sang together.

The nurses also smiled when they heard us singing. They probably like having a little levity in this dreadful place where everyone dies, I thought.

Dr. Koster was visibly upset when the woman from Ralph's original room died after receiving a third liver transplant. Then, another woman from his original room in ICU died. I felt grateful to have a bit of peace and quiet, away from all the gruesome scenes, now that Ralph was quarantined in a separate room. Although I believed the nurses had tried to shelter me from some of the horrors, how could they when I was there so much of the time in the ICU where so many people died?

Previously, Dr. Koster's boss, Dr. Wyman, who was the Head of Surgery, had rarely visited the patients in ICU. Yet since the meeting when Ralph's status was changed, I saw him often, particularly visiting Ralph.

"It's my duty to tell you," he said, "that you could move your husband to another hospital, preferably to the university hospital where he had his previous surgeries."

"He wouldn't make it there alive," I said.

"We could keep him alive until he got there," he replied, as if that were the end goal.

"You've done your duty," I told him, totally dismissing the idea. "He would be starting all over. He wouldn't stand a chance."

"A special meeting has been called tomorrow to review your husband's case."

A few minutes later, Ralph's minister friend Anne walked into the hallway. "Ralph started crying the minute you left the room," she said. "He said you had a new boyfriend. I kept telling him it wasn't true, but he said he had seen it with his own eyes. He said it was the man who had been standing at the foot of his bed. I thought you should know."

"Honestly, Anne, sometimes I can't believe the connection between us. For a fleeting moment when I was in Ralph's room, I looked at Dr. Wyman and thought he was an extremely handsome man. That's all. I feel so bad to have added to his misery."

When I walked back into his room, Ralph made kissing noises like a baby.

"Honey, you know how much I love you, don't you?' I asked.

The one interesting thing about this whole nightmare, I thought, is that I have gotten to know Ralph as few wives have the opportunity to know their husbands: through most of our twenty-year marriage as a kind, thoughtful man; when his liver started failing, as a stubborn adolescent; when we first came into this ICU, as a young boy dependent on his mother; and now, as the sweet baby boy everyone said he once was.

Minutes later, another doctor from the gastroenterologist team examined Ralph. She was a large woman with a brusque, harsh manner.

"I don't know why you're putting your husband and yourself through all this," she said in a disgusted tone. "Can't you see it's futile?"

"You don't know him. You don't know how strong he is. If his case is so hopeless, why was he scheduled for a transplant last week?"

"I can't comment on that situation," she said haughtily. "There will be five gastroenterologists and four surgeons at the meeting tomorrow."

"So, you're telling me the odds will be against Ralph ever being returned to a Priority 1?"

"I'm not telling you anything," she said in a harsh voice, "and even if we decided to put him as a Priority 1, it could be weeks before he is operated on."

I wanted to slap the woman in the face. The good thing about her insensitivity, however, was that she propelled me into action.

SIXTEEN

The next morning, I put on my best business suit, walked into the ICU, and handed Dr. Koster the letter I had written the night before. It had been an easy letter for me to write because of the detailed notes I had taken ever since we entered the ICU.

"I think this will get their attention," Dr. Koster said, looking up at me after he had finished reading.

The letter, which was addressed to the hospital's President, Dean, Director, and the heads of the surgical and gastroenterologist teams, explained in simple terms the escalating conflict between the two teams of doctors and what had specifically happened with Ralph's priority status since he had been admitted to the hospital. After receiving Dr. Koster's approval, I dropped off copies of the letter at the addressees' respective offices and went to the cafeteria to get a cup of tea.

As I stood in the cafeteria line, a young woman approached me. "I am Dr. Polowski's assistant," the young woman said. "She would like to speak to you. I'll pay for your tea and bring it to you."

Dr. Polowki was the primary director of the hospital. As I sat down outside her office, I felt calmer and stronger than I had in a long time. The hysteria I so often felt pushing against my chest, the panicked voice I heard screaming inside my head, and the tension I felt throughout my body had subsided for the first time in weeks. I knew what I had to do, and I believed it was Ralph's last chance.

"Dr. Polowski is on the phone," another secretary said, as she handed a phone to me.

The doctor greeted me pleasantly. "I've read your letter, and I suggest we have a meeting today to clear up this situation. I will bring in two independent doctors if that will make you feel more comfortable."

"I'm sorry," I said, "but my husband doesn't have time for meetings. The surgeons and the gastroenterologists need team building in order to learn how to work together, and that doesn't happen overnight. Emotions are running way too high over the transplant system. I want to talk to the President of the hospital, whom I assume has the final decision-making authority."

"He's a very busy man, and I doubt he'll have time to meet with you."

"That's fine. I'll wait," I said, and hung up the phone.

I arrived at the President's office a little after 8:30.

"He's been on vacation for ten days and is fully booked today," the President's assistant told me in response to my request to see him.

"I'll wait as long as necessary," I said, sitting down on a sofa next to her desk.

Less than a half an hour later, another assistant directed me into the President's office.

I saw a short man looking out the window with his back to me, dressed in suit pants and a white jacket. For some reason, I hadn't expected to see a doctor.

"Please sit down, Mrs. Fridrych," he said, turning around and directing me toward his conference table.

Sitting down at the long table, I suddenly felt nervous and decided to let him begin the conversation.

"I have just been briefed by Dr. Polowski and have heard some of the medical facts about your husband's case. I have also read your letter. It appears you have done a fairly good job of assessing your husband's situation."

I tried not to let my feelings of surprise and relief register on my face. At least he's not going to patronize me and act as if I don't know what's going on, as I feared he might do, I thought. He must be concerned about

Ralph's case. Otherwise, why would he have seen me so quickly?

Silence hung in the air between us. I had the feeling he was trying to decide the best way to deal with me, so I waited for him to speak.

"I understand the committee changed your husband's status last Thursday due to the identification of a new infection," he said.

"His infection had been treated and his lungs were clear as of last Thursday," I said quickly. "And, this ridiculous TB threat had not been identified yet."

"Furthermore, I understand the surgical team did not accept the decision of the committee," he said, seeming to ignore my input.

"There was no valid reason to change his status last Thursday," I said, unable to conceal my anger any longer. "Nothing changed from the night before when I signed consent papers for a transplant. Do you know that Dr. Wyman has threatened to resign over this?"

"I hired Dr. Wyman. He is a fine surgeon," he said, seeming perturbed.

Then he leaned back in his chair and looked up at the ceiling. "Your husband is in an unusual situation," he said, after what seemed like several minutes of contemplation. "Normally, your husband would have been placed in a regular hospital room when he entered the hospital and been overseen by the gastroenterologist group. It was highly unusual that your husband went directly into the ICU and, therefore, the surgeons had control over his case from the beginning. The points he gained by being placed directly in ICU are part of the issue here."

"All I know is that both the gastroenterologists and the surgeons agreed from the beginning that my husband needed a transplant as soon as possible." I paused to be sure he was listening. "I also know that I'm being used by both sides," I added.

He smiled. "I was trying to think of a nice way of telling you that," he said, "but I guess you beat me to the punch." His acknowledgement and the look on his face made me believe I had gained some respect from him because of my admission.

"However, I really don't care how I'm being used," I said, after another brief, uncomfortable pause. "I just want my husband to have a fair chance for a liver transplant."

Then he launched into a lengthy discussion of how the transplant system worked and how important it was to stay within the system.

"I couldn't agree with you more. Given the life and death decisions that must be made every day due to the organ shortage, I believe it is important to follow an objective system. That's my point. The system is not being followed in my husband's case. He entered the hospital under the current system, and he should be treated according to the existing rules. He is near death, and has been accumulating points for weeks in ICU; he should be a Priority 1. This talk of TB is ridiculous and just an excuse for not making him a Priority 1. No one…and I mean no one… believes my husband has TB. The nurses don't even put masks on when they enter his room. The nurses understand what's going on in this hospital. You should talk to them."

"You understand the system is in transition?"

"I don't care. My husband is grandfathered under the old system. He was a Priority 1 on Wednesday, and he was changed on Thursday for no apparent reason."

"Two of our doctors have told me your husband may never have been a Priority 1."

I remembered how I had seen with my own eyes that Ralph had been designated a Priority 1 status, but chose not to mention that fact as I knew I had no business looking at the hospital's computer system.

"Then why was he prepped for a transplant last Wednesday, and why did I sign the consent papers?" I asked in a challenging tone. "Why was I called at three in the morning and told the surgery was cancelled because the liver was not in good enough condition to be transplanted? Those are facts," I said, in a louder voice than I had intended. "Also, everyone in the ICU knew he was the transplant candidate that night. That's what everyone was talking about, even the other patients' families."

"I need to do more research on your husband's case," he said, again looking perturbed. "I've been gone for ten days, and I oversee ten hospitals."

He has no idea what goes on underneath him in this hospital, I thought.

"As I said, Mrs. Fridrych, I need to do more research about your husband's case. There's obviously much I don't know about it. I will get the facts and get back to you as soon as possible. I understand the urgency."

I stood up to leave the room, believing I had done a good job of making my points and pleading Ralph's case, even though I had been somewhat confrontational. At least I hadn't started crying, I thought.

When I reached the doorway, I turned around to face him. "One more thing," I said, pausing to be sure he was listening to me. "I'm not interested in filing a lawsuit. All I want is for my husband to have a fair chance."

When I walked back into Ralph's room in the ICU, two Infectious Disease doctors were standing on either side of his bed. I noticed that neither of them was wearing the required masks for quarantine. For God's sake, I thought, you would think they would at least put on a pretense.

"We expect to be able to confirm the results of the culture in a few days," the younger of the two doctors said, "and we don't expect to have to recommend treatment for TB or any other infection. We're sorry you've had to go through this," he added, seeming sincerely apologetic.

I decided to leave the hospital, because I didn't want to be seen sitting around appearing anxious. It may have been implausible for me to think that hospital management would feel threatened by some lady who was upset about her husband's treatment, but I believed I had touched on issues that went beyond my knowledge.

When I returned to the hospital later that afternoon, I was surprised to hear that the President had requested to see me again. I walked hurriedly to his office and was immediately ushered inside by his secretary.

"I am asking a trusted friend and doctor, who has had much experience with transplant operations, to examine your husband tomorrow," the President said. "The Dean was supposed to be off, but I have asked him to come in as well. Since several doctors are still concerned about an infection, we will take another culture from your husband's lungs. It is most likely, however, that he will be returned to a Priority 1 status immediately," he said, pausing to ensure his comment had registered with me.

I couldn't have been more elated, but I tried to keep the expression on my face neutral.

"If a liver becomes available, however, we will not perform the surgery unless he is stable and free of infection. Furthermore, we will not use your husband's Priority 1 status to get a liver for another patient. Your husband was, in fact, taken off of Priority 1 status on Thursday because of the identification of a new infection."

This was the only fact that didn't match up with what Dr. Koster had told me. I didn't say anything in response, because all I really cared about was that Ralph be returned to a Priority 1. For this to happen would be an exception to the rules, because the culture results had not been finalized by the Infectious Disease doctors.

If Ralph were not returned to a Priority 1 status, I didn't know what I would do. I frequently thought about various forms of disruptive action I could take, especially while driving back and forth to work. I was angrier than I had ever been…even angrier than I was over my father's inept hospital treatment. Before my meeting with the President, I felt so battered about by the warring factions of doctors that if the President had not listened to me and treated me with respect, I was seriously thinking about some form of public protest.

After leaving the President's office, I walked quickly to Ralph's room. "I think you're back at the top of the list, baby," I said, as tears of happiness and relief streamed down my face. "Do you understand? You're going to get a healthy liver and get better."

Ralph smiled and grabbed my hand. "Thank you, Donna-Girl," was all he said, in an adult-sounding voice and with a look of gratitude.

"You still want to live, don't you, sweetheart?" I asked, as my tears continued to flow.

He nodded his head in the affirmative.

For months I had been worried that Ralph would ask one of the doctors to take him off life support when I wasn't around. Although he seemed to want to live and receive a liver transplant, the quality of his life by most standards was poor, and he was, in fact, being kept alive by various machines. I remembered how he had twice signed a living will form before previous surgeries, indicating he didn't want to be kept alive by extreme measures. Perhaps the difference was that in spite of the many machines keeping him alive, there was hope for a transplant and recovery. I also realized that the decision to take someone off life support is much more complicated than merely looking at a piece of paper that has been signed at an earlier time and under different circumstances.

"I'm surprised the President spent so much time with you," Dr. Koster said when I told him about both my meetings that day. "He's a very busy man. I've never met with him," he said, sounding envious.

"Well, I think the only reason he met with me was because he knew something wasn't right with Ralph's case. I now think Ralph being placed as a Priority 1 because he earned so many points by being placed in the ICU, instead of a regular room, is the key to the controversy. But who knows how quickly he might have been placed into the ICU anyway for a myriad of reasons and started gaining points quickly?"

"You're absolutely right. By the way, Ralph has been returned to a

Priority 1 status."

The next morning, I paged Dr. Koster to let him review a note I had written to the President.

"There's no reason to send this now, Donna. Things are looking up."

"I want to send the note for myself," I told him. "I want to thank him for his support and also put in writing the fact that Ralph did not have a new infection last Thursday."

"Actually, there were results that came in on Thursday that identified a possible new infection. The results, however, were not conclusive. I immediately started treating Ralph for an infection until he could be retested."

"Then why did you jump to the conclusion that my insurance company was at fault on Saturday?"

"Because I thought only I or Dr. Wyman could change his status. And, since neither of us approved the change, I thought the only logical answer was your insurance company."

I decided to forego questioning or arguing with him further, because now I didn't fully trust what he told me. The only thing I knew for sure was that Ralph had been losing precious time during this period of controversy. And, even though Ralph had been returned to a Priority 1 status, how could I know the doctors wouldn't tell me one thing, but have no real intention of giving Ralph a chance for a liver transplant?

The next day, I sat with Doreen in the waiting room, while Mack went in to visit Ralph in his room. A few minutes later, Mack returned to the waiting room.

"It was like the old days," he said, smiling and crying at the same time. "Ralph actually sat up and talked about the time we burned down the tree in the town park and how we didn't get blamed for doing it. All these years it's been our secret."

I found it incredulous that Ralph had been in such a good mood. I was glad that Mack had had the opportunity to see a rare surge of energy from his best friend, though I was a bit jealous, because I couldn't remember the last time Ralph and I had had such a fun conversation.

SEVENTEEN

"My neck and my back hurt so much," Ralph complained. I had stopped in to see him before leaving for home on Saturday morning, my usual day to go home for a few hours.

"I'm sure it's the excessive fluid in his abdomen that's putting pressure on his back," said Dr. Sanchez, an assisting surgeon. "We'll perform an abdominal tap and drain the fluid again with a needle. Dialysis is no longer effective on him."

An abdominal tap was a routine procedure for patients in the final stages of renal failure and one that had been performed numerous times on Ralph. Dr. Koster had already told me that Ralph now needed a kidney as well as a liver transplant and that there was a chance both could be done at the same time.

After Dr. Sanchez left the room, Ralph and I were alone. Even though the concern about Ralph having TB had been eliminated, he remained in isolation in the same large room.

"I'm going home for a while, honey," I said.

Suddenly, he pushed himself up on his elbow, in spite of the many tubes connected to his body, demonstrating a strength and energy I hadn't seen in months. Then he grabbed my left shoulder and braced himself in a half-sitting position.

"Take me with you," he pleaded. The desperation in his voice and the beseeching look in his eyes tore at my heart.

"Honey, I couldn't possibly take you out of here. You couldn't live without these machines. You couldn't walk." He seemed so rational that I decided the best approach was to try reasoning with him. "I'm living in a hotel room now, not at home, remember? I'm just going home to do errands."

"I'll stay with you in the hotel," he insisted.

"No, Ralph, I can't take you with me. I'm sorry, honey," I said, feeling terrible even though I knew it was an irrational request.

"I'll be back before you know it," I said, and then kissed him good-bye. "As soon as you get your new liver, then you can come home." I forced myself to leave the room quickly before he became more upset.

"Please check on my husband," I told one of the nurses near his room, while I tried to keep from crying. "He seems unusually agitated and is asking to go home."

That was awful, I said to myself, as I drove home. I don't ever remember seeing him look so desperate. And he seemed so sane. But just remember how logical he sounded when he talked about babies being killed in the hospital's basement, I told myself.

After a brief visit with Janice and the puppies, I drove over to Body & Soul where I had booked an appointment with my favorite esthetician, Laura.

Of course I enjoyed having a facial, but the real reason I relished my treatments was because of Laura. There was a strong connection between the two of us that frequently allowed us to understand each other's thoughts without verbalizing them. She had a remarkable ability to help me relax, and the headaches I had started experiencing again usually disappeared by the time she finished.

I had fallen asleep when the spa manager knocked on the door, woke me up, and handed me a portable phone. "A Dr. Koster says he needs to talk to you," she said.

"Oh, my God, now what?" I said, grabbing the phone.

"Ralph's intestine was punctured while removing fluid from his abdomen," Dr. Koster said calmly. "Depending upon where the puncture is and how severe it is, surgery may be necessary. I doubt, however, he would survive the operation. It will be a difficult decision for you, Donna."

"He will pull through," I told Dr. Koster with strong conviction. "He always does."

"Dr. Sanchez feels terrible about what happened. We will let you know if he gets any worse."

"I'm coming back to the hospital right away. Call my cell phone if you need to."

I tried to keep myself from panicking. This is just one more thing to surmount, I told myself. Imagine how guilty I would feel if he died while I was having a facial. God just couldn't do that to me after all these months of trying to be there for him as often as I could.

After Laura wiped my face quickly and I had dressed, I was walking by the back office when my cell phone rang. It was Ralph's head nurse. "I think you better come to the hospital right away, Mrs. Fridrych," she said.

Laura, who had followed me, caught me as my knees buckled for the second time in my life, and I fell backward into her arms. She held me upright, as I tried to catch my breath and gather my strength.

"Get a hold of yourself, Donna. Don't fall apart," Laura told me sternly. The manager and several other members of the staff had gathered around us.

"That was one of Ralph's nurses," I told them, and then started to cry. "It must be pretty serious if she called. Ralph begged me to take him out of the hospital this morning," I said, remembering his desperate pleas of only a few hours ago. "Somehow, he must have had a premonition this was going to happen…just like my father had a panic attack the morning before he had a minor surgery. They know…they know…I know they know before something terrible happens," I said, on the verge of hyperventilating.

My body trembled, and I sounded hysterical to myself. I don't know what a nervous breakdown feels like, I thought, but if I'm ever going to have one, it'll be now. Then I slipped under my glass cover.

"She can't drive," I heard Laura tell our manager in a voice that sounded far away to me, as if she was in another room, even though she was standing next to me.

Normally, I would have protested that I could drive myself, but I felt as if I was in a trance and had to do what I was told. By the time I arrived at the hospital, I was calm but frightened. During the trip, I had slipped out from under my glass cover.

"I feel very badly," Dr. Sanchez said, after I walked into the hallway of the ICU.

Without responding, I went into Ralph's room and looked at him. His eyes were bloody, his legs were leaking fluid, and his face was swollen to twice its normal size. I felt numb and found it hard to believe that it was really Ralph in that hospital bed. He looks like Frankenstein's monster, I thought. How could that beautiful body turn into this?

Dr. Sanchez came in and asked me to leave the room and wait outside.

About twenty minutes later, Dr. Sanchez found me in the waiting room. "His breathing is smoother and his oxygen level is up," he said, and then looked down at his hands. "I tapped on his abdomen four or five times before doing the procedure, and entered his abdomen near the same point as other times."

It was obvious to me how bad he felt. "I know it was an accident," I said. "I don't blame you, because I've seen how hard you work and how you care for your patients."

I did blame hospital management for the mistake, however. Except for Dr. Koster, Dr. Sanchez worked more hours than any other doctor there. Who in their right mind would let an overtired assistant perform an abdominal tap? To me, this was just one more sign of poor management.

Ralph was unresponsive when I went back into his room. He was intubated, and his eyes were shut.

Dr. Koster walked into the room and stood next to me. "I don't think we should perform any more surgery," he said. "Even if we find the source of the bleeding and he survives the surgery, he couldn't survive a transplant."

"I want you to do everything possible to keep him alive and give him an opportunity for a transplant. Even if there's only a small chance, I don't want to give up. I'm not sure what the right medical decision is, but I want you to do everything humanly possible to save him," I said firmly.

"I don't want to put you or Ralph through anything more."

"Don't worry about me. And I don't think Ralph has given up."

As Dr. Koster was leaving the room, I wondered if some of his ambivalence about performing surgery on Ralph was because he already had another operation scheduled early the next morning. I had gotten into the habit of keeping tabs on the three head surgeons' schedules, so I would know when there was a window of opportunity for another transplant operation. I also continued to take notes to cover everything that had happened since we first entered the hospital.

By that evening, Ralph was bleeding profusely from his eyes and mouth. Three nurses worked frantically giving him blood transfusions. Sweat poured from their brows, even though the temperature in the room was quite cool. I jumped back as a pair of bloody surgical gloves was flung across the room and landed on top of my briefcase.

This can't be real, I thought to myself. Soon I will wake up and know this was only a nightmare. My body felt disconnected from my mind again—trancelike, as if I could no longer react or feel anything.

Desperate calls from the nurses for more bags of blood were followed by more transfusions. Surely, I shouldn't be in here, I thought, unable to take my eyes off of the nurses' tense faces.

I suddenly became aware of someone standing next to me. I turned and looked into the steely eyes of the gastroenterologist who had let me know in no uncertain terms that she didn't think Ralph should have the opportunity for a transplant.

This really is a nightmare, I thought. How could she be the one on duty tonight? I felt a chill run from my head to my toes and hysteria rise in my throat, as I clasped my arms around my waist.

"I can do a scope on him to see where the bleeding is originating," she said, "but you need to realize that it may be his last memory."

I felt paralyzed. How could I make such a decision?

"He'll never be able to survive a transplant now," she said, "so why put him through another ordeal?"

This doctor is the last person on earth I want to touch Ralph, I thought, feeling trapped. Although I knew that it probably wasn't true, I actually feared she might do something subtle to let him die.

"Look," she said in a harsh voice, as if she had read my mind. "No matter what you think of me, I am excellent at doing this procedure. There's probably no one better."

What choice do I have? the voice inside my head screamed. He will surely bleed to death if this continues. I'm so scared. God, help me!

"Go ahead. Do the procedure," I said, bursting into tears and walking away from her. Please, God, don't let this be his last memory, I prayed.

After I walked into the ICU waiting room and sat down, the hospital chaplain sat down next to me. Throughout our entire stay in the hospital, she had never talked to me, but I had seen her with other families, usually before their loved one died.

They know! They know! They always know when someone is going to die, I said to myself, and buried my head in my hands.

I had seen the routine many times. The doctors, knowing within a few hours of a person's death, would move the patient to an isolated room where their family could be alone with their loved one for the last few hours of their life. I feared that Ralph had been kept in isolation partly because the doctors saw no sense in putting him in a room with other patients and then having to move him again to die.

In spite of my fears, I found myself soothed by the chaplain's loving words and prayers as she held my hand. She was a beautiful, middle-aged, black woman with a gentle touch.

About an hour later, the gastroenterologist who performed the procedure on Ralph came into the waiting room with a smirk on her face and her hands on her hips. "He is one tough guy," she said, shaking her head from side to side. "Much to my surprise, we found minimal internal bleeding in his abdomen. The bleeding must be coming from someplace else. But, he came through the procedure fine. I am truly amazed."

"I keep telling everyone how strong he is," I said vehemently.

"I'll give my report to Dr. Koster," she said, then turned and walked away.

When I returned to Ralph's room, the same three nurses were still there, frantically giving him blood transfusions. I was convinced the gastroenterologist hadn't performed the procedure effectively.

At 7:30 the next morning, Dr. Sanchez approached me in the ICU waiting room.

"Dr. Koster has scheduled Ralph for surgery in a few hours to try to identify the source of bleeding," he said.

"What?" I exclaimed, almost unable to believe what he had said. "I thought he was in a transplant surgery."

"That surgery was cancelled and now the operating room is free. I'm surprised Dr. Koster is doing this," he added.

"What would you do," I asked, "if a member of your family was in our situation?"

"I'm not the right person to ask. I personally think most families would have given up long ago. My background and beliefs do not encourage pain and suffering. You should talk to Dr. Koster. I am just here to learn."

His words bothered me immensely. I felt as though he was accusing me of allowing Ralph to be tortured. How could I explain that I knew Ralph was fighting to stay alive, even though for years he had always said he didn't want to be on life support systems? Had I truly believed there was no chance he could survive a transplant, I would have given up hope and let him go, I told myself. No one really understood how strong he was. Despite Ralph's discomfort during the past months, I believed he had never been in severe pain. As Dr. Sanchez walked away, I forced myself to stop worrying about what he had said and put my mind on the surgery ahead of us.

Dr. Koster came out to the waiting room to see me before Ralph was taken into surgery. "The odds are very low," he said. "Even if he makes it through this surgery and then receives a transplant, we're talking about at most a one or two per cent chance for survival."

"It's better than zero," I said without emotion, hoping I was making the right decision. It was just so hard for me to give up and admit defeat.

A few minutes later, Janice walked into the waiting room.

"It's been too long since I see my boy," she said with her hands on her hips.

We hugged and walked into Ralph's room. To her credit, Janice didn't wince at Ralph's appearance. She walked up to his bedside and began singing a gospel tune.

This is exactly what Ralph would have wanted, I thought, as tears rolled down my cheeks. No one could have sung better that morning than Janice.

Ralph was taken into surgery at about eleven.

"It couldn't have gone better," Dr. Koster said late that afternoon. "His heart came through the surgery as strong as ever. We found a small hole from the perforated intestine against his abdomen wall and an enormous amount of blood. I think we got most of the blood out. Time will tell."

I started crying—this time, tears of joy.

As I stood in Ralph's room, my eyes were fixated on the monitor above his head, which, among other things, registered when he breathed on his own. On those few occasions when I saw he actually breathed instead of letting a machine do it for him, my heart soared with hope.

"I'm exhausted, Janice," I said, after watching the monitor for a while.

"Why don't you stay with me tonight? There's an extra bed in my room, and I don't want you to take public transportation at this hour. Your daughter can take care of the puppies tonight and you can go home in the morning."

About one o'clock the next morning, I woke to hear Janice moaning and thrashing in her bed. Then she fell onto the floor.

"What's wrong?" I asked, jumping out of bed and shaking her shoulder.

"A bad dream," Janice answered. She went to the bathroom, got back into bed, and fell asleep. So did I.

Two hours later, the same thing happened again. Only this time I couldn't wake her. She was thrashing on the floor between the two beds.

"Oh, my God!" I screamed, as I tried in vain to pick her up. "I can't lift her." She had to weigh well over two hundred pounds.

I called the hotel operator. "I need help!" I screamed into the phone. "I have a woman here who is very sick. She needs to be taken to a hospital right away."

"I'll send the security guard on duty right up to your room," the receptionist said.

My heart was racing. As I opened the door for the security guard, I started to cry. He was at least 6'5" and looked thin but muscular, like Ralph used to be. He was a black man with a beautiful, gentle smile.

"Everyone calls me Big John," he said.

"We need to go to the county hospital," I told him. "I know she's been there before, and I don't think she has insurance for a regular hospital." He moved quickly, and between the two of us, we dragged Janice to the elevator and out to his van.

Within minutes, we arrived at the county hospital, which was only a short distance from the hospital where Ralph was. Two men lifted her onto a stretcher and took her into a room with many other patients.

"She had an epileptic seizure," a young male doctor told me after examining her. "She'll be fine. We get a lot of experience here."

Feeling almost lifeless from exhaustion, I walked out to the reception area to call Janice's daughter, because I had left my purse and cell phone in the hotel room.

"We don't have a phone here for public use," the receptionist told me. "Go back outside and turn to your right. Then walk along the passageway until you come to another building. There will be pay phones in the lobby of that building."

"I don't have any money with me."

"Call collect," she said, sounding as if she was used to hearing this dilemma.

That does it, I thought. I can't take anymore. I just want to scream and stomp my feet and hit somebody. But, as was typical these days, I just started crying.

As I walked along the dark passageway, I saw two men lying on the pavement. Oh, my God, I said to myself. I don't know if they're alive or dead or drunk or waiting to rob someone. I ran the rest of the way to the next building, lifting my legs as high as I could to jump over the rubbish strewn in my path.

"Your mother is all right," I told Janice's daughter, breathing heavily into the phone from the exertion of running and the panic I felt. "She had a seizure and will need to be picked up at the county hospital downtown. How soon do you think you can get here?"

"I can't," her daughter said. "I have no transportation."

"Call your friends," I said. "This is an emergency. I can't stay here. I need to get back to my husband's hospital."

"I can't miss school today. It's an important day."

"For God's sake, this is your mother!" I yelled at her. "This is your duty. Get down here right now."

"No, I can't," her daughter said and hung up the phone.

I was beside myself, feeling once again an awful surge of panic and sense of entrapment. This is too much, I said to myself. I can't handle it. Ralph could be dead for all I know. I tried to calm myself by taking deep breaths, but I wasn't sure how much longer I could keep myself under control.

"Give me your cousin's number," I told Janice's daughter when I called her back.

I quickly learned that Janice's cousin had an appointment at the county hospital later that morning. At one minute things couldn't get worse, and then, just like with Ralph, they suddenly looked up, I thought. These ups and downs that I had no control over were driving me crazy.

Running back outside through the dark corridor, I saw the two bodies were still there in the same place where I had seen them before. Oh, God, I hope they're just sleeping, I said to myself. I'll have to tell the receptionist.

Janice was propped up in bed when I returned.

"Do you know what wrong with me?" Janice asked.

"Yes, the doctor told me. You'll be fine."

"I didn't have medicine with me. I don't think one night not taking pills would cause problem. I'm sorry for do this to you."

"That's okay," I told her, touching her hand. "You're fine. I need to get back to Ralph. Your cousin will be here shortly."

I went back to the hotel, relieved to find that no one had left me a message, and I showered and changed. By then it was daylight, and I went to the hospital to see Ralph and Dr. Koster.

"Everything is moving along okay for right now, Donna," Dr. Koster said. "We're going in the right direction. The next day or so will determine if he develops an infection. That's our biggest worry right now."

I sat next to Ralph's bed for a while, holding his swollen hand and talking to him. "I hope you're okay with what I've done, baby. I know you're tough. I know you can make it. Please make it. I don't want to live without you. I'm going to work for a few hours, and then I'll be back. I love you." I hoped he heard me.

Later that morning, I drove to work like a zombie. As I walked into my office building, a manager whom I was close to asked how Ralph was doing. I started crying. It took only one kind word now, and I was in tears…especially after the stress and lack of sleep from the night before.

"I'm not sure he'll make it," I admitted.

He looked shocked. It was the first time I had acknowledged out loud that Ralph might die. I had kept up such a stoic facade at work that no one except Lana was aware of how close he was to death. "I can't talk about it now," I said, trying to stop crying.

When my boss Randy popped his head into my office, I told him about the previous weekend's happenings: the puncture of Ralph's intestine on Saturday, the surgery on Sunday, and the episode with Janice the night before. I wanted him to stay abreast of what was happening because I valued his ongoing advice.

Randy just shook his head when I finished bringing him up to date.

When I arrived back at the hospital late that afternoon, Mack and Doreen were sitting in the ICU waiting room. Although I had tried to prepare Mack for how Ralph looked now, his face looked red from crying,

"I'm sorry, Mack; I know he looks awful. Maybe it would have been better if you could remember him as he was the last time you visited."

"No, I'm glad I came. I just hope he isn't in pain."

"The nurses told me he does react to poking and prodding, but otherwise does not appear to be in discomfort."

"Why is his body so bloated?"

"He's no longer able to eliminate fluids except through the pores of his skin. Dr. Koster says he needs a kidney transplant, too, but the liver is the most critical. I know how horrible he looks and smells."

Mack started crying again.

Later that evening, Dr. Koster and I stood together watching the monitor in Ralph's room.

"He should have had a transplant as soon as he came into this hospital," he said vehemently.

Then Dr. Wyman walked into the room. "It would be a good time to call in family," he said. "I assure you we will do everything we can to keep him alive, but I don't expect him to recover. We will not cross the line, however, of being inhumane," he said firmly.

They all think I've crossed that line, I thought, but they've let me do it because I've pushed them and threatened them, and some of them love the thrill of experimenting against all odds. Perhaps, I have gone too far, but I know Ralph wasn't in intense pain…and then the puncture happened. I tried rationalizing to myself all the extreme measures I had pushed the doctors to take to save Ralph's life—to save my own life.

Every time I thought about Ralph begging me to take him with me on Saturday morning, I started crying. I'll never forget the look on his face, I said to myself. I just can't bear the thought of that awful moment. What if that is the last memory I will ever have of him being awake and coherent? God, please don't let that happen.

On Monday night, I saw on the monitor that Ralph was occasionally breathing by himself—very infrequently, perhaps one out of thirty breaths. But he showed no other signs of responsiveness.

"Please don't leave me, baby," I begged him.

On Tuesday, I stared at the monitor, hoping to see it register at least one voluntary breath from Ralph. It didn't. The nurses continued increasing his dosage of blood pressure medication.

Randy had told me recently that the sense of smell was the last to go before someone died. So I bought some mint leaves for Ralph, because he had always liked the smell of mint, which he grew in his garden. But when I placed the leaves under his nose, he didn't respond.

"You can do it, honey. Please come around. You've done it so many times before. I know you will...." I kept up a continuous stream of positive chatter, as I always did when I was in his room with him, hoping he could still hear me.

Then I went under my glass cover once again.

EIGHTEEN

"I don't think he can recover," Dr. Koster told me on Wednesday. "I could be wrong; there are always exceptions, but I'm usually right. I'm afraid he's in a syndrome of lowering blood pressure, fluid retention, and possible infection. If there is any window to operate, it will be infinitesimally small."

"How can you say that when only two days ago you were sounding hopeful?"

"Perhaps, I was just overly optimistic because I was encouraged he made it through surgery on Sunday. I don't want to crush your hopes, but I usually know when a patient is nearing the end."

No more questions, I said to myself. I'm not going to ask him anything because his answers only upset me. I just have to think positively. But I do believe he is being honest with me because he isn't acting or talking in his usual boastful manner.

When I left work on Friday afternoon to go to the hospital, Lana followed me in her car because she planned to stay with me during the weekend.

When we walked into Ralph's room, she went to his bed and touched his hand. "Hi Ralph. How are you doing?" she asked in a soft voice. "We're ready to get you out of here. Let's hope it will be soon.

"I'm not sure how much lower his blood pressure can go," I said to Lana, as we watched the monitor in Ralph's room. "I'm afraid to ask. His nurse told me he's being given almost the maximum amount of blood pressure medication they can give."

"If she said almost, that means they can still give him more," Lana said.

At times she was as ridiculously optimistic as I was. "Are you all right?" I asked, as we walked out into the hallway.

"You prepared me well," she said in a calm voice, although she looked a little sick.

One of the surgeons walked up to us. As I introduced him to Lana, he gently placed his hand on my cheek and held it there for a few seconds, almost in a caress. Then without saying anything, he walked away.

"Doctors usually don't act like that," Lana said.

"That's because I've been here for so many months and have seen and talked with many of them daily. Even though they know it's been my decision to put Ralph and myself through all this torture, I think they feel sorry for me."

Ralph's sister had been trying for some time to persuade me to talk to a psychic friend of hers. Finally, I agreed. What harm can it do, I decided, if it satisfies Sarah and gets her to stop bugging me?

When the phone rang the next morning in my hotel room, I placed the psychic on the speakerphone so Lana could listen, too.

"It's totally up to Ralph what happens," the psychic said. "He needs to go back and clear up some things he's been carrying around since he was a little boy. You can help him by visualizing a golden light while placing your hands over his head and moving them down over his body to his feet, as if you were sweeping away the hurt and disease with the light. In the end, however, it's his decision."

"He's in very bad shape," I said. "It's hard to see how he could rally even if he wanted to."

"It's his decision," she repeated. "He must address his past. He has not reached his potential."

Lana was crying as she took notes about what the psychic said; I just felt numb.

"I don't think that conversation was particularly helpful," I said, when we finished the call. "Who doesn't have things to resolve from their past?"

"I agree," Lana said, "but I guess it won't hurt if we try the procedure she suggested over his body."

Before Lana and I were ready to leave for the hospital, Dr. Koster called. "I think it will be this weekend, Donna. I thought you should know."

"Thank you for calling," I said after I had taken a deep breath. I didn't cry. I felt I had permanently moved under my glass cover, and nothing was going to make me come out from under it.

"I refuse to believe what Dr. Koster said about this weekend," I told Lana. "Ralph has always rallied when no one thought he would. Perhaps, the psychic was right and he just needs to decide he wants to live."

Lana and I stood in Ralph's room most of the day on Saturday with our eyes glued to the monitor, which showed his blood pressure continuing to slowly drop.

"He's now on the maximum amount of blood pressure medication we can give him," one of his nurses said.

Oh, my God, I thought, as I was jolted out from under my glass cover for a moment. This is what I've been worried about. Then, I retreated back under my glass cover. No more tears, no more hysteria, I told myself. If I get upset this time, I will lose my mind.

Lana had made a reservation for Saturday evening at a nearby restaurant. Although I didn't think I had the appetite to eat, the meal was excellent, and we both ate most of our food.

"I feel so guilty that I'm enjoying this food and just the time away from the hospital," I said. "You know, I think I've finally used up all my tears. That psychic didn't make me cry this morning like you did."

"You know you can't feel guilty. That's not what Ralph would want. Life goes on."

"I don't see how it could go on for me without him. I wish I could believe life would go on, but I honestly don't care anymore."

"It will go on. You're just a little used up right now. Let's think positive thoughts about Ralph recovering."

We looked at each other skeptically. I knew in my heart that the charade we were acting out was becoming more and more difficult to sustain. Otherwise, why would Lana be staying with me this weekend?

When we came out of the restaurant, thunder crashed, lightening flashed, and rain poured down, flooding the streets. Our taxi driver told us that it was one of the worst flash floods the city had ever experienced.

As soon as we got back to our hotel, I called the nurse on duty.

"I think you should stay overnight…here in the waiting room," she said in a solemn voice.

The mere thought of that scary waiting room, with lightning and thunder reverberating back and forth in the six-story atrium made me shudder. But, I knew I had to go. What if Ralph does die and I'm not there? I asked myself. I would feel terrible.

Lana and I put on sweat pants and walked through the rain over to the hospital. Before we went to Ralph's room, Lana pushed chairs together to make a bed for each of us, while I went into the ICU and got extra blankets and pillows from the nurses. Before lying down, we stood on either side of Ralph's bed and watched his inert body, as the graphs on the machines dropped dangerously low.

Oh, my God! What have I done? the frightened voice screamed inside my head. Panic mounted within me as we stood there watching the gruesome sight that had once been my beautiful beloved, but then it quickly subsided, and I felt peaceful once again, moving back under my glass cover where my body could just shut down. I didn't know what to say to Ralph or what to do. I had said everything I could think of but to say good-bye—and that was something I refused to do.

"I'm not going to sleep," Lana said, as we walked out to the waiting room. "I don't like the looks of that guy sitting over there," she whispered.

"You don't suppose he had anything to do with the robbery we heard about last week?"

"I don't know. I've never seen him before." A quick death by murder might be a blessing, I thought.

Lana wasn't normally skittish about anything, but I guessed the horrible circumstances had finally gotten to her. Just as I had imagined, lightning flashed and thunder reverberated throughout the empty atrium with dramatic intensity. I don't think I could have conjured up a worse setting, but, somehow, I felt safe and removed from everything.

Lana and I fell asleep for a short time in the early hours of the morning. When we awoke, we lay in silence. The violent storm had subsided, but I could tell it was still dark outside because no light shined through the atrium skylights. My watch said it was about 5:30.

I had only been awake for a short time, when a nurse walked toward me. "You should come now," she said softly. "It won't be long."

Instead of immediately going to Ralph's room, I went to the bathroom next to the waiting room and washed my face and brushed my teeth. I remembered how I had sewn a hem in a pair of slacks during the flight after my father died. Why is it that in times of crisis I find comfort in the mundane, routine aspects of life? I wondered.

When I finally walked into Ralph's room, I first looked out the window at the heavy fog that surrounded the buildings like a shroud. The view looks more like a typical, foggy London morning than one in a city in the Midwestern United States, I thought.

Then I forced myself to look at Ralph's inert body.

Lana and I were each holding one of Ralph's swollen hands when he was officially pronounced dead at 5:45 a.m.

NINETEEN

After one nurse had pronounced Ralph dead, another recorded the time of his death in a notebook; then they both walked out of the room with Lana, leaving me alone with Ralph's body. I felt dead myself. What can I possibly think of to say in this unearthly silence, I wondered? Besides, he's not here. I don't know when he left, but I know he's gone now, maybe somewhere in that mist rising up into the sky. Maybe he even left before we came into the room this morning and that whole process of pronouncing him dead was nothing but a charade.

The deadly silence was making me uncomfortable. Although I thought most people would be crying now, I had no tears left. Looking for a final time at the grotesque image that had once been my beloved, I walked out of the room and found the hospital chaplain waiting for me. She took my hand and led me to a sofa where she began praying.

I listened intently. "Could you write that prayer down for me?" I asked.

"Of course, I can do that," she said, looking surprised but graciously consenting. "I think I can remember most of it."

While the chaplain wrote down the prayer, a nurse asked me to sign papers to have Ralph's body sent to our home county fifty miles away.

Afterward, Lana and I walked silently back to the hotel, where I began packing the many clothes I had worn during my three-month stay, while Ralph had been in intensive care.

"You sure have a lot of clothes to pack," Lana said, making small talk in a normal sounding voice. "Let me help you."

"I'm fine, Lana, really. Now that it's over, I'm perfectly fine. I feel totally in control."

"Well, I'm sure you are," she said in a much sweeter voice than she normally used, "but I think I should drive you home, and then Keith and I can pick up your car later."

"I don't want you to drive all that way twice. You haven't had much sleep either. I told you I'm fine. Don't I seem perfectly normal? I haven't even cried since yesterday morning."

"Look," Lana said firmly. "Will you just listen to me for once and do what I say? Rely on my judgment right now."

Her sharp tone of voice surprised me, but I knew Lana had to be thinking more clearly than I was. And actually, I couldn't believe how calm I felt—almost lifeless.

We didn't talk much as Lana drove me home. I felt there was nothing more to say.

"I feel so badly for you," Mom said, throwing her arms around me and hugging me tightly when I arrived home. "I know you'll never find anyone else like him, so bright and kind and good to you."

Although I knew she meant well, I couldn't stand the thought of never having someone like Ralph in my life. She loves me more than anything in the world, I thought, but right now I just need to be alone. There's nothing she or anyone else can say to make me feel better.

My body felt disconnected, as if I was sleepwalking. The day droned on as I went through Ralph's and my address books, calling only those people that I knew fairly well and asking them to call other friends and acquaintances. Even though Mom and Lana encouraged me to start thinking about funeral arrangements, I couldn't bring myself to do it; I was just too tired. Surprisingly, even though Ralph had been given a death sentence thirty years earlier, not only had we never talked about death, we had never discussed funeral arrangements either.

"Have you thought about having Ralph cremated?" Keith asked the next morning while he drove Lana and me to look at a funeral parlor near our antique shop.

"Not really. I suppose he wouldn't mind being cremated just to be rid of his diseased body, but I think my Catholic upbringing prejudices me toward a normal burial."

"It seems more natural to let the body decay in its own time," Lana said.

"I think I'm afraid of doing something that isn't right for him," I said. "I guess I'm still struggling as to whether I prolonged his life too long."

"You did everything the best you could," Lana said protectively. "No one could have done more."

"I think what would be most important to Ralph is to have his friends have as good of a time as possible at the wake and funeral," I said. "He always thought about others."

"I sure liked how this place looked on the outside," I said, as we toured the first funeral parlor, "but the inside reminds me of a cheap hunting lodge."

Keith looked disappointed. "I don't know, Donna. I think it's kind of nice."

"She doesn't like it," Lana said firmly, probably understanding far better than her husband how picky I could be and how I would search endlessly to find what I wanted. "Let's move on."

Next we went to another funeral parlor in the same town. There was a charming Bed and Breakfast across the street from it, which I thought could accommodate some of the out-of-town guests.

"What's unusual about this home," the funeral director told us, "is that you can have the entire place to yourselves and not be bothered by other wakes."

"This is it," I said, looking around the homey rooms with their old-world charm. "I'll call back in a couple of hours," I told the funeral director. "I'd like to check out one more place."

"Why do you want to see another place if this one is perfect?" Keith asked.

"C'mon, Keith. Don't fuss," Lana said.

As we drove to the next funeral parlor, I looked out the car window, reflecting on how unemotional I felt. Occasionally, a wave of grief rose within me, but then it seemed to quickly subside. I wondered whether I was in some kind of state of shock, or whether the mundane focus on funeral arrangements was keeping my mind occupied. Or maybe it was that I truly didn't care about anything but making the funeral nice, now that the struggle for Ralph's life was over.

Shortly, we arrived at the main funeral parlor in the wealthier town where we lived.

"No, this one is too formal, too stuffy," I said. "It's not like Ralph."

"Okay," said Keith, seeming relieved that the search was over.

On the way back to the other funeral home, we stopped at a cemetery that I vaguely remembered seeing one time when I took an alternate route home. Adjacent to an old church, the cemetery was enclosed by an intricate black iron fence with a gate that we managed to pry open. Although the cemetery was small, I loved everything about it—the setting, the trees, and the old gravestones.

"This place reminds me of how Ralph and I grew up, surrounded by nature and reflecting a simple way of life," I said to Keith and Lana. "Keith, will you contact the overseer and buy plots for both Ralph and me?"

It was not an easy job. No one had been buried in the cemetery for many years, and, just as I had suspected, most of the people buried there had died in the late nineteenth or early twentieth century. The problem was that when Keith contacted the overseer, she admitted that no one had an accurate map of the burial plots, so she didn't know if there were any empty plots. Fortunately, Keith was able to persuade the overseer to do some excavating, and two available plots were found.

"How did you find a cemetery with a basketball hoop?" Ralph's best friend Mack asked when I showed him the plots that had been found.

"I didn't even see it," I said, looking to where he pointed across the parking lot. I saw the quaintness of the church and cemetery; Mack saw the basketball hoop.

Then I picked out an outrageously expensive, simple oak casket with brass fittings, which I knew Ralph would have also chosen until he saw the price. Although a part of me wondered what difference it made what kind of casket was buried in the ground, I was determined to make everything the best I could for Ralph. Because of the grotesqueness of his body, the casket would be kept closed, with one large floral arrangement and several enlarged pictures of him setting on top of the casket.

As Mom and I culled through photos, we listened to music from a CD called "The Secret Garden", which contained soulful tunes with titles like "Nocturne", "Heartstrings", and "Ode to Simplicity".

"Honey, are you sure you should play these songs at the wake?" Mom asked, in a tone of disapproval. "You'll have everyone in tears."

"Well, what do you expect at a funeral, Mom? This is not a party," I said, more sharply than I had intended. There I go snapping at her again, I thought. I just want this to be over.

"I've decided to wear that old black skirt and jacket that I showed you," I said, changing the subject and trying to speak to her more gently. "At least it fits."

But then, I changed my mind and drove to a boutique, where I bought a new black skirt and top. I just wanted everything to be perfect; I didn't want to overlook one detail.

I had to smile and shake my head when Lana said she had convinced the funeral home director to let us have candles burning during the wake, despite what he had said about a fire ordinance restricting their use.

Having a last-minute idea, I arranged a display of Ralph's favorite antiques at the entrance of the funeral home.

Three friends and I were still putting photos in picture frames when guests began arriving at the funeral home on the day of the wake.

"Everything looks so lovely," I said to Lana and my mother as I looked around. "I couldn't have done this without you two."

Hundreds of people mingled throughout the three large rooms. Ralph's father was conspicuously missing from the crowd, because his sister was afraid he might make a scene if he was drinking, and so she chose not to tell him about the event.

Even with all the tears and soulful music, it seemed more like a party than a funeral. There were only a few times when I thought I might totally break down (such as when Dr. Williams approached me), but then I just retreated back under my glass cover. I was worried, however, about how I would hold up at the burial ceremony the next day.

The late summer day dawned unusually chilly, but at least the sun shone brightly. Most people drove directly to the cemetery, while my relatives, close friends, and I drove behind the hearse carrying Ralph's body from the funeral home to the gravesite.

When we arrived at the cemetery, I felt overwhelmed by the throngs of people milling about inside and outside the old iron fence. In the crowd, I saw my boss Randy wave and smile at me. That gave me courage—I knew he had faith in me and believed I could handle this.

When I walked up to the gravesite and saw the large hole that had been dug in the ground, however, I felt nauseated. Then I counted five chairs placed on the ground in front of the hole. Who ordered those five chairs? I wondered. And who is supposed to sit in them with me? No one told me I was going to have to sit right in front of that hole.

For the first time since Ralph had died, I felt shaken—a small crack had worked its way into my glass cover. You wouldn't think that such a small thing as someone else deciding the number of people who should sit in front of the grave with me would upset me as much as it did, but I felt I should have had a say-so in determining where I sat and how many people sat with me. The tight control I had kept over everything (including myself) had been taken away from me. Then I looked up and saw my brother Bill and Mack walking toward me.

I grabbed my brother's hand first and then took Mack's hand. "Sit there," I said, as I pointed at two chairs on either side of the middle chair. They were the two people I was counting on to give me strength; I felt I needed their strong, masculine support and I didn't care who sat in the other two chairs.

As the three of us sat down, my brother held my hand tightly. That's exactly what I need, I thought. We were not a handholding family, but if ever I needed support, I needed it now.

Ralph's friend Anne began the ceremony with an opening prayer, but no sooner had she started speaking, than she had to stop and gain control of her emotions—her struggle was obvious from the tortured look on her face and the gulping sounds she made.

Oh, no! I thought. This was a mistake. She's too close to Ralph and is far too emotional to do this ceremony. I held my breath as she struggled to regain her composure. After a short while, she resumed her opening remarks and prayer.

Then the vocalist whom Anne had recommended began singing her first song, "Wind Beneath My Wings." Even though I had chosen the song, I felt as if I was hearing the words for the first time when the soloist began singing with soulful passion:

    "Oh, oh, oh, oh, oh

      It must have been cold there in my shadow

      To never have sunlight on your face.

      You were content to let me shine, that's your way.

      You always walked a step behind."

Suddenly, I felt as if a stone had been thrown against my glass cover, shattering it all around me. I felt exposed. My chest hurt with each and every word. Of course, I said to myself, I know Ralph supported me in everything I did and even put his needs and achievements secondary to mine. Why do these words upset me so much? I wondered.

"So I was the one with all the glory

While you were the one with all the strength."

I never once questioned who was stronger, even at the end. He had the strength to hang on for so long, not for himself but for me. He knew I would be terrified without him.

"A beautiful face without a name for so long

A beautiful smile to hide the pain."

Ralph's smile was special. Everyone said so. Suddenly, I wondered if the psychic had been right. Maybe, his smile had hidden much of his pain since childhood—the poverty, the fighting between his parents, his dad's drinking…going to school with holes in his shoes.

Oh, my God, I thought. I can't take this. These words hurt too much. Why can't I escape from these painful feelings again? Why can't I disappear?

"Did you ever know that you're my hero

And everything I wish I could be?

I could fly higher than an eagle

For you are the wind beneath my wings."

He really was my hero, I thought—the one who gave me the confidence to be successful, who made me feel beautiful, and who was always there for me. I can't imagine living without him. It will be a death sentence. I wish I hadn't spent so much time on work, when now I would give anything to have another precious moment with him. The song seemed to have unleashed so many painful thoughts.

"It might have appeared to go unnoticed

But I've got it all here in my heart

I want you to know I know the truth, of course I know it.

I would be nothing without you."

I felt as if the soloist was singing each word slowly, loudly, and clearly, just so I would remember the truth. I knew with all my heart and soul that I wouldn't be half the person I was without Ralph. I sat with my heart pounding and listened to several more stanzas of the song, including the piercing high notes when she sang, "Fly, fly, fly…." When the song ended with the words "Thank God for you, the wind beneath my wings", I wanted to throw myself on the ground and thank God for having given me Ralph. I didn't. Instead, I sat there rigidly while my brother gripped my hand, almost as if he was willing me to hang on.

After the song finished, muffled crying could be heard throughout the crowd. The soloist's voice and passion had touched many people.

"Would anyone like to share their memories of Ralph with us?" Anne asked.

Anne and I had talked about making this request, and even though I had mentioned it to a few people, I had no idea what they would say.

Immediately, Mack jumped up and faced the crowd with a small smile on his face. "I've probably known Ralph longer than most people here because we grew up together as kids. I don't know if this story is appropriate at a funeral or not, but it's typical of the fun we always had together."

Then Mack proceeded to tell several stories about how they had tormented their driving teacher: once, by making him believe the car they were in was burning by staging a fire in a trash can along their usual route, and another time, by encouraging a slightly retarded classmate to drive erratically and scare the teacher out of his wits.

When Mack finished, most everyone seemed to be laughing or smiling at his stories…even me.

Next Ralph's brother-in-law jumped up.

"Well, the last time Ralph visited me, I short-changed his sheets one night. Then, he tied my shoelaces together. So, I guess he didn't change much from when he was fifteen to fifty."

Those who knew Ralph well smiled. We all knew how he loved a practical joke.

Then Shelley, Ralph's childhood friend, stood up and said some nice words about how he had been such a good friend and always supported her. And, finally, Ralph's most recent boss stood up and said some kind words.

In the midst of the silence, while everyone waited to hear who else might want to speak, I suddenly thought that perhaps the audience expected me to say something.

No, I told myself. I wouldn't even consider talking because I know I would just cry. That song made me lose my ability to bury my emotions. And here I thought I was doing so well.

After a few moments of silence, Anne said a few more prayers, which although meaningless to me, added some dignity to the ceremony. The soloist ended the burial ceremony by singing the song made famous by Celine Dion—"Because You Loved Me".

When she finished the song, I felt pain in my chest worse than I had ever felt, as if my heart was bleeding. I'm sure it's just from tension and trying not to cry, I told myself.

"I think I want to stay here for a little while," I told Mack and my brother, as I watched the guests leaving the cemetery.

"I'll wait in the car to drive you home," my brother said.

Home was the last place I wanted to be, although I knew I had to go there to see the guests who would be visiting. As I walked around the cemetery, I reflected on the ceremony and thought Ralph would have liked it. Unfortunately, I didn't think he was there, because I had an empty feeling…as if an umbilical cord had been severed between us.

When I arrived home, I thought that everything looked awful from having been neglected for so many months. Normally, I would have been upset, but now I was too tired to eat or talk or feel anything.

I watched as pictures were taken of guests with smiles on their faces. They're probably relieved that the ceremony is over, I thought, as I wandered around aimlessly. I would be, too, if I were them. Now, they can go back to work and their homes and their lives.

I watched as one person after another left, until the only people remaining were my mother, Shelley, and Ralph's sister.

Mom tried to act upbeat and make small talk in the quiet that ensued. I became irritated with her because I didn't want to feel better—I just wanted to die. Certainly, death would be preferable to this awful sick feeling I have throughout my entire body, I thought.

Then my tears started as Ralph's sister Sarah and I wandered around the yard, neither of us able to contain our grief any longer.

Surprisingly, the person who helped me most that night was Shelley, someone I didn't know well and of whom I had been a bit jealous over the years.

"You know, I always feared Ralph still had strong feelings for you," I said, as Shelley and I sat alone upstairs in a bedroom that Ralph had used as his office.

"He did, but only as a very good friend. We knew each other even before grade school."

I looked at her suspiciously.

"I suspected you were concerned about how Ralph felt about me," Shelley acknowledged, as we sat together on my bed, "but, believe me, although there were many other women interested in him, you were the only one he cared about. He adored you. You were everything to him."

"Thanks for telling me that, Shelley. I value your opinion, and I needed to hear that."

"I knew there was a reason I was awakened out of a sound sleep when Ralph died. You know, I have fibromyalgia and take heavy medication in order to sleep. Normally, I wake up in the late morning, but I awoke that morning at almost the exact time of his death. I know because I looked at the clock. I felt uncomfortable, woke up my husband, and walked outside."

I stared at her. "That's interesting," I said, "because I was surprised I found your number or even thought to call you."

"You need to get out of this bedroom and pull yourself together for Ralph's sake. You know that's what he would want."

I looked around the room. I had slept there on an uncomfortable sofa bed ever since Ralph had entered intensive care the first time. Books and papers were in every corner, but this small room was the only place where I now felt comfortable. "Maybe I'm comfortable here because Ralph spent so much time working in here on his computer," I said to Shelley. "This was the last place I had any communication with him before I moved to the hotel downtown."

"Ralph would want you to move on with your life. Your mother and even your close friends don't know how to help you right now. Maybe, that's why I'm here. You can push back on them and brush off their suggestions because you know them so well. It's harder with someone like me whom you don't know well."

I had to smile, knowing she was probably right.

"I feel like I've lost a daughter, not just a wonderful son-in-law," Mom said the next morning with tears in her eyes as she got ready to go home.

"Oh, Mom, don't say that. I'm still here. I just need some time to sort things out."

At some level, however, I knew she was right. Things would never be the same between us, or with anyone else for that matter, because I would never be the same. A big part of me had died, too.

Then Shelley left. Only Sarah planned to stay for a few days.

I'm glad she's here, I thought. She'll know what to do if I lose my mind. I don't know how I'm going to make it. I doubt that I will.

TWENTY

It's not that I had never felt emotional pain, but the way I felt after Ralph died was far worse than anything I had ever experienced. Crying was the only thing that seemed to relieve my physical suffering. My chest hurt with a stabbing pain much of the time; my arms and legs bristled with an uncomfortable tingling sensation, and I frequently felt nauseated. Nothing, however, seemed to relieve my emotional pain. That was something I thought I would live with for the rest of my life.

During that first day after the funeral, I sat outside in the warm sunshine, sorting through unpaid bills and sales receipts for our businesses. That night, I sat on my living room sofa, playing over and over again the songs sung at the burial ceremony. If anyone telephoned, I cried so much that I was barely able to talk.

As I sat reading the many sympathy cards that people had sent, there were a few that particularly touched me. One was from a supervisor who had previously worked for Ralph. He wrote: "Many of my good work habits are because of Ralph's leadership and his compassion for his fellow workers." A coworker of mine wrote: "I only met him a few times but feel I know him better after that beautiful ceremony at the cemetery. People's description of him as a coach, mentor, and person of integrity with a great sense of humor are reflected in you and will stay in your heart forever." I liked that the authors had recognized some of Ralph's best traits.

Most surprising of all, however, was a hand-written note from Dr. Noyes: "I was so sorry to hear of Ralph's passing. Obviously, we were all hoping for a better outcome. Ralph certainly did his part. It was a pleasure to know him. I'm glad his suffering is over. A liver transplant is a difficult course, but I'm sorry he did not get the chance. Thanks for all of your support of me as a physician." Each sentence had great meaning for me, as no one had been harder on Ralph than Dr. Noyes. I remembered the night he had slowly buttoned Ralph's shirt and now understood that the tough stances Dr. Noyes took with Ralph were probably meant to test how strong he was and how much he wanted to fight to live.

I learned that, although it was nice to know people were concerned about me, what I really wanted was for them to remember Ralph as the special person he was. I even received a surprising phone call from the head surgeon who had performed the experimental surgery on Ralph over five years ago, thanking me for Ralph's participation, although neither of us had had any input into the decision or knew at the time that it was the first surgery of its kind

I knew that addressing the financial mess I was in, plus paying back my company for all of its support would take years, and yet I also understood that focusing on these problems would help me survive.

Just work, I told myself. Don't think! Work until you're exhausted. The only problem was that I couldn't go back to my corporate job until I could stop crying.

Two days after the funeral, I stepped outside my back door and was startled by two, small, light-colored butterflies. First they flew toward my face, almost touching it, and then they swooped down behind me toward my ankles. As they fluttered around my ankles, I thought of Ralph, probably because they took me by surprise and made me smile, just as Ralph used to do.

"Why, you silly things," I said out loud. "Are you trying to play with me or what?" For a fleeting moment, my grief had lifted.

After working for an hour or so on tax forms, I stood up to get a drink of water. Two yellow butterflies swooped toward my face again, lingered close to my arm, and then flew toward the back of my ankles, just like the first time, though I had no idea if these were the same butterflies or not.

At least, I had the presence of mind to note that they were both yellow—something I was too startled to notice the first time. I smiled, wondering if this could possibly be the year for crazy butterflies. Ralph would like that, I thought: the year of the butterfly.

Since neither Ralph nor I had lived at home for months, we hadn't talked about what to name this year. For many years, we had a tradition of naming the year after the species that seemed more prolific than usual, not necessarily for the way the animals or insects acted. I could distinctly remember the year of the fox, the year of the deer, the year of the rabbit, the year of the bee, the year of the ladybug, and the year of the ant.

The strange phenomenon with butterflies happened several more times that day. They always flew in pairs. Some were white, some were yellow, and some looked like a monarch or painted lady. Whenever they swooped at me, the warm feeling of Ralph's presence surrounded my body and relaxed the area around my belly.

The next day, as I helped Sarah carry her suitcases to her car, two butterflies dove toward my face and then flew behind me.

"Why are they flying at you like that?" Sarah asked.

"I don't know. It just started happening yesterday. I honestly think they're trying to make me feel better."

"Oh, well. I hope they do," she said, with tears in her eyes, as she gave me a hug.

That night I listened to the songs sung at Ralph's service once again. Suddenly, at the very end of "Wind Beneath My Wings," the CD got stuck, and the words "Fly, fly" kept repeating, making horrible, pounding sounds.

I restarted the CD, but the same thing happened again, in the exact same place.

It's a good thing this happened now, I told myself, because I really should have extra copies of these songs. Who knows when they might be discontinued? There is obviously something wrong with this CD.

I wiped the disc with a cloth and shook it, but when I tried to play it, the CD got stuck in the same place again. Although I could recall other CDs getting stuck, I had never heard such a loud, pounding sound as this one made, which was very disturbing to me. At the same time as I was telling myself that something was wrong with the CD, an inner sense told me that Ralph was trying to get my attention—to tell me he didn't want to fly away. I worried that he might be stuck somewhere.

The next morning I bought new CDs, and when I returned home, I decided to play the original CD with "Wind Beneath My Wings" one more time. The pounding sound and the repetition of "Fly, fly," didn't happen; the song played normally to the end. The speck of dust must have fallen off, I said to myself, but another part of me wondered if Ralph was now going to fly away and leave me, although I knew he didn't want to.

Although it was a little over a week since Ralph died, I didn't feel ready to go back to work. After I woke up that Monday morning, I lay in bed, feeling too exhausted to get up. Suddenly, I heard the sound of Ralph's favorite recliner chair falling backward, just like it had done hundreds of times when he was alive.

I hurried downstairs and found the recliner in its upright position, just as it had been since the day Ralph left home for the last time. Yet I knew I hadn't imagined the sound of the recliner falling backward and that Ralph was telling me he had not gone away, as I had feared.

Since it was raining outside that morning, I made myself a cup of tea and sat down on the sofa in my living room to struggle once again with my bills and tax forms.

After working for a while, I looked up from my paperwork and was shocked when I saw that two of the four globes in the old brass ceiling light fixture in our entryway were shining.

"Oh, my God, Ralph. You fixed it!" I exclaimed out loud, staring in awe at the light fixture. I remembered complaining to him, on numerous occasions, about how I missed being greeted by the warm glow of the light fixture whenever I came home. Yet, he had never gotten around to fixing it. If, by chance, someone flipped on the light switch by mistake, as I had done on numerous occasions, electricity in half of the house would short out. When we had put our house up for sale earlier in the year, a potential buyer's electrician had made such a fuss about the fixture being dangerous that my realtor taped a sign over the light switch that read: DO NOT TURN ON. The sign was still taped over the switch.

For me, the light fixture starting to work was the pivotal event that not only confirmed Ralph lived on, but changed my whole concept of death. I was elated. There couldn't have been a more positive sign to prove Ralph was still here taking care of me.

No wonder people use the word "passing" instead of "death," I thought. He's not really gone at all. He's just in a different zone or place or space…I don't know what to call it. But I know he still exists and is able to communicate with me.

From that day forward, I found it hard to use the word "death" in thinking about Ralph or anyone else who had departed from this world. From that day forward, I also found it hard to feel totally forlorn and inconsolable. I no longer felt so alone.

Later that momentous day, our realtor and good friend stopped by to offer her condolences. After we had talked for a while, I pointed to the illuminated light fixture.

"Oh, you had it fixed," she said.

"No, it just came on by itself this morning and has stayed on ever since. I didn't touch it. No sparks flew and no fuses have blown."

The realtor looked skeptical. After recovering from her initial surprise, she just shrugged. "Well, that's good. It needed to be fixed," she said in a neutral voice.

By now, I was becoming not only familiar, but comfortable with these strange incidents that were happening in my life. I sometimes felt like a child anticipating the next ride at an amusement park. The friendly butterflies, the strange noise from the CD, the sound of Ralph's chair falling backward, and now the light fixture being fixed were accompanied by an instantaneous knowingness. There was no time to think between an event's occurrence and my reaction to it. I knew exactly what was being communicated or what the intent of the communication was: the butterflies were meant to make me feel better; the noise from the CD was meant to let me know Ralph didn't want to fly away and leave me; the loud thump from his chair falling backward let me know that he was able to stay near me; and fixing the light fixture was a sign of how he would continue to take care of me. I decided to call the events "soul-to-soul communication", because it made no difference what my rational mind thought about the events; my knowingness and absolute certainty about them superseded any thought process.

How am I going to explain this to anyone? I wondered. Surely, people will think that my grief is causing me to imagine these things are happening—that it's only my imagination, not communication from Ralph. Or, they might think I am just assigning meaning to the event to make myself feel better.

Then I decided that I didn't have to explain anything to anyone. I knew what was true, and these incidents made me feel better.

My days continued to be filled with endless battles with my insurance company, hospital billing departments, the IRS, and collection agencies. For the most part, they were not a pleasant group to deal with, although I must say that the IRS and Department of Revenue were unbelievably supportive in giving me time to pull together all the tax materials, once they understood my situation; I explained to them that I would have to review every sales receipt from Alouette over the past year—a daunting task. It was the insurance companies and collection agencies that gave me the most difficulty; one hospital even billed me for surgeries that were performed on patients other than Ralph—bills, which, of course, ended up with collection agencies during the time that I disputed them.

I had often wondered how people managed to survive after a spouse's death. Although I knew that a certain percentage died within the first year, I was surprised the statistics weren't higher. Even with resources, assets, an accountant, and decent financial and business sense, I was barely able to cope. Of course, I had complications because of the multiple houses and businesses I owned, but then I had butterflies and other signs of Ralph's continued existence, which made me laugh and feel good.

My boss Randy, knowing much of what I had gone through during Ralph's illness and hospitalizations, had urged me to see a psychiatrist to help me through the grieving process. I didn't feel I needed one, but I decided to comply with his suggestion. What did I have to lose? I thought.

During my first session with the psychiatrist, I told her about Ralph's soul-to-soul communication and how much better it made me feel.

At the beginning of our second session, she asked me again if I felt depressed. "No, I am not depressed," I told her. "How can I be depressed when the minute I start feeling really bad, Ralph does something to make me feel better?"

"You mean like the butterflies and lights," she said.

"Yes, and now he works with the third light on our entryway fixture as his primary communication tool with me. It's different than the other two lights that stay on all the time. For example, I was feeling pretty low the other morning before going to work."

The psychiatrist sat quietly, with a neutral look on her face, seemingly listening to me.

"After putting the dogs in their pen and carrying out the garbage, I made one final trip upstairs to get my watch that I had forgotten to put on. As I walked downstairs, the third light at the foot of the stairs came on for a few seconds and then went off. It was as if Ralph winked at me and told me good-bye, wishing me a good day. He used to always tell me to have a good day when I left for work."

"See, that's what I mean," the psychiatrist said. "You're depressed and should be on antidepressants."

"Well, it's true I was depressed for a while, but then Ralph made me feel better. Why should I take antidepressants when I can count on him to make me feel better? I can tell him anything. I'm not alone. I told him to have a good day, too, when I left for work."

She gave me an exasperated look. "How do you know it's not just a loose wire in the light fixture?" she asked. "And how do you know exactly what he's saying if you can't hear him?"

"I just know. That's part of this whole deal…I instantly know what he's telling me, more clearly than if he was talking."

"Well, my religion does believe in the afterlife," she said, "but I've never had the experiences you describe myself. Nor have any of my patients," she added, "although it appears you are able to carry on with your executive job and attend to your business affairs."

"I've never heard of such things either, but I'm telling you these incidents are not in my imagination. They are as real as you and I sitting here talking."

"You don't feel suicidal, do you?"

"No, I don't," I said, feeling it was now my turn to feel exasperated with her because she kept asking me the same questions. "I've told you before that my problem is that I don't know intellectually whether I want to live or not. Of course, I can survive if I want to, and I don't feel depressed now. I'm not going to do anything rash, but I suppose at some point I will make a rational decision whether I want to live or not."

"Any idea when that time might be?"

"Not really. I now understand how easy it is to give up on life and die. I learned this from how much energy it took to keep Ralph alive for so many months and how hard he had to fight to stay alive."

"You're depressed and need to be on medication."

"Don't worry. From everything I've read, the worst thing a person can do is to commit suicide; every religion seems to profess that things are much harder for those individuals in the afterlife," I said, trying to appease her, "or they have to come back and address the same issues again in their next life."

Actually, I thought, if someone had told me about their afterlife experiences before I experienced them myself, I would probably have been as skeptical as she was. I was amazed at myself—amazed at how I had so readily accepted Ralph's communication and the fact of an afterlife.

I decided that I didn't really need the psychiatrist's support, because I felt so protected and comforted by Ralph. Actually, instead of helping me, I thought I may have helped her to think about the healing experiences that are possible with deceased loved ones.

TWENTY-ONE

Exactly three weeks after Ralph's passing, I spent the day, working on bills and taxes—an activity that I still spent much of my free time doing. I went outside that night at about 9:30 to lay by the pool on one of our chaise lounges. The night was warm and still, with hardly any wind; Mattie and Buffy lay on the concrete floor by my side, peaceful and content.

I thought about how Ralph and I had often sat there together at night, listening to the wind rustling through the trees and myriad of sounds from the crickets, the frogs, the foxes, and other creatures. Although I had often been afraid of some of the animal noises, particularly the terrible screeching of the foxes or the wail of the coyotes, since Ralph's passing, I had lost all fear of both the dark and strange noises, animal or otherwise. I felt a deep peace, whereas previously, I would have been frightened to be alone outside at night on our remote property. And, not only had I lost all fear, I felt strongly protected from any harm.

Sitting by the narrow side of our kidney-shaped pool, I continued to think about how much I had changed since Ralph's passing. As I gazed into the darkness, my thoughts were suddenly interrupted. Right across from me, just above the top of two of the pool railings, a brilliant cluster of small multi-colored lights, which twinkled like little stars, appeared out of nowhere in a formation similar to a large exclamation point, but flipped horizontally, and parallel with the ground.

My mouth dropped open in surprise. In my mind, I heard Ralph say, "Ta da!" It was as if he were saying, "See what I can do! Isn't this fun?"

The light formation was so spectacular and colorful; it was not more than fifteen feet away and maybe four feet off the ground. The dogs didn't stir or make a sound, which they surely would have done if they had heard or seen anything. After about ten seconds, the red, blue, yellow, and white lights vanished into the darkness.

"Well, that was truly unbelievable," I said to Ralph. "It must have taken a lot of effort on your part. You probably were saving up your energy all week to do this." Of course, there was another little voice inside of me that said, "Are you kidding? This can't be for real."

"It was well worth your efforts, honey," I said out loud, wanting Ralph to know how much I appreciated him. "Now, I am more convinced than ever that you're still here."

I suspected that some activities took more energy on his part than others. For example, I thought that communicating through the third globe in the hallway was an easy thing for him to do. He did it frequently and signaled to me, whenever I was feeling depressed. I suspected that this latest trick took a lot of energy.

I spent another hour outside, enjoying the night and thinking about all the implications of this most recent event. Maybe, someone would argue that the light fixture in the entryway had somehow rewired itself, or was fixed without my knowledge, yet still had a loose connection causing it to blink on occasion; maybe someone would argue that my body emanates a scent that attracts butterflies; maybe someone would say that I imagined hearing Ralph's favorite recliner chair fall backward. But this light show wasn't easy to rationalize…it was so unusual and, in my mind, defied any logical explanation, other than being a paranormal event.

No wonder I'm not afraid of the dark anymore, I said to myself. I feel so loved and protected. If only everyone could have these experiences and believe in life after death, this world would be a much more peaceful, happier place. And, I thought, isn't it strange that so many people profess to believe in an afterlife, but are afraid of so many things here on earth? Once a person has truly accepted death, what else is there to be afraid of? Perhaps pain and suffering? But then death would be even more appealing, because it would finally end the pain and suffering of the body, just as it did for Ralph. I know he is so happy now. I slept well that night.

The next day, Lana stopped by for a visit.

"Are you sure you didn't turn your head around too fast?" she asked, after I told her about what happened the night before. "You know, sometimes you see stars out of the corner of your eye when you turn your head too quickly."

"Absolutely not," I said in an irritated tone. "I was looking straight ahead, and I didn't just see a few stars; there were hundreds or thousands of them. It was definitely Ralph showing off and entertaining me."

"Well, what about some kids playing with fireworks?"

"I've never seen a firework like this, and there was no loud sound accompanying it. The dogs would have heard it, too. You know how they fly off the handle at the slightest noise."

Lana said no more, but she continued to look pensive. If the situation had been reversed and Lana was telling me such a story, I conceded that I would probably have reacted even more skeptically than she had. I had become so certain of Ralph's presence that I felt there was nothing or nobody that could change my mind—not a psychiatrist, not Lana, though I trusted her so much—no one.

"Honestly, Lana, sometimes I think Ralph not only wants me to feel better, he wants to entertain me and show me how clever he is. I think he is not only happy and feels well, but I believe he's having the time of his life."

In an effort to better understand what was happening, I bought several books about grieving, but I became frustrated that I couldn't find a good explanation for Ralph's continuous and varied communication. I read about individuals who had an occasional communication from a deceased loved one telling them they were well and happy; sometimes, a flower unexpectedly appeared or a lost article was found. I did read about some incidents with flickering lights and an occasional actual appearance by the deceased person, but they were usually isolated incidents. I was looking for confirmation about the diverse and continual events that were happening in my life.

About a week after I told Lana about the spectacular light formation in my backyard, I stood outside my front door, waiting for her to pick me up to go to lunch.

"Where are you, Ralph?" I asked teasingly. In response, a white butterfly flew up from some bushes and paused while fluttering, inches from my face.

"That's my Ralph," I said, as I jumped backward, smiling.

Soon afterward, Lana drove up my driveway, and I got in her car. She seemed quiet, as we drove. I decided to wait and let her begin the conversation.

"Ralph woke me up last night and gave me a hug," she said solemnly. "He thanked me for helping you."

Now it was my turn to be skeptical about what Lana had said. "Are you sure it wasn't just a dream?" I asked my friend.

"I'm positive," Lana said. "This was different. He woke me up, and I knew it was him. I could feel his presence."

"I know what you mean. And I'm sure he is very grateful for everything you did," I quickly added, not wanting to give her the impression I doubted her.

Lana's experience with Ralph made me feel even more comfortable about talking about my experiences with him to others. Although both of us were highly analytical and somewhat cynical, Lana was even more grounded in facts and skepticism than I.

I started traveling again for my job, taking long trips to Asia and Europe. No incidents occurred while I was away from home, no communications from Ralph, which made me sad. Had it not been for my busy work schedule while traveling, it's likely that I would have started the grieving process during that time away. It's hard to grieve at home when the person you're supposed to be missing was making you laugh.

As the weeks went by, I looked forward to the weekends when I could work outside with my handyman and now good friend, Greg. The beauty of nature filled me with a sense of peace that I hadn't experienced since childhood. The simple pleasure of mowing the lawn—listening to the drone of the tractor, smelling the freshly cut grass and looking at the lush green color—was the highlight of my week. Walks in the nature preserve behind my house with Mattie and Buffy, while listening to the rustle of the wind and the birds singing, filled me with awe. I wondered if I enjoyed nature's nurturing so much more now because of the emotional pain I had experienced during Ralph's hospitalization and passing.

I noticed the change in my relationships as well. Ralph had been the center of my life for over twenty years. Work, travel, and our small businesses had left me little time to spend with friends. And that was okay then. Now that climbing the corporate ladder had lost its importance to me and I had started simplifying my life by divesting of our businesses and houses, I valued my friends as never before. I felt not only loved by new and old acquaintances, but I had a greater love for them as well.

Arriving home from a long business trip overseas in the fall, I heard hammering sounds in the basement. I walked downstairs, assuming that Greg was working down there as planned while I was away.

"The first time I came over when you were gone," he said, "the front hall light blinked twice when I drove up the driveway. I thought about what you've told me, and it made me happy to think Ralph was thanking me for helping you."

I had told Greg how Ralph liked to communicate through the third globe on the entryway light fixture.

"You don't seem very happy about it now," I said, noticing that he didn't seem like his usual, upbeat self. "How did you know he was thanking you?"

"I just knew. It felt really good."

"Is there something else wrong?"

"I've only told my wife about this because I was really scared," he said. "I've never had anything like this happen to me."

"What happened?"

He looked hesitant, as if he was trying to decide whether or not to tell me something.

"I don't think there's anything you could tell me that would shock me," I said, trying to support him.

"I was working in the basement when I heard heavy footsteps walk across the kitchen floor upstairs. I ran upstairs, thinking maybe that painter you hired had come over to paint or something. There was no one there," he said, with a bewildered look on his face.

Greg was obviously upset, but I didn't know what to say to him. "What do you think it meant?" I asked.

"Ralph didn't like the way I was fixing the ceiling."

"Oh," I said, immediately knowing it was probably true. When Greg didn't like doing something, he often didn't do the best job. I bet repairing the ceiling isn't something he likes to do, I thought. "Are you afraid to come over now and work here?" I asked out loud.

"No," he said, finally giving me one of his typical, broad smiles. "I just have to be careful that I do a good job."

I laughed. "See, that's how it is with this soul-to-soul communication," I said. "You know exactly what he's telling you instantaneously. It's not like you have to think about it."

We both shook our heads and smiled at one other.

I was dreading the holidays, having heard how difficult they can be, particularly the first year after losing a loved one. I didn't want to make it hard for family and friends, or myself, so I decided I would just go along with the plans that everyone else made for me. Mom as well as my niece and her family were planning to go to my brother's house for both Thanksgiving and Christmas.

Before Christmas, I had made an appointment for a massage at Body & Soul. My favorite esthetician, Laura, was booked and I didn't want to bump paying customers, so I had foregone having a facial.

After my massage, I sat on the waiting room sofa feeling relaxed, when a troubled-looking Laura came out of her treatment room and walked determinedly over to me, and stood there with her hands on her hips. By the stern look on her face, I thought she must be angry about something.

In her usual direct fashion, without any greeting whatsoever, she said in her broke English with a Russian accent: "Ralph come to me in dream last night. He whisper in ear and tell me to tell you. I don't know what. I very, very sorry. Do you know what he tell me?"

I burst into tears and walked out of the room so the other customers wouldn't see me crying. I didn't doubt for a second what Laura had told me. Ralph and Laura were fond of each other and had a special relationship, just as I had with her. Ralph had always teased her, whereas most people were afraid to approach her because of her size and threatening demeanor.

This was the first time when someone whom Ralph contacted didn't know instantly what he was trying to communicate. Lana knew that Ralph was thanking her for helping me; Greg knew Ralph was first thanking him and then cautioning him to do a good job. I always understood. How could I possibly know what he's trying to tell Laura if she doesn't know? I wondered.

On my first day back to work after the holidays, I came home that evening and felt Ralph's presence for the first time since before

Thanksgiving. He didn't show me any signs; I just strongly felt him there.

A few days later, I figured out why Ralph had probably left me alone over the holidays. If I had felt his presence before leaving for my brother's house on Thanksgiving or Christmas day, I doubt if I would have gone; I would have wanted to stay home to be with him. Like always, Ralph seemed to think of me first, and he wouldn't have wanted me to spend the holidays without my family.

Several days later, I was feeling depressed as I walked upstairs to get my eyeglasses before leaving for work. My toy frog, dressed in Christmas clothing, was sitting with its feet dangling over one of the steps of the staircase; suddenly the frog started croaking its little Christmas tune. Ever since I had gotten the toy several years ago, he had been my favorite of many Christmas animals.

"No way!" I shouted out loud. "There's no way that could happen by itself. No way!" To make the frog play its tune, someone had to push hard on the frog's toe. Neither I, nor the dogs, were anywhere near it. I tried bumping into it and jumping up and down on the steps to make it play again. It didn't. The frog remained silent.

"Okay, Ralph, I've had it. You're driving me over the edge. Enough is enough. This is no longer funny." Although I said the words, I didn't really mean them. I had just been surprised, that's all. I actually enjoyed the variety and playfulness of his communication.

"You know I'm not really mad, honey," I said a few minutes later. "That was kind of cute." Suddenly I realized that I had been knocked out of my depression once again.

That evening Lana and I ate dinner together. I told her about the most recent incident with the Christmas frog, knowing she was familiar with the little guy because she had one exactly like it.

She didn't comment but continued eating, seeming distracted and unusually serious.

"Is something wrong?" I asked her.

"I didn't want to tell you this until I figured it out for myself," she said, "but it's been over a week, and I don't think I'm going to understand it. About a week ago, Ralph was in one of my dreams. He kept whispering in my ear, trying to tell me something. I kept telling him I couldn't hear him. I couldn't understand what he was saying," Lana said, looking upset.

I was taken aback by the resemblance to Laura's dream and wanted to tell Lana about it, but hesitated before speaking because I knew that Lana felt that Laura manipulated me. "That's the exact same dream Laura told me she had the week before Christmas," I cautiously told my friend. "I know you're not particularly fond of Laura, but your dreams were identical, from the continual whispering in your ears to both of you being frustrated because you didn't understand his message. I didn't tell you about it because I don't like bringing Laura's name up around you."

We looked at each other, neither of us knowing what to make of the identical dreams.

The next day Lana called me. "He's not trying to tell Laura or me anything," she said. "He's trying to tell us to tell you to listen to him. You must be blocking him."

I hated to admit it, but I knew it was true. For all my talk about enjoying the communication with Ralph, I didn't want the incidents to go any further than they had up to that point. Or rather, I was afraid of what my reaction would be if I heard his footsteps or saw his ghost.

"I think if I actually saw him, I would totally freak out," I admitted to Lana. "I can handle everything that's happened so far, but nothing more. Everything he's done has been fun and comforting, not scary at all. I don't think I could even handle the sound of his footsteps—like what happened to Greg."

"I can understand that, but there must be something he wants to tell you. Just try to be open."

That very night, I had the most poignant dream I had ever experienced since I was a young child. First, I felt Ralph lying next to me with his cheek against mine. His cheek felt so unbelievably smooth…like a baby's, and his mood was sweet and loving. I felt so peaceful with his body lying next to me, just the way it used to feel before he got so sick. Nothing has changed, I thought; he still loves me very much.

When I awoke, I remembered and felt every moment of the dream. Now I knew what Lana meant when she had described her experience with Ralph as being more real than an ordinary dream. There was a physical aspect to it that I actually experienced. The lingering sensation of his smooth cheek on mine stayed with me throughout the day. Usually, after being awake for a while, the sensation of a dream quickly faded. How interesting, I thought, that this incident happened the very night after Lana told me I should be more open to Ralph, and it's particularly interesting how vivid it was since I rarely could remember my dreams.

The next night, I was awakened by Ralph's voice slowly and deliberately saying my name, "Doooonnnnnaaa…." That's all I heard. It reminded me of the time he had come out of a coma the previous year and yelled my name; although this time the predominant emotion was love, not anger or anguish. Again, there was a physical element to it that was more real than a dream, and the feeling of his presence stayed with me throughout the next day.

A week later, I had a dream that began in the house where I had grown up. I was hiding inside from a gang of people who were outside trying to get into the house. They were a tough-looking group—young girls, looking worn beyond their years, and older men who looked like they drank a lot. One of the older men became ill, was proclaimed dead, and was carried inside the house. The dead man was then taken away, and later I learned he was okay. That was the end of the dream stage.

Then I felt myself move outside of the dream, and I saw Ralph's body for a fleeting moment. I can't say for sure that I was awake, but the sight of him was more real than a dream. It felt as if I was in a liminal space—somewhere between dreaming and waking. He looked as he had when I first met him, thin but healthy, with shiny dark hair and a serene composure.

"I…have…to…stay…here," I heard him say, slowly enunciating out each word.

Although similar to the other experiences when I had physically felt his presence, the difference this time was that he seemed sad. I concluded he was sad about not being able to come back and be with me in the physical sense.

Perhaps the dream was my way of trying to rationalize what happened to Ralph. After he lost his job, he made the wrong friends and started drinking. Then he became ill and died. After his death, he realized that life goes on, but he had to leave me and couldn't come back.

I wondered how long my struggle to make sense out of Ralph's drinking, his illness, and his passing would continue. We had had so much going for us. How could this have happened? I wondered. What's more, how can I ever truly accept what happened?

Despite Ralph's antics and communication, which made me feel loved and protected, I struggled to overcome the feeling of futility about what had happened to him. Although I will probably never know what happened for sure, or why, I believe the most likely scenario is that he just slipped into casually drinking too much as he watched television, waiting to find a new job.

TWENTY-TWO

I had procrastinated for more than six months about selling Ralph's car—an ordinary, white Subaru station wagon that was just a little over a year old when Ralph passed. I never drove it because the battery was dead and didn't keep a charge after letting the car sit idle for so long. It's not that I didn't want to sell it…I just hated to take the time to bother with getting it ready, because I had so many other pressing problems— like collection agencies, for example, because I refused to pay bills that weren't accurate.

Finally, I replaced the battery, had the car detailed, bought a couple of "For Sale" signs, and planned to place the car in the driveway of our antique shop the following Saturday morning.

On Friday night, I drove the car to do some errands and then stopped at a new car wash in our neighborhood. Getting out of the car, I looked around, searching for a change machine or a token dispenser. Just then, a car pulled up behind me, and the driver stepped out and walked straight toward me.

"Do you know where the change machine is?" I asked the man as he approached.

"I have no idea," he said. "I never come here." He was an older man, extraordinarily good-looking and well-dressed, with the bluest eyes I had ever seen, so vibrant they almost made me uncomfortable.

"How do you like your car?" he asked, moving closer to me. "I'm looking for one like it. I saw you over at the shopping center and followed you here."

I stared at him suspiciously.

"Do you mind if I look inside?" he asked.

My car door was already open, so I stepped aside as he looked inside the car.

"If you're really serious about buying this car, it will be for sale at this address tomorrow morning," I said, handing him a business card with the address of my antique shop.

He bought the car after the antique shop opened the next morning.

Perhaps it was just a coincidence that this stranger followed me and decided to buy a very ordinary car. I knew there was no possible way he could have known the car was for sale, because I didn't have the "For Sale" signs in the car that night. And perhaps the man's wife, who had bright blue eyes similar to her husband's, was just being kind when she told me my husband would be happy that I sold the car. Both the man and his wife had an otherworldly aura about them of peace and serenity, an aura that I had never encountered.

Yes, perhaps this was nothing but an extraordinary coincidence, but it didn't feel that way…not for one second. I believed that Ralph had just decided to give me a little help.

As soon as it became warm again outside in early summer, butterflies began their antics, diving toward my body and fluttering in front of my face. Only now, they had become much bolder; they actually touched me.

One day, I took a friend's eight-year old granddaughter to a county fair. The little girl ordered a pizza with special toppings, so we stepped aside to wait for the pizza to cook.

Suddenly, a butterfly started running up and down my right leg—first, it ran up the front of my bare leg to the bottom of my shorts; and then it circled my knee and ran down the back of my same leg. The little girl and I watched as the butterfly continued to run up and down my leg for several minutes.

"Are you wearing some special perfume?" the little girl asked.

"No, honey, butterflies just like me."

"Doesn't it tickle?"

"No, I like the way it feels."

We both smiled, as we watched the butterfly play. It was a special moment to share with this little girl I loved.

I found it hard to believe that almost a year had gone by since Ralph's passing—a year filled with many playful signs and communications from him that had eased my pain. Nonetheless, I dreaded the upcoming first anniversary of his passing, not knowing how I would react to memories of that dreadful time a year ago. I took the day off work, because I wasn't sure if I would become overwhelmed with sorrow, and I also wanted to honor that special day. Ralph had always been particularly sentimental about birthdays and anniversaries.

It was a beautiful, warm, sunny day as I lay outside by my pool, dozing on and off. After several hours of feeling lazy, I forced myself to get up. I had decided to build a rock garden for Ralph around the butterfly house that I had received from a friend who knew about how butterflies acted around me. I had never seen a butterfly house before this one; it was made out of wood, narrow in width and not quite two feet tall, with a hole in the front where butterflies could enter.

After carefully choosing rocks of different shapes and colors from around our property, I carried them to the backyard and carefully placed them around the butterfly house. Then I found some small twigs and branches and placed them inside the butterfly house.

Once I was satisfied with what I had done, I walked around to the front of the house and sat on the lawn next to a white iron settee. By then, it was late afternoon, and I felt pleased that I had not become terribly emotional during the day and had done something productive. As I sat on the grass, two butterflies with their wings interlocked, a white one and a yellow one, flew together and landed on the settee.

I stood up, because I wanted to sit near the butterflies. "May I sit down with you?" I asked.

After I sat down, I placed one hand on the settee, and the butterflies flew together and landed on the back of my hand, resting there for a few minutes before flying away. Peaceful, loving feelings washed over me…. There couldn't have been a more perfect event to celebrate the first anniversary of Ralph's passing.

Ralph continued to play his little tricks in the year that followed, as I intensified my efforts to simplify my life. I think he played with every lamp and light fixture in our house at least once, either to make a point or to make me feel better. As always, I knew exactly what he was communicating with the lights. The employees at Body & Soul said he often played with the lights there as well.

Occasionally Ralph would try something new. One day, a clock that sat on the fireplace mantel in my living room—a room that I sat in most days to watch television—started working for the first time in years. I think that particular incident was done strictly for my amusement.

Other times, I think Ralph did things for my protection. One day after I had been at Body & Soul, I walked out to the parking lot, got into my car, and looked up toward the rearview mirror, as I started my car. Except…there was no rearview mirror. It was gone. I found it on the floor of the car. I was unnerved, because I had always relied on the rearview mirror for most of my driving, having never really learned to use my side mirrors very effectively. I was also surprised because the car was not that old and was still under warranty.

I put the car in reverse and backed up. This feels so weird, I thought. I can't drive the car very far this way. I decided to take the car to the dealer, which was about twenty minutes away. After driving for about ten minutes, a terrible, screeching noise began somewhere under the hood. Now I was really unnerved and scared. I didn't know if I should continue driving or pull off the road. I continued driving and thankfully made it to the dealer, where I was promptly told by one of the mechanics that the car was unsafe to drive.

Some people may see my mirror falling off as just a fortunate coincidence, which it was, because it forced me to go to the dealer to attend to a more serious problem. But, was it just a coincidence or was Ralph guiding me to the dealer? I chose to thank him for watching over me.

Often, I felt as if I lived in another world than most people…and in a certain sense I did. I lived in a magical world where I was loved and protected.

I awoke in an anticipatory mood on the second anniversary of Ralph's passing, like a child on Christmas morning, wondering what surprises he would bring me that day. I walked into my dressing room and turned on the radio. "Wind Beneath My Wings", the first song that was sung at Ralph's burial service, began to play. Just another coincidence? I knew it wasn't. If anyone had told me I could feel this good only two years after Ralph's passing, I would never have believed them.

I couldn't help but wonder why these things were happening so frequently to me. Realistically, I knew that millions of people had lost loved ones, and yet I had never heard much talk of similar experiences. Surprisingly though, whenever I cautiously mentioned one of my experiences to someone, they appeared at least outwardly to be understanding, almost as if they knew such things happened; and occasionally, someone would mention an incident with his or her deceased loved one.

But why? I wondered…why this ongoing, prolific communication from Ralph in so many different forms? Ralph had let me know right from the beginning that he was well and happy so I wouldn't worry about him. Even though we had had a good marriage for almost twenty years, we'd had our share of difficult moments, like most couples, especially after I found out about his drinking.

Lana said I needed Ralph's communication to survive. Perhaps I did. After the many nightmarish months when Ralph was in intensive care, followed by the financial burdens and stress of managing five houses and two entrepreneurial businesses, while traveling all over the world with my corporate job, I had little emotional or physical reserves. I wasn't sure that I wanted to continue living.

As I said in the beginning of the book, I initially started writing because I had to. I look back now and realize I had to write this book for several reasons. First, I needed to get the horror of Ralph's illness and death down on paper…so I could make sense of what we went through. I found that putting things down on paper, not only helped me to understand the past, but it helped me to "let go" of the past. Second, I needed to try to make sense out of all the extraordinary after-death communications from Ralph. I had never heard of such events, and it wasn't until the book *Hello from Heaven* fell at my feet many years later in a bookstore that I read about all the different kinds of after-death events that other people had experienced. Surprisingly, I found that I had experienced eleven of the twelve widely-documented categories of after-death experiences.

Even with those probable reasons for needing to write my story, I believe there is one more prevailing reason that I felt this overwhelming urge to write: Ralph gave me all these after-death experiences, because he wanted me to write about them…to encourage others to watch for signs from deceased loved ones and not to be afraid but to be comforted by them. I believe Ralph wanted to help me as well as others, because once a person has had some of these after-death experiences, he or she can no longer believe in the finality of death. Better than any sermon about heaven, or any words from a spiritual or religious guru, having an after-death experience confirms the existence of an afterlife. There is no question about it.

I also look back and realize that the worst thing that ever happened in my life—Ralph's passing—became one of the best things that ever happened to me. That may sound shocking and strange, but in spite of my grief, with Ralph's help, I now have a spiritual belief and an understanding about life that I never knew was possible. The butterflies and other soul-to-soul communications began my spiritual journey. This may not have happened if Ralph had not passed. I may have stayed on the path of worldly pursuits to the exclusion of spiritual goals.

TWENTY-THREE

Seven years after Ralph's passing, I retired and moved to a warmer climate, first to Arizona and then to California. I was then able to work fulltime on finalizing this book and begin my other five books, which I had begun to write simultaneously. This first book opened up the floodgates and the other books became equally compelling for me to write.

Butterflies continued to play a major role in my life. According to Native American teaching, butterflies represent transformation; they certainly began my transformation. From the day that butterflies started swooping at me when I walked outside the week after Ralph's passing, I began to believe that life goes on…that Ralph was behind these beautiful creatures acting as they did.

One day, while on the patio of my California condo, a little yellow butterfly flew onto the back of my hand and stayed with me for almost three hours, moving back and forth from one of my hands to the other, as I tried to perform my household chores. Only once did she (I just knew it was a "she") flap her little wings and possibly get mad at me when she became stuck in a T-shirt I was trying to put on. My next-door neighbor obliged me by taking several pictures of me and my little butterfly. After those three hours with her, I knew this book would eventually be published and it would be called *The Year of the Butterfly.*

Over time, my experiences with butterflies and Ralph's communications began happening less and less frequently…until many years went by when I didn't have any such experiences.

I mostly think of him now with gratitude…for all the love and wisdom he gave me—for the butterflies, the lights, and the toy frog singing. Of course, I still miss him, but I have learned that life goes on for everyone—whether it is here on earth or after this life ends.

AFTERWORD

It is hard for me to believe that twenty-three years and two months have now gone by since Ralph's passing. I have not only moved to several different states and homes, but I have been in a long-term relationship with another wonderful man for ten years.

Having moved back to the Midwest part-time, I decided to visit the cemetery where Ralph had been buried. Not having visited the cemetery for at least a decade, I didn't know how I would react when I got there. I expected to feel guilt for not having visited the gravesite for many years, and a sense of deep sadness.

As I drove into the deserted parking lot next to the cemetery, I felt tears barely in check. I parked my car in front of the old iron gate that was the only entrance to the cemetery, and immediately saw a padlock by the gate's door handle. It was a familiar site that I remembered seeing years ago when I would visit the cemetery on my way home from work. After Ralph's burial, the gate was always locked with a padlock. I assumed few people ever visited the cemetery because most of its inhabitants had been buried there in the 1800s. The township had finally given me a key to the padlock, but I had forgotten about it and had no idea where it might be. Twenty-some years ago, I might have considered climbing up over the gate and jumping to the ground on the other side of the fence. But now, at seventy-five, I doubted that I could climb the gate or fence without getting impaled on the pointed spikes on top of the fence.

As I stood there, I noticed that the gate's latch and door handle looked newer—its brass color did not look as old and tarnished as I remembered. Instinctively, I pushed down on the gate's handle and, much to my surprise, the gate opened. Then I saw that the padlock was actually in a locked position beneath the gate's door handle.

I slowly pushed the gate open and walked inside. Everything looked much the same as I remembered…there were just a few more dried leaves and walnuts on the ground because it was October. There were no flowers or signs of visitations that were usually visible in most cemeteries.

I walked to the plot of ground where Ralph had been buried and where I had bought a plot for myself. I chided myself for the umpteenth time for not having gotten a gravestone and promised myself I would do so next year. At the time of Ralph's burial, I had put all my focus and energy into the wake and burial service. I remembered that immediately after the burial service, I felt Ralph had left the cemetery. I never sensed his presence there during the following years when I visited, and felt no urge to buy a gravestone.

As I walked around the small cemetery, I paused to read the dates on some of the gravestones. It took only a few minutes for me to reach the opposite side of the cemetery, because the entire site is not much more than 12,000 square feet. Then I had another surprise. For seemingly no reason at all, I started feeling joyous and exuberant…not just a little bit happy…but really ecstatic. This is the last thing I ever expected to feel here, I said to myself.

I began talking out loud to Ralph, as if he were right there in the cemetery. "I am so happy you're doing well," I said in a loud, excited voice. I looked up at the sky and could feel Ralph's happiness. I felt his energy. I felt as if I could almost see him. I envisioned him flying above me in the sunshine, smiling broadly, happy and carefree. This sudden change in my feelings reminded me of how Ralph used to surprise me and delight me whenever I was feeling depressed.

"Look at us!" I said. "We're both so happy and doing well. I know you are proud of me for moving on and finding another man to love. I looked around at the beautiful trees and the sunshine sparkling on the gravestones. I remembered the sadness and despair that I felt twenty-three years ago when I walked around the grounds of the cemetery after his emotional burial service. Now, I felt only joy—for him and for me. Twenty-three years ago, I didn't want to leave the cemetery to go home and face the loneliness I knew I would feel there. Today, I didn't want to leave the cemetery because of all the happiness and joy I was experiencing with Ralph.

But I had errands to do and a long drive home. Shortly after I got back into my car and started driving, I turned on my car's radio. The first song that played was a song from the movie *The Bodyguard*, "I will Always Love You". I have always had mixed feelings about that song. Ralph had bought the CD for me several years before his passing. It is the only CD that he had ever bought for me, and I hadn't asked him to buy it. As much as I liked the movie and the soundtrack from the movie, I was uncomfortable with the words of the song that was now playing on my radio. I have always believed that Ralph bought the CD, so I would hear the strong words and message of the song:

> "If I should stay, I would only be in your way
> So I'll go, but I know I'll think of you every step of the way
> And I will always love you…."

To me, it has always been a song of bidding farewell. It tore at my heart almost a quarter of a century ago, and it did so again now. It wasn't long after he bought the CD that I felt Ralph had changed, and then shortly afterward, our relationship became worrisome. So hearing the song played again, especially after my jubilant feelings at the cemetery, made me sad. Yet, I suspected it was a sign from him…another message that he would always love me.

I drove another hour or so to a grocery store near my new home. As I pulled into the store's parking lot, the song "Wind Beneath My Wings" began to play on the radio. I sat in my car and listened to the song. I was no longer suspicious…I knew this was another sign from Ralph. For whatever reason, Ralph has frequently communicated to me with songs playing in unusual or coincidental circumstances—like this same song being the first one I heard when I turned on the radio on the second anniversary of his passing. One meaningful song playing after I visited the cemetery was perhaps just a coincidence. Two such meaningful songs, not popular for decades…an unlikely coincidence. As I said at the beginning of this book, I no longer believe in coincidences. But twenty-three years is a long time to be still getting messages from the other side. I guess love really never dies.

It was because of my experience at the cemetery and the songs playing on my radio that I decided to not only print this book, but to distribute it as well…not just stash it in my garage, which I had done for years.

One last message from Ralph and me: Notwithstanding objections due to religious beliefs, please consider signing up to provide organ donations in order to save more lives, if you have not already done so.

DONNA FRIDRYCH was one of the first female consultants in the field of computer technology. Starting as a computer programmer, she climbed the corporate ladder to act as Chief Information Officer for United Airlines, and later became CEO of the United Airlines Employees' Credit Union. As a marketing director, she traveled around the world conducting business in many foreign countries and relished the opportunity to get to know people from different cultures. As an entrepreneur, she owned an antique business in a four-story Victorian house for twenty years, and was also co-owner of a day spa. True to the "Renaissance Woman" label given to her by friends, she is the author of six other books. In addition to *The Year of the Butterfly*, her book *Women Must Save the World! A Call to Action* was published in 2020, and *Reflections from the Glass Ceiling* is scheduled to be published in 2022. See RenaissanceDonna.com for further information.

Donna currently spends winters in Arizona and summers at her lake home in northern Illinois with her long-term partner William and their two dogs—Valentino (Tino), who got his name when he was rescued on Valentine's Day, and Natasha (Tasha) his adorable playmate.